I0770026

Forbidden Captive
Legends & Predators I

Ashley Earley

Earley Literary Press, LLC

Earley Literary Press, LLC

Forbidden Captive

Copyright © 2025 by Ashley Earley

All rights reserved.

First Edition

Published by Earley Literary Press, LLC

Publication Date: September 25, 2025

Paperback ISBN: 979-8-9879815-4-2

Exclusive Hardback ISBN: 979-8-9879815-5-9

eBook ISBN: 979-8-9879815-3-5

Book Cover by Wolfe Fantasy

Translations by James C.

Formatted using Vellum

Map illustration by Fantasy Fox Maps

Line Editing & Proofreading by Dee's Notes

Developmental Editing by Earley Editing, LLC

To everyone who felt they never fit in or have too little confidence. Pick up your ax and cleave your way through those who shame you for being different or tarnish your badassery.

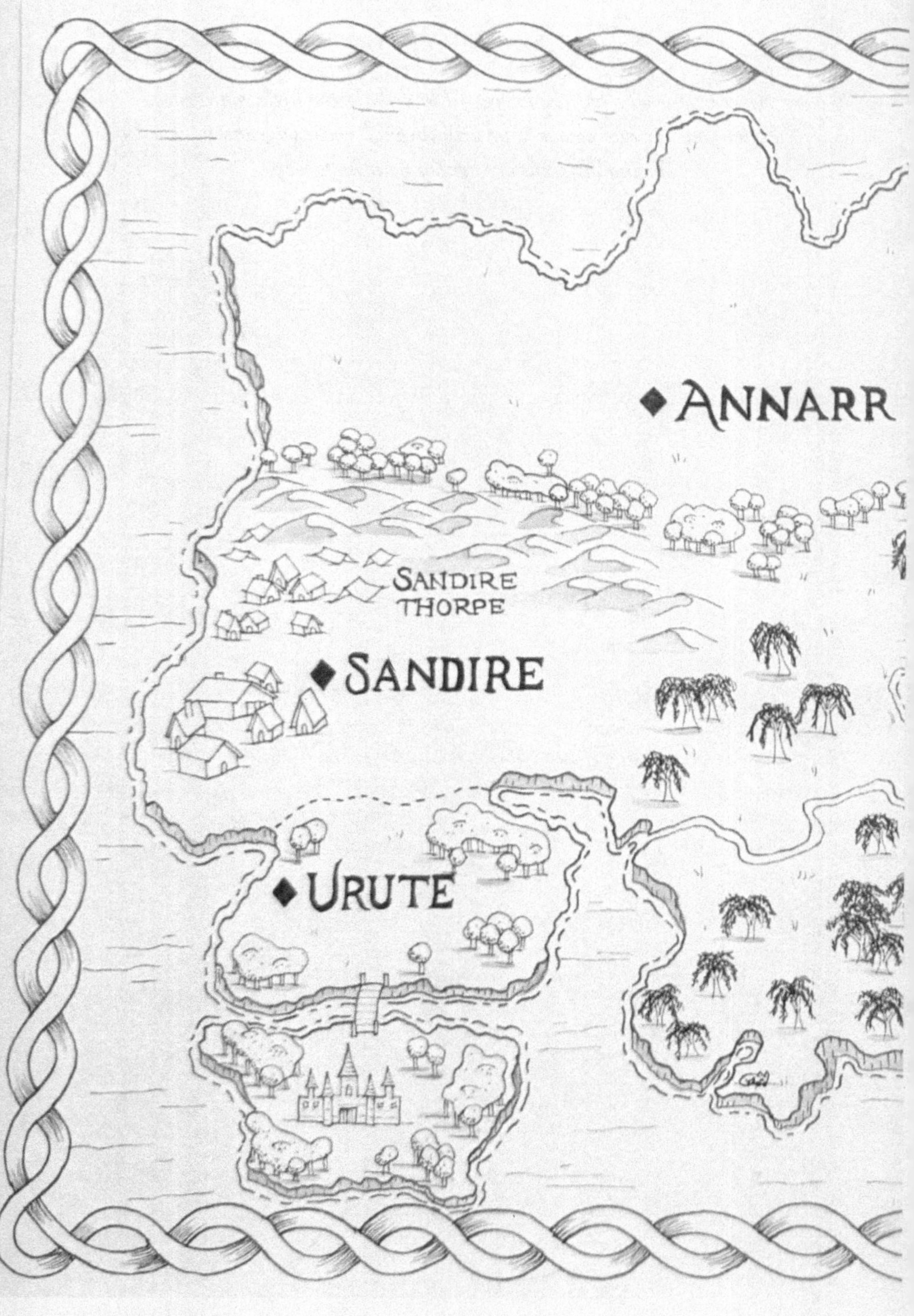

ANNARR
SANDIRE THORPE
SANDIRE
URUTE

N
W
E
S
NEDFIN
WAYLRIA
WAYLRIA BOROUGH
REALM
TOWN

Translations

<u>Words & Terms</u>

- *Elðr* — the Old Norse word for **fire**.
- *Fórn* — the term refers to a **sacrifice**, especially one made in a ritual or religious context.
- *Hjarta* — the word for **heart** in Old Norse.
- *Hjarta ðýrs* — translates to "**beast's heart.**"
- *Loganda reykr* — translates to "**burning smoke.**"
- *Øx* — **axe/ax**.
- *Sanðr* — this Old Norse term translates to **sand**.
- *Varúlfur* — **werewolf** (a later Icelandic term).
- *Hel* — the word refers to both the **goddess of the underworld** and the **realm of the dead** itself, depending on the context.
  - **Hel** (the goddess) is the daughter of **Loki** and **Angrboða**, and she rules over the realm of the dead, which is also called **Hel**.
  - **Hel** (the realm) is the destination for those who did not die in battle and were not honored in Valhalla, where warriors go after death.

- *Völva* — this Old Norse term translates to **seeress** or **prophetess**. A *völva* was a female shaman or seer in Norse mythology and culture, known for her ability to practice *seiðr* (a form of magic or divination).
- *Seiðr* — this Old Norse term translates to **magic**, **sorcery**, or **witchcraft**. It refers to a specific type of Norse magical practice associated with prophecy, shaping fate, and influencing the natural or supernatural world. It was often linked to rituals, spells, and trance states.

<u>Sentences</u>

- *"Dauði er með þér. Øx þín mun rísta háls þinn í dagan."* — "Death is upon you. Your ax shall cleave through your neck at dawn."
- *"Ek mun ekki nafn mitt þik gefa."* — "I will not give you my name."
- *"Góðan dag, bróðir."* — "Hello, brother."
- *"Nei! Þú mun ekki hann finna!"* — "No! You will not find him!"
- *"Nøkkut at segja?"* — "Anything to say?"
- *"Svikall sonr minn ok varúlfr fúll hans."* — "My treacherous son and his foul werewolf."

More translations in the back of book for Part III. Flipping to that page means potentially encountering spoilers for Part III.

Prologue
Riker

Showing fear was a weakness.

A death sentence.

Vikings could not be afraid.

But when I heard my sister's desperate shouts ... my entire world stilled with fear.

I hurled from my cot, scrambling for the door as fast as I could. Identical footsteps thundered from behind me as I ran down the hall.

Annora's bedroom was the room beside mine, but her shouts were coming from farther away.

At the other end of our house—our parents' bedroom door was wide open. As I ran toward it, I saw it was draped in darkness, but the very marrow in my bones knew Annora's voice was coming from inside.

Rather than letting fear grip me, I reached for anger until I was surging with it—until I felt like I could tear the entire house apart with my bare hands.

At their bedroom, I saw red.

There was so much blood—Annora's blood.

My heart withered in my chest. A breath heaved through me.

She looked so small, I was afraid to touch her.

And I could do … nothing.

There was too much blood.

Helpless and useless. The realization was so consuming and weighed me down so fully, it was nearly suffocating. Tears racked through me, each drop landing at the knees of her nightgown.

By the time her eyes found me, she couldn't speak. I watched how the light left her crystal-blue eyes. Still, when her eyes became lifeless to the world around us, it seemed so sudden.

I didn't care if I was showing weakness.

I let fear swallow me whole. Agony suffocating my heart, I allowed my tears to fall.

FORBIDDEN CAPTIVE

PART 1

TREASONOUS TERRITORY

Chapter One
Zyra

NO SHAPESHIFTER HAD EVER TAKEN me seriously. And with mashed strawberries trailing down my cheeks and stuck to my hands, I didn't blame them. I groaned, more than a little tempted to turn around and head back to the warmth of my bed. Then with a slight snarl, I forced my feet to move.

I wiped the fruit from my face, the scratchy rag flushing my cheeks. The shelves facing my kitchen held every nut, berry, herb, syrup, preserve, pickled vegetable, and even oil any one person could ever need. Each one brightened the small space. Light peeked through the windows on either side of the front door, casting rays across the hall and into the kitchen. I stepped around the wooden countertop more often used as a kitchen table than the actual table beside the shelves. After grabbing a jar stuffed full of jam, I stood at the counter, ready to pop open the lid, and the door burst open. I paused but didn't need to look up to know who it was.

Corinna slammed the door, shutting out the murmurs of the borough and blocking the light.

"Too loud. Too early," I mumbled when I found words, speaking for the first time that morning.

"Too cold, too," she offered, removing the hood shadowing

her face. Sharp, red tattoos snaked up her right hand, traveling across her arm to her shoulder, then winded up the side of her face before disappearing into her dark hair. "Thank the Great Spirit you keep this place warm."

I fought not to roll my eyes. The borough stayed plenty warm, thanks to the tree and how the cavern narrowed the closer one got to the entrance. We had drafts, but it wasn't like snow blew inside.

Before I could finish opening the jar, Corinna had sauntered across the room and snatched it from my hand. Hopping onto the counter, she crossed her legs, tossing the jar from hand to hand.

I wouldn't dare mention the pureeing incident to her.

Upon catching my disapproving glare, a slow smile spread across her face. "You invited me to breakfast."

"I didn't realize you would be stealing my jam."

"I'm stealing your bread, too. Hand it over."

I sighed. Despite having grown up together, the friendship between Corinna and me had its limitations. I was nothing more than a glorified apprentice, while she had grown into a warrior for Haiden's bidding. Navigating whether she was speaking to me as a friend or as my superior left me on edge at all times. Even when we weren't under Haiden's thumb.

"I could just tell you to get over it and go hunt for your food."

That. That right there was why I walked on eggshells.

I could only imagine how she would react if I said something similar to her.

I scoffed, unwrapping the loaf of bread I had traded for the day prior and cut a slice for each of us. The jam was a mixture of berries, which would pair perfectly with the sourdough. Most of my nights were spent right where I was standing. Typically, I was alone, though.

"What are you doing today?" I asked, for a change in topic, handing her slice over to let her spread her own jam.

"No idea," she said, spinning the lid of the jar off and flicking it to the floor. "I haven't seen Haiden yet."

I nodded, taking a bite of plain bread. I nearly spat it back out, but Corinna handed over the jam before I had to take drastic measures.

Haiden, the Chief of Waylria, played favorites. While I mostly pickled vegetables and made fruit preserves for trade despite working under Haiden, Corinna and Nabil were Haiden's esteemed shadows and warriors—because they followed his every command. He rarely made me report to him anymore, but Corinna and Nabil were under strict orders to meet with him every morning.

"I think I'm just going to head out, then." Averting my eyes, I popped the last bite of jam-covered bread into my mouth before heading to the shelves again.

Corinna took a massive bite as she scanned the cramped space, taking in the cooking pot over top kindling, a water basin, the wooden countertop she sat perched on, and the table from where I had grabbed one of my bags to stuff the day's necessities inside.

Corinna released a long sigh. "Do you get bored of pickling and jamming?"

Do you get bored of following Haiden's every whim? I kept grabbing things off the shelf but glanced at the door periodically.

Inside, it was impossible to tell whether it was early or late morning. Either way, I was ready to make my way down to the trading stalls. Afterward, I would be ready to come home and isolate myself with more pickling. The realm of Nedfin—since they were a realm that stood for healing, farming, and peace—was the source for all crops and orchards. Our realm, Waylria, often traded for their fruits and vegetables by offering them back as pickled or preservatives. Food kept longer, and farming could continue without guilt of waste.

"No. Why would I? It's not like there's much more to do."

Aside from portioning food to help it last longer and

helping Waylria and those in other realms, the trading stall provided a sense of community. It was a place where everyone stood on even ground. While there were favorite items for trade, there was no favoritism of those doing the trading.

Everyone had a stall, and everyone supported each other's stalls. If one person didn't have something, they would direct to another's dealing.

It was one of the few places I didn't have to walk on eggshells.

Corinna let out another long sigh, then I watched from the corner of my eye as she pushed off the counter and started for the door.

She pulled up her hood when I turned to her. "I have to leave, but thank you for breakfast ... You could try standing up for yourself one of these days, you know, when you get bored."

I stuffed the last jar into my bag before meeting her at the door. She kept a careful eye on me the entire way, as if waiting for something. This time, it was my turn to sigh. "I don't think it's in my best interest to start making demands."

I was unsure what would happen if I approached Haiden about expanding my responsibilities again. I had already asked to be more involved once, and that had gone worse than anticipated. What more could I do anyway? My own parents hardly spent time with me. Why would Haiden treat me as anything more when even they didn't?

I shook my head, struggling to swallow around the lump in my throat.

Corinna merely nodded, then opened the door. When I stepped out behind her, I swallowed again. She moved to the edge of the top step leading up to my front door, then didn't even look back before she flung herself forward, shifting into a raven. Furiously flapping her wings, Corinna glided through the borough until she reached the waterfall, where she disappeared into Haiden's quarters.

I stood envious of her effortless shift into flight.

Running, growling, and hunting was all my shift seemed good for. A mere wolf. No wonder Haiden thought me beneath Corinna and Nabil.

I shoved those thoughts to the shadows of my mind and, rather than shifting to race to the market on all fours, walked down the endless stone steps on human legs. Murmurs met my ears, growing louder the farther into the borough I went.

Stairs upon stairs had to be descended before reaching the split paths. All the winding footpaths joined at the center—where the Great Spirit upheld the ceiling with sturdy branches stretched across all corners of the vast cave, alighting the dome with its orbs of fruit and bright-green leaves.

Myths told of how we were birthed from the tree, having burst from its roots and climbed from the ground. And tradition upheld ritual blessings where we discovered what animal form we could shift into. The tree was Waylria's source of light and life.

Memories of having the glowing fruit spread across my forehead did anything but bring a smile to my face.

But I refused to think about that when I was stepping into the market.

Each stall resembled that of a cramped home. Each one barely fit more than two people. Once squeezed through the door, someone would be met with a small wooden block for a counter and walls packed with items for trade. With a few already setting up for the day, I offered a tentative smile as I passed. Lizeth, whose stall was beside my own, was the only one who noticed as she set a handcrafted bowl on a table just outside.

My walls were lined with shelves, and some still had a few leftovers from the previous day. I didn't bother setting my bag down; I kept it braced on my shoulder while refilling the empty space on the shelves. While others offered things such as bowls carved with intricate designs, or weapons or even clothing and draperies, I offered preserves and pickled foods. Others traded fresh fruit, vegetables, and spices from Nedfin, too, but I was the only one who had mastered preservatives. My ability to balance the sweetness and bitterness within preserved foods was what Haiden used to claim I was more of a necessity when it came to trade. Not only with our people but with Nedfin, to continue the back and forth of goods between our communities.

That was where I was an asset.

The glass of the jar in my hand splintered beneath my palm, and my teeth gritted to hold back a snarl.

My animal skin was not that of a raven like Corinna and Nabil, but I was his messenger whenever a produce runner came to Waylria. That was when I was allowed in Haiden's chambers. That was my time of importance. And yet, though I dealt with trade between realms for Haiden, another world felt like an impossible reality. Nedfin's runners came to us since it was too dangerous for shapeshifters to leave Waylria.

Our lands were where we were safest from Vikings.

Chapter Two
Riker

DAYS AND NIGHTS BLENDED TOGETHER — NEVER ending. And I only ever stopped running when I absolutely had to. When the exhaustion became overwhelming and I had to sit or I would collapse. I never experienced a quiet moment, a constant roaring in my ears kept me moving. My mind was chaos, replaying everything that had taken place, beginning with the night of my sister's death. Even with my eyes closed, I saw the spear shooting through her body.

To beat back the images, I thought of everything I was leaving behind. I would never be forgiven. I would be blood eagled if I ever stepped foot in Sandire again. My ribs severed from my spine; lungs pulled through the opening to create a pair of wings.

My entire life had been stripped from me in the same way, it felt like, leaving me with only one possession — the ax clutched in my hand.

I may not see my friends again, let alone be accepted by them.

Never seeing my mother again was also a possibility. And my last image of her sobbing over Annora's lifeless form stained in blood was all I had left to cling to.

I ground my teeth, locking my jaw to fight back the grief overwhelming my every breath.

My father's men weren't far behind. I had spotted them in the distance a few times, usually at sunset or sunrise when their silhouettes stood out against the light. They intended to capture me, but it went beyond that. It was also to stop me from speaking of his plans. I would have to go into hiding, become someone else; take on a new identity in a new realm.

I couldn't ever be the Viking Prince of Sandire again. I was an outcast, forced to blend into a new and foreign culture. They couldn't find me. I had to escape them and start a new life. Beginning anew was the only way to have a life at all, but to avoid my old life was to abandon. Walking away forever when my family was in shambles and needed me to put them back together was outrageous.

Never returning wasn't an option. Not when they needed me to keep them safe from the war my father was about to ignite.

Letting them catch up to me couldn't happen. Not when I needed to stop him from setting these plans in motion. Not when my family needed me and my ability to go home relied on my father's failure.

Chapter Three
Zyra

"Got tired of organizing by vegetable and jam?" a voice asked from behind me.

With my jars organized by color on my shelves, I was satisfied by the look of my trading stall by the time Lizeth peeked her head inside with a smile.

I shrugged. "Shopping should be a challenge sometimes."

Lizeth wandered inside, picking up a jar of nuts and setting it beside a jar of almond spread for a smoother cohesion of color. Hands on hips, she gave a nod, as if she had put in the same amount of time and energy as I had. A laugh nearly burst from my lips, but when she turned back to me, I was smiling and shaking my head at her. "You put it in the wrong place. Don't make my eyes bleed like that again."

"Careful … you're starting to sound like Corinna."

Lizeth grinned. "As if Corinna could be gentle enough to carve pretty bowls like I do."

"As if you could handle abiding by—"

"Oh, I certainly couldn't."

With Lizeth's unique animal skin, it was surprising Haiden had never offered her a position in place of Nabil or Corinna, especially since both had identical animal skins to that of ravens.

Lizeth's animal skin took the form of a fox. Her red hair already took on a life of its own in her human form, with how every bushy strand wove its way around her neck and shoulders. In her fox skin, it was still beautiful but more contained. Smart, curious, and intuitive — Lizeth was talented at hunting and always had to be on the move. One could only imagine what she would be capable of if Haiden took her under his wing.

Ravens could only do so much to protect us from our enemy.

They were sneaky enough to gather information and could fly high and quick enough to drop messages from their talons, but if a true invasion and attack ever ensued … I feared it would not be enough.

Then again, Haiden could just sideline Lizeth the same way he had done me. Despite her skin being far more unique than my own. Despite her talent.

I had no use outside of pickling and trade.

"Do you want to go hunting tonight? Oh! Can I show you the new bowl I just made?" Before I could answer either question, Lizeth bounded out the door to make for her stall, only to rush back with a large serving vessel in her hands.

I pressed my lips together to keep from laughing at how frantic her mind worked at times.

Lizeth held the wooden bowl up by her palm and spun it to flaunt the designs she had carved. Various animals were etched around the bowl, each small and intricately detailed. My jaw nearly dropped as I pictured Lizeth sitting stooped over the bowl for hours without so much as blinking away from her art. Birds, big cats, and even canines like us appeared to be racing around the bowl, aiming for a destination that would never come.

I opened my mouth to tell Lizeth how gorgeous her work

was and what she might want to trade for it, because I might need it for my kitchen, but I never got the chance.

"Haiden sent me to ask you something, but it seems you're rather busy."

Her scent hit me the second before Lizeth and I whirled.

Corinna—one of the few who could sneak up on me—sat perched on the wooden slab near the door, her talons digging into the counter beneath her. Her yellow eyes moved from Lizeth to me and back again. A heaviness settled into the pit of my stomach.

"It's just Lizeth and I. No one is here to trade," I said. "What does Haiden need?"

Her expression was impossible to read, making my heart jolt against my chest.

"I thought you would be excited to know he was asking for you."

Lizeth tensed at Corinna's words, knowing their effect on me.

Haiden was asking for me specifically. He'd sent Corinna to seek me out. Him wanting to speak to me, the unknown of what his question could be and what it could all mean, had me in a chokehold. I was left to my own devices often—only called upon when it was beneficial to Haiden.

Corinna also knew the clutch her words had on me.

"Of course I want to hear what he has to say. What does he need?"

Corinna nodded before saying, "He wants to know when Nedfin is supposed to have its next runner arrive for trade."

I frowned at the peculiar question. "The last exchange was a month ago, so we won't see another for another two months. Why is he asking?"

She pushed off from the counter, silently landing on her feet. "I'm not entitled to say."

I clenched my jaw, and my stomach plummeted. I was one of the three shifters Haiden trusted enough to have under his command yet was treated as anything but a confidant.

"I'm sorry, Zyra," Corinna went on, finally showing a glimmer of guilt. "He wanted me to ask you but didn't want me to share any details. I have no choice. I'll see you outside tonight."

"But you don't hunt," Lizeth pointed out with the tilt of her head.

"I'm a raven, not a pigeon."

With that, Corinna was gone as quietly as she had arrived.

I stared out the door after her until Lizeth came up beside me. "What was that about? I hate it when Haiden messes with you like this. He treats you—"

I shrugged, trying to ignore the way my heart sank to my toes. "Who knows. I'm not privy to the same information they are ... evidently."

Biting my tongue, I tuned out what Lizeth said following that. I did not need reminding of how Haiden treated me; it was blatant enough. Two people came in to trade for preservatives, and one followed Lizeth out to her stall after seeing the bowl she'd shown off to me.

I traded for the bowl before someone else could take it for themselves, planning to pile my unpreserved fruit inside it.

Still, sundown could not come soon enough.

WITH MY STALL closed for the night, I stepped out to head to Lizeth's stall, and she burst out the door. "I'm ready to catch myself some mice!"

I couldn't help but smile. "Mice? Dream bigger. I'm after a rabbit."

She gasped, and her eyes grew wide. "No! They're so cute

and fluffy! Don't eat a rabbit. You'll get their fluff stuck in your teeth."

Hunting and eating raw animals wasn't necessary. We could survive off human food, and often did, but hunting kept our animal instincts sharp. It also curbed cravings from our predator forms, quieting the itching.

I grinned at her, flashing my canines. "I'll pick the hair out with its bones."

"You're cruel. I'm not watching you eat a bunny."

We meandered down the paths, heading toward the stairs that led to the borough's exit. The steps were steep and seemingly endless with how they ran into the mouth of the cave. On two feet, climbing such stairs was exhausting, yet Lizeth and I pushed to walk side by side as we discussed our day.

I hadn't been able to get Haiden's question out of my mind.

Even as I talked to Lizeth, I wondered why he'd asked it. What was the purpose of the information? He knew our trading deals with Nedfin, so why ask a question he already knew the answer to? If he asked it for the sake of making sure, why was there a need to? Sending Corinna to ask it rather than summoning me to his chambers didn't make it seem urgent, but Haiden didn't overlook details. Especially when it came to outsiders crossing into our realm.

As we neared the top step, a chill wrapped around my arms, bringing with it an itch that spread across every inch of my skin and snapped me from my thoughts.

The change of seasons did not apply inside the borough. Our Great Spirit kept us warm. This left only one season to prosper: spring. Inside, the cave was always warm, thriving with luscious green, always thrumming with life. Fall did not seem to exist, and it never snowed. Cold air never made it past the first steps inside.

Outside the borough, the ground was covered in snow; the forest blanketed in white flurries.

My every exhale misted into a fog. Flurries fell from the

trees, making it seem like snow was still coming down. Either way, snow would get caught in my fur and keep me just cold enough while I ran free.

Lizeth grinned, her canines extending before her skin morphed and shed to replace the human with a fox. Her gorgeous red hair was replaced with that of a beautiful red coat. Her black ears perked at attention; she looked up at me with a mischievous grin of sharp teeth.

I flashed my own elongated smile, relishing in how they dug into my bottom lip.

A raven appeared in a flapping of wings, landing in the snow in front of me. Corinna cawed, and I knew if she had been gifted with a different skin, she would have likely been something ferocious. Her raven skin did not match her furious and rigid personality. To match her animal skin, I feared she would have to be one of the made-up animals from Urute, like a dragon. Then she would breathe fire in both human and animal form.

I shredded my human skin in a stretch of discomfort, my clothes transforming into fur. Afterward, I stood before them as a wolf.

I nipped at Corinna, pretending I was after one of her feathers. When she screeched and hopped back on her short legs, Lizeth squeaked and panted with laughter. I whirled before Lizeth rolled with laughter, releasing a frisky bark as I leaped over her and snapped at her tail. Her beady eyes narrowed, but when she took a step toward me, I took off. Blood pounding through my veins, my heart soaring, forcing my paws to beat against the snow-covered ground.

With my thundering heart echoing in my ears, I almost shut my eyes to take it all in. The smell of the dense evergreens, the soft crunch beneath my paws, the chill that clung to my fur but didn't penetrate it—this was where I thrived. No matter what anyone said or did, everything about me felt fierce once I was in my wolf skin.

Corinna flew overhead, her winged shadow racing above me, and Lizeth's steps sounded from behind me. Yet, the surrounding night was quiet. Our paws left a soft crunch and a print where they landed, but no sound or sight caught our attention until we were miles into our hunt.

Slow down, Corinna called to Lizeth and me through her mind, followed by an image of a few rabbits. With the three of us in our animal skins, projecting our thoughts to each other was effortless.

No, Lizeth groaned while I sent laughter to their minds.

Stop your complaining, Corinna bit out. *All of us get a meal this way.*

You're a fox, so start acting like it and eat a delicious rabbit, I told her as I crouched close to the ground, careful to stay hidden behind a tree. Corinna disappeared to land somewhere, and Lizeth scurried to the tree closest to mine.

From behind the tree, I saw four rabbits bounding through the snow in search of something edible, but nothing would bloom green again until long after the snow melted. I tried not to think about how cute their little twitchy noses were; Lizeth was getting in my head.

Somehow, my thoughts settled on how Haiden had sent Corinna to ask about the next trade with Nedfin.

Crouched with my belly touching the snow, I wanted to ask Corinna about it. My curiosity was burning for me to. Corinna must have felt it through what bonded our thoughts because she cawed from somewhere in the distant trees. I shrank farther into the snow, my nose nearly buried as I turned my focus back to the twitchy bunny noses.

This time, my mouth watered at the thought of catching one in my maw.

A few heartbeats later, at the precise moment my instincts told me to, I burst into a run. My hind legs kicked up snow from the force of how quickly I took off. They scattered, eyes wide, and their limbs flailed with the visceral need to get away.

Lizeth was behind me, but I could hear the hesitancy in her steps.

I didn't wait to see what she would do. The moment I had a rabbit within reach, I clamped down. Lizeth flinched at the crunch of bones, failing to catch her own.

I dropped my limp rabbit in the snow in time for Corinna to land on its neck, aiming her beak at its head to give it a poke. *Just eat fruits and vegetables,* Corinna snapped at Lizeth.

Lizeth's yellow eyes narrowed at the black bird. *I just don't like killing cute animals. Ravens are not on my list of cute animals.*

I couldn't contain my snicker, then forced Corinna away from my meal to dig in.

When Lizeth, Corinna, and I stepped back down into the borough's cavern, it was on human legs. I took in the wide, thick trunk of the Great Spirit, my eyes alight at its fruit. The streams wearing around the base of the tree reflected the glowing orbs as each trickled beneath a few of its raised roots. Lush, green, and strong—nature had its own pattern in Waylria, but the tree represented our people. A symbol part of our very essence. Everything was sacred, precious.

Standing among the streams and roots, grass and encompassing flowers was my mother, a force compared to the other shamans and healers, striking as she worked to crush herbs with a pestle. Since we hardly spoke, I did not know how involved she was with Haiden or what her duties were. Even as a healer, I assumed she was more involved with Haiden than I would ever be. I could only guess as to whether the herbs she was crushing were meant for healing or as an offering to the Great Spirit.

She probably made a point to visit with Haiden regularly to spite me.

Ever since my blessing in discovering my wolf skin, both my parents had distanced themselves, slowly turning their backs on me. Once I moved out on my own, I stopped talking to them.

It was the fact they *let* me stop talking to them that hurt the most.

I inhaled a shuddering breath to fight the tight ache in my chest.

Not wanting to think about where my father was, I tore my gaze from her before my thoughts could spiral further.

Chapter Four
Riker

Fighting for breath, I stopped at the top of a hill surrounded by trees that appeared to bloom purple leaves, but I couldn't trust my vision when a haze still consumed my mind. With the sun rising, I turned, squinting to get my eyes to focus. I fought hard to keep on my feet, afraid of collapsing if I let my mind wander from that blurred focus.

My father's men were drawing closer. Their distant figures were still somewhat small, but they were closing in. Their pace made me question whether they were even stopping to sleep. If they were, I doubted they were getting much. I moved until exhaustion overpowered my will and drowned my mind in the depths of unconsciousness, but I couldn't control how long I was under.

With them drawing closer, I wouldn't be able to sleep again for some time.

After turning into the woods, my footsteps were calculated as I maneuvered around twigs, roots, and patches of dirt. I watched the ground, searching for any sign of tracks. Eventually, sunlight spread through the forest, glistening the dew on the plants. I waited, scouring every inch of the forest until my prey revealed itself. Then I beheaded the rabbit with my ax before tearing through its fur to get to the meat beneath.

I wrestled with the haze to figure out what to do next.

By the sight of the purple leaves, I knew I was at a crossroads.

With Urute being an alley to Sandire, they would turn me over the moment it was asked of them. Even if I told them of my father's plans to overtake the realms, they would not believe a traitor.

I could hide—blend into a society until my father was done hunting me and turned to his greater plans. The mountains of Nedfin would provide the seclusion I needed to lose my father's men.

Only, there was a strong possibility my father would never forget the betrayal I had been accused of and wouldn't turn his back on having me hunted down and blood eagled. Then, of course, I was loose and aware of his plans. He would do everything to bring me back in chains.

My only other chance …

I rose to my feet, refusing to let my legs buckle beneath me.

There was only one place I could go where my father's men wouldn't follow—Waylria. The land of shapeshifters. The land of our enemy.

I gritted my teeth at the mere thought, my hand tightening around the hilt of my ax. The trek would wear at me, and the savages would be at my throat the moment I crossed into their realm, but it was the only way. Perhaps I could convince them to be on my side after they knew of how determined Slate was to eradicate their kind. On a deeper level than ever before. The moment Vikings were the ultimate power among the realms.

Perhaps their survival instincts would overshadow their eagerness for bloodshed.

Chapter Five
Zyra

After seeing my mother the night before, I went home to throw myself into preserving. I refused to say anything to either Corinna or Lizeth because Corinna would've offered to stay the night with me, and I couldn't stand the thought of her feeling like she had to spend time with me. All I wanted was quiet time to myself.

Mashing fruit helped extinguish the surge of emotions that surfaced.

Sometimes, it felt like reopening a wound. Other times, seeing either of my parents sent me spiraling into anger. Then there were the times I felt like locking myself away to cry. I craved the moments where I felt detached in an indifferent way. Most days, I relied on them.

But for now, I crushed and squeezed and mangled until everything was a splattered mess in the giant bowl.

I worked until the empty spaces on my shelves were filled. Once I was too exhausted to stand, I collapsed into bed.

The next day, I got up to do it all over again. Only, this time, I put my head down to keep my emotions at bay. I had every intention of avoiding looking around the borough, busying myself with helping the other stalls, until I spotted my mother out of the corner of my eye. Neither Corinna nor Nabil was with her. No, she was alone as she made her way behind the waterfall to Haiden's chambers.

I gritted my teeth. My mother had been summoned by Haiden when there wasn't another blessing for weeks, if not months. Corinna was keeping secrets from me but asking strange questions per Haiden's request.

For the remainder of the day, I stayed in my stall.

I kept myself and my emotions under control when people came in for trading, but otherwise, I was slamming jars and drumming my fingers against the counter. With every breath I took, I was more ready to tear the shelves from the wall. What was meant to calm, only seemed to fuel the heat in my veins.

It wasn't until nearly nightfall, when I was putting everything away, that I saw Corinna. She bounded through the door of my stall, grinning from ear to ear. "What are you planning for the rest of the night?"

The moment she walked in was the moment I should have been ready to tear the smile from her face.

But every emotion collapsed within me.

Corinna was acting under Haiden's orders, but she was also my friend.

Somehow, there was a hierarchy—and I was at the bottom of it.

I had not done anything to deserve it, but perhaps my mother's influence had gotten to Haiden. I'd heard the murmured myth. Even still, I was one of the few under his direct rule, and my mother only garnered me negative attention. While she was likely the only reason I was under Haiden, she also had the ability to snatch it away.

I sighed a hot breath. "I don't know, Corinna. I'm still trying to wrap my head around your question earlier."

She frowned. "I can't tell you anything further, you know that."

I couldn't help but push. "Why does Haiden need to be reminded about when Nedfin is supposed to arrive next?"

Her jaw clenched. "I told you. I'm under strict orders not to say anything further."

"I told you—"

"I asked a question. You gave an answer. I cannot say anything more on the matter."

I forced myself not to flinch at how she cut off my words.

With anger heating my blood, my nails elongated to claws that could rip through life. "I'm going hunting. Don't follow me."

There was no bite to my words. If anything, I deflated the moment they left my mouth.

Leaving Corinna there, in my stall, I had no desire to close up for the night. She was one of Haiden's top warriors; she could figure out how to blow out the candles and shut the door. Locking doors seemed unnecessary when her whole purpose was to protect the borough.

I raced up the stone steps, shifting in time for my paws to land on the final step.

I RIPPED through a few rabbits and now have a raccoon clenched between my teeth. The moment I shifted, my skin stopped itching under the sway of the moon. I had been itching to detect movement. Itching to release the predator growling inside me.

A howl built in my wolf throat, my fur standing on end as my thoughts whirled.

Shapeshifters originated from wolves, so my animal skin was anything but special. We began as wolves when we climbed from the Great Spirit, slowly evolving into other animals over time. Most represented a shifter's personality, but a wolf was viewed as nothing special.

That was where the dismissal and disgust from my own people began.

But it was a myth that further damaged me.

The last wolf shifter to me had fallen in love with a Viking. Somehow. By some revolting tragedy. Since my blessing from the Great Spirit, murmurs about Vikings having some sort of power over shifters spread through the borough. As if another wolf shifter could be influenced to look past an ancient rivalry to fall in love with another.

The thought made bile rise in my throat, silencing my howl.

That was why Corinna couldn't tell me anything. Why Haiden barely paid me any heed. Disappointment spread the day of my blessing, and I continued to be punished for something beyond my control.

My fate was up to the glowing fruit hanging from the limbs of the Great Spirit.

As the hours wore on, night turned into early morning, when the stars were given the chance to shine as brightly as they wished. Although I couldn't see the moon, the light breaking through the trees was enough to send shudders rippling down my spine. Enough to feel its pull, causing my blood to thrum while my heart thumped in my ears.

Each breath I released floated away in a whisper of curled frost, and each intake singed with the frigid air. I breathed the cold deep into my lungs, searching beyond the silent entanglement of trees and subtle shimmers, the flurries painting the branches, and the leaves and glistening forest floor. Snowflakes twinkled when they passed the rays of moonlight peeking through the branches. They clung to my fur and melted beneath my paws.

Still holding the limp corpse of the raccoon between my maw, I scrutinized every shimmer my eyes caught when the smallest of breezes swept through the trees, and a shudder ricocheted down my spine.

As the breeze glided by, I sniffed the air and was again met with the cold, wateriness of snow with a tinge of pine.

Then … a hint of sand.

I stiffened, my paws digging into the snow as I nearly dropped my catch.

There wasn't a grain of sand in Waylria. Forests and soil covered our land, not desert wastelands. Hardly anyone traveled so deep into Waylria unless they planned a trade, let alone did anyone threaten Waylria.

I tasted the air again to get a sense of where it was coming from, but without the breeze, I couldn't catch it and didn't have the restraint to wait for another. Heart pulsing, I studied past the trees in front of me, every muscle in my body stiff with focus.

Perhaps it was nothing. Perhaps no one was here.

But my senses were gripped with attention, warning me to be cautious.

I hadn't heard approaching steps in the snow. I hadn't smelled anything out of the ordinary until now, or so much as sensed another presence.

Focusing on every detail around me, I waited for the slightest hint of movement. My entire body was thumping, warming my blood and escalating the thrill that stole all feeling from my legs. Every part of me was wound tight, and my surroundings were so still, I began to question if I had imagined the whispered scent of sand.

Slowly, ever so slowly, I crept behind a tree with a cluster of bushes and continued to watch through the shrubs, ducking low as I waited for the slightest of sounds. I had stopped breathing to keep my breath from stirring the air. Though, there was no movement in the shadows beyond where I stood.

Luckily, the faint brush of snow came before my patience wore thin.

Only a few trees separated me from the sharp intake of breath that came.

I tore from my hiding place, my heart stuttering with a surge of excitement.

A towering figure burst from a cluster of trees and underbrush a few yards away.

The sudden movement stirred a feral growl from the depths of my chest, but I didn't hesitate, taking off into a run to catch the intruder. I only ground my teeth when I skidded across the snow.

Twigs snagged at my clothes; snow fell from pine needles as I ran past. Otherwise, the forest around us echoed with tense silence.

Between the needled branches, I caught glimpses of the broad figure whenever they dashed through the pockets of light. Long, unbound hair. Worn and dirty clothes that appeared to be wet in some spots. A weapon in hand. Moonlight reflected off the ax clutched beneath white knuckles.

When I breathed in the air again, a male's scent mingled with the sand.

I bit back a growl, a confident need coursing through me. A need thrilled with the chase and whirling scents. A need begging me to catch him. I wouldn't let him get away.

I couldn't. Not when so much was at stake.

Panting through a clenched jaw, I pushed my legs harder, my lungs burning.

How long had he been there before I detected him? How did he get so close without giving himself away? How had I not heard or sensed him?

Cursing under my breath, I pushed my body harder until the trees around me were a blur of contorted shadows. I darted around them without seeing them, my instincts telling me exactly where each tree stood. My eyes were on the intruder, my target, my prey.

Closing in, I moved from behind to loop around the trees

beside him, knowing once we reached the small clearing ahead, there would be nothing to separate us. Once he broke into the moonlight, there would be nowhere for him to hide. Only the dense forest kept me from reaching him now.

Looking through the trees between us, I saw the intruder burst into the clearing, then hurtled into him, feeling as if I'd thrown myself against a wall of stone as my breath left me. He crashed to the ground, gripping my legs, taking me with him. We rolled—both of us sharply inhaling before he landed on his stomach with me braced above him, having righted myself.

I was panting even though my body wasn't crying out for air. My lungs were merely trying to calm the blood pounding through me like wildfire, from the chase and the shock of catching my intended target.

Before he could move—before he could take in a single, shuddering breath—I shifted into my human form. I kept my nails elongated to claws, though, and held them against his neck hard enough to warn him but not hard enough to draw blood. Not yet.

Straddling him, my knees dug into his sides to keep him trapped, I glowered at him even though his face was half hidden in shadow by the ground. The clench of his jaw on the other half was illuminated, along with the tension of his body beneath mine. It wasn't from fear, though. He wasn't intimidated by me or the claws against the sensitive skin of his neck.

When he looked back up at me, the ire in his eyes scorched through me as they assessed me. Relying on my adrenaline to keep my confidence, I bent as close as I dared with him pinned below me.

A snarl ripped through my teeth. "Now, why don't you tell me why you are in Waylria before I kill you."

Chapter Six
Riker

I GROUND my teeth as my chest heaved, fury barreling through my veins. Snow had soaked through my shirt. I didn't feel the sting of it or register anything other than my raging blood and the revolting creature above me.

Her snarled words were still rebounding off the trees, quieting as they traveled through the forest. Though I couldn't fully see her, I felt the sharpness of her gaze and her revolting claws biting into my neck with equal malice.

I swallowed the repulsion of having her so close, my fingers eager for the ax lying just out of reach. It would take little effort to grab for it and wield it against her. Then, at least my anger would have a release.

"Are there more of you?" she went on when I stayed silent, pressing her sharp nails harder against my neck. "Are you the only one, or are there more of you?"

I bit back every horrid answer I could've given her. My blood bellowed hotter the more I struggled to breathe, my lungs unable to pull in enough air with her weight above me.

The whiteness of her bones would blend with the snow.

That had been my first thought after spotting her wolf form

trotting through the snow with a raccoon between her fangs. Before I quickly ducked into the densest underbrush.

I had hoped she would eventually leave so I could continue on.

But something had triggered her senses.

And my slip in the snow had sent her straight for me.

I wouldn't make that mistake again. My next strike would not miss.

"That is none of your fucking concern, foul wolf," I spat in her language.

Her eyes blew wide, but I wrenched one of my arms out from under her, reaching for my fallen ax as I propelled to my side. Her nails scarcely left my neck unscathed. I slammed her against the ground, my fingers grazing the hilt of my ax, and pinned her arms before climbing on top of her to trap her. She tried to recoil, blinking rapidly when she found herself immobilized.

She snarled up at me the only way a disgusting shapeshifter could.

I pushed her into the ground harder, roaring in her face, matching her savage expression. I was practically trembling with rage, my body hot despite the bitter-cold air cutting through my clothes.

"Let me go!" she gasped out.

Her eyes blazed, and my mind clouded over.

She tensed as I perched myself on her legs with my knees, the full weight of my body holding her to the ground. She hissed in warning but did not flinch or cry out, barely having time to process what was happening before my hands were at her throat.

My hands tightened, digging hard into her trachea. Fingers clawed at me, scratching down my arms. The cuts stung, leaving trails of angry skin.

I savored the sight of her contorted expression as I grasped harder, my nails leaving indentations at the back of her neck, and satisfaction coursed through me at getting to use my bare hands against the foul creature foolish enough to believe she could win against me.

"You're all the same—just as barbaric as the legends portray your kind," I bit out, my face inches from hers. I wished I could demolish her under the torment of my ax instead.

Her body stiffened, but instead of trying to speak around my unwavering grip, she writhed beneath me.

Then, before I could react, the girl morphed into a wolf. My eyes bulged as a heaviness fell into my stomach, chilling me. The creature bared its teeth with a convulse and buck of its body.

I fell back, disoriented from watching the shift so closely— from having touched it during. But I did not move in time. Not before her teeth caught my wrist.

The pain was sharp, piercing and as strong as her unrelenting canines.

I swallowed the shout threatening to burst from my throat. I wanted to lash out, scramble away from the beast, but I couldn't show weakness.

It could smell fear—sniff out inferiority.

Her teeth tore my flesh as she shoved me away. I landed on my palms, ready to jump to my feet despite the ache seething up my arm. My gaze shot to the ax resting out of reach behind her, the ghost of her teeth embedded in my skin.

With her on her feet, the moon glistened off the snow and revealed my blood coating her mouth.

Clenching my hands into fists, I held her deadly stare. I *would* make her bleed before this was over. I didn't care about her animal skin, only about crushing her until she was nothing but powder in the snow.

Her body warped again, and she stood on two feet as a human, heaving to catch her breath.

She eyed me up and down, waiting, knowing I would make

a move for it, analyzing everything she could to pinpoint a weakness.

"Are there more of you?" she demanded. Again, I didn't answer; I didn't react to her. She couldn't speak to me unless in her humanlike form, but I didn't have to answer. In this moment, I dared not think of anything outside of surviving.

Her eyes briefly fell to the emblem ingrained in the handle of my ax a few feet away. "What's wrong, Viking? Not much of a talker?" She grinned. "That's all right. I'll get you to talk soon enough."

I saw red and lunged straight for my weapon, snatching it up to whirl on her.

The weight of my battle-ax was a reassurance. The smoothness of the wood against my palm hardened my confidence, had me wielding its weight as I turned to send the curved blade straight for her.

I heard her sharp intake of breath—the only surprise she revealed before she went rigid and twisted to avoid my blow. Except, the momentum of her whirl fell short, so the hook of my blade grazed her left shoulder.

She staggered forward slightly, clutching her razored shoulder and breathing heavily, her canines still stained with my blood. Upon lifting her head, her green eyes locked with mine, burning with hatred as she cursed under her breath.

In an instant, a wolf was left standing in the girl's place, canines still bared, hackles raised to kill. The wolf's green eyes were trained on me, a low growl rumbling through her body.

The grip on my ax tightened.

Varúlfur.

Nothing laid discarded in the snow around her. Not a stitch of the clothing she'd been wearing. Only the large brown wolf that had shredded through the girl's skin, the thin cut on her shoulder turning her fur crimson.

I had hunted many of her kind before.

Shapeshifters were disgusting creatures that thrived off savage bloodlust.

Beasts with centuries of our ancestors' blood coating their fur.

Our stories spoke of packs raiding our clans with vicious intent to spill and taste the blood of our loved ones. Each and every one of us had committed plenty of these stories to memory, as they'd been passed down the moment we could take our first steps.

I was ready when she leaped, propelling my ax in front of me to keep her at a distance. She crouched, fur standing on end while her focus stayed locked on me. When she backed away from my swinging blade, I hurled it at her again.

That seemed to be the very thing she wanted, as it gave her the opening to lunge for my wounded wrist again.

I flinched back at the closeness of her bloodstained mouth. But I wasn't quick enough to avoid her wrestling the ax from my hand. She threw it, wasting no time to charge at me.

Chest rising and falling with lethal rage, I was ready when she did. With her jaw snapping inches from my face, I caught her thrashing body and flung her into the nearest tree.

She didn't have so much as a second to brace herself. Then she slumped to the ground, half propped against the base of the trunk. Light swallowed her limp form, and she was human once again, clothed and still armed with her vile ability to lengthen her claws and fangs.

"I'll get you to talk soon enough." I scoffed, retrieving my ax before stomping toward her. Of all the shapeshifters I had hunted and captured for sacrifice, I wanted this one to be conscious. I wanted her to look at me as I bashed her head in.

But her eyes were closed, and most of her features were shrouded in darkness. No breath was visible. No movement. Her eyelids didn't so much as flutter open.

With the ax above my head, I paused, needing to find a way to speak to Waylria's chief. Killing one of their kind was not going to convince them to side with me against my father. My scent would be all over the girl at my feet. They would hunt me rather than listen —

The girl shot up, locking her legs around me and hurling me to the ground. She forced my ax from my grip again as she tackled me to the forest floor, flinging snow.

Her chest rapidly rose and fell as I fought to get her off me, but she held fast, grabbing my weapon, then slamming the hilt into my face.

I blinked against the rattling in my skull and reached for her through the darkness swallowing me, needing to get my hands around her neck.

My head swam when she brought the hilt down a second and then a third time, blackness bordering my vision. Before it could absorb the remainder of my sight, another figure came racing up behind her. My eyes shot back up to the girl's before everything faded into darkness.

Chapter Seven
Zyra

LIZETH CAME up beside me in the same moment the invader's head hit the ground, nearly missing a protruding root. I gasped, wringing my hands together before looking up at her. When I'd shifted forms earlier, she had been the only one close enough to hear my calls through our linked minds. I had worried about overpowering him before and knew I could call someone for aid.

"What is he doing here? Where did he come from?" Lizeth asked after shifting into her human skin, worry radiating from her. She warily approached, keeping her eyes locked on him.

My heart was pounding furiously, making it nearly impossible to inhale a full breath. Unable to believe what I had done, I couldn't bring myself to look down at him.

"We need to get him to the passage and down to the cells," Lizeth continued, tearing her gaze from the intruder to face me. There was no fear in her eyes, only determined interest. "Help me?"

The thought of carrying his hulking frame sent my heart into my throat. I had chased, attacked, and won against him—my instincts taking over to protect me and mine—yet the thought of touching him again made my skin crawl.

We needed to know why he was here. What was coming. We would need to be prepared for whatever threats we might soon face. Lizeth, too, seemed to be aware of the sickening possibilities.

Flinching from my own thoughts, I refused to allow my mind to wander to those possibilities. Not yet. Nor would I allow myself to consider what might have happened if his strength had won out against my own. Such thoughts of being so close to our enemy, so close to becoming a sacrifice, caused my body to tense and my nails to bite into my palms. Bile rose in my throat at how the gash in my shoulder throbbed.

The throbbing only worsened when I helped carry him from the bottom of the forest hill up to the cave. With the intruder's weight burdening each of our shoulders, the snow sloshed beneath our feet, causing us to stumble and nearly drop him several times. Our heavy breaths clouded the air in front of us, and I failed to answer nearly all of Lizeth's questions. I didn't know anything, and I could hardly think past the pain. Then the glowing warmth of the cave made our breaths invisible once again.

There were stairs upon stairs to climb down with this brute before we would even reach the paths that split off throughout the borough. But there was only one place we could take him.

Lizeth and I walked down each step, awkwardly carrying the intruder, hoping not to skid and tumble the rest of the way. Snow melted off our boots, making the steps slippery. I bit back against the discomfort spreading through my shoulder, straining to hold his weight and focus on my steps. Stares fell upon us. Shifters looked our way, gazed out of homes, or openly gawked from the paths. There was too much —

A screech ricocheted off the walls above us. Our heads snapped up, and a familiar raven glided over us, leisurely drifting to the far side of the cave.

Even more stares fell upon us.

Soon, either Nabil or Corinna would be screeching to

Haiden, feeding him everything their beady eyes had observed while flying over us. My heart sank at the thought of Haiden waiting for us. We would have to move quickly—before he grew impatient for the details his spy couldn't gather.

Reaching the final step, we rushed down the far-right path, his feet now dragging across the stone floor. Then we crept behind the waterfall and down the passage there.

Although none of the cells lining the wall were full, we chose to throw him in the second chamber. Fidgeting with the key, I turned away from our caged enemy.

Lizeth stepped back, her mind seeming to be reeling as much as mine. Her eyebrows were pinched. Every part of my body felt both alive and numb.

What if there were more—others? Could we fend off their brutal attack? Would Haiden want those beneath him to fight, or would he command all shifters to defend the borough?

A red-cloaked figure appeared before my mind could spiral further.

"Caught yourself a new plaything?" Corinna asked with a smirk, crossing her arms over her chest.

Lizeth jumped at the sudden human appearance of Corinna, which made me flinch beside her.

Corinna noticed her weakness. "Go back to patrol. You need to be on the lookout. We don't know if there are more. Be on high alert but don't spread word about this."

Lizeth only nodded before turning on her heel to head for the forest. Corinna barely looked at her. Instead, her stare was locked on the cell behind me.

I followed her gaze to the sprawled figure cloaked in the shadow of the cell. I could only make out his dirty clothes and the rapid motion of his chest, assuring I hadn't accidentally killed him when I slammed the hilt into his skull.

"I didn't sense anyone else," I said to Corinna. Though I was not involved in much between Haiden, Corinna, and Nabil, I knew enough to understand my reassurance meant little. Either no one would believe me or an invasion from the Vikings was around the corner.

Our eyes left the prisoner to lock on one another. Her next words came out in an almost growl. "Then why else is he here? We need to know if Sandire is planning an attack."

"I didn't exactly have time to ask questions while I was taking him out, and then he was unconscious the whole way here."

Her smirk returned. "I'm sure we'll find out more about our guest once he wakes up."

Corinna turned to start down the passage leading to the other end of the waterfall, where Haiden was undoubtedly waiting in his quarters. He would have several things to snarl about when I walked in. The thought of his massive tiger form stalking around his desk provoked the tension in my body. I straightened my shoulders, holding my head high as I prepared myself for his questioning.

Noticing my rightened posture, Corinna's glare went to the cut on my shoulder. "You let him get close."

I paused, my thoughts whirling. "He had an ax."

Corinna nodded gravely, her mouth set in a serious line. "He can't be the only Viking. They've never advanced this far onto our lands, and they always hunt us in groups. Sandire wouldn't be foolish enough to come without an army. They wouldn't come to the heart of Waylria without a plan."

A figure glided to the ground before feathers fell away to be replaced with pants and a tunic. The change from bird to man was sudden as a voice echoed from the other side of the passage.

"I informed Haiden that you were on your way," Nabil said when we drew closer, his voice straining to be louder than the waterfall. No one outside the passages could hear us over its steady plummet. "Did you take the prisoner to the cells?"

I gave a timid nod.

He spun on his heel to lead the way—as if we hadn't been to Haiden's quarters hundreds of times before.

Corinna kept pace behind him, each stride long and strong —powerful, like Corinna herself. I had always envied my friend's strength. She did not need to rely on her animal skin to be tough. She worked to make herself fierce in both her human and animal skin.

As I tried to match her speed, she caught me watching her and smiled. Her dark hair swirled around her body, standing out against her pale skin while somehow brightening her tattoos. Corinna pointed to Nabil and feigned plucking feathers. I snickered as we reached the doors of Haiden's quarters, his two guards standing watch on either side.

Inside, Haiden was pacing behind his desk, nearly as I had imagined. Except he was on two legs rather than four paws. He looked up, momentarily halting to narrow his eyes. His mouth went slack, making the scar disappearing into his dark beard look considerably rigid and pale.

He stiffly gestured for us to take the chairs before his desk, though he didn't speak or move to take his own seat. Rather, he picked up where he left off with his pacing.

I swallowed, sitting still in my chair, watching Haiden's mind work. Beside me, Corinna sat on her hands and looked everywhere but at Haiden. Attempting to sit still under the tension plaguing the room, I ran my hands along the armrests of the chair and fought the urge to dig my claws into the wood.

With the doors closed, the trickling of the waterfall was faint, like the drops sliding down the slick walls of the office. The alcoves, untouched by the precipitation, were filled with books, jars, and other trinkets.

Haiden stopped behind his chair, bracing his hands on the back of it, claws digging into the material. His voice was strained when he finally looked hard at me and spoke. "This could end up being a bloodbath. Are we checking to make sure there aren't others?"

There was no swallowing around the sudden dryness of my throat before I answered.

"I didn't detect others, but in any case, we sent Lizeth to run the parameters to be cer—"

"How did you know he wasn't one of our allies from Nedfin, or even Urute?"

I nearly bit my tongue at the interruption while Corinna scuffed beside me. "I didn't need to see him up close to know he wasn't from Nedfin," she told Haiden. Then, quietly to me, she added, "He certainly doesn't have the body of someone from Nedfin. Definitely a Viking."

Ignoring her comment, I said, "The scent. I smelled sand; it was the first thing I noticed."

Haiden waited, his catlike eyes piercing.

Brawling with the Viking had left me drained, my limbs heavy as I struggled to keep my mind focused. Now that I was free of his weight, my shoulder had dulled to an ache that was barely noticeable.

"He also had the build of a warrior, was wearing dirty clothes, and had long hair," I went on under Haiden's demanding gaze. "The Fey are too vain to wear such filthy clothes, and Nedfin does not produce weaponry or chance wielding one for fear of breaking their vow of peace. None from either realm would have felt the need to run from me either. That left only one option—which was that he was a Viking." I pressed my lips together and sat back in my chair, hoping my answer was satisfactory.

Haiden's hands tightened on the back of his chair, his knuckles nearly white. Still, the material did not split. His eyes became slits as he prowled from behind his desk.

My stomach dropped, and Corinna went rigid beside me.

He took in a long, calculated breath through his nose, but his eyes remained slits. A few moments passed before he spoke again. "Sandire could be planning an attack. We need to find out what the Viking is doing here. Can he understand our language?"

I gave a slight nod. "I don't know how, but yes."

"I'd imagine they learned so they could slander us in our own language before slaughter."

After hunting us for their sick sacrifices to their gods, it was not at all that surprising. Any who drew close enough to a Viking did not get away alive. Because of that, we had never gained the opportunity to learn their language.

"If he can speak the tongue of his enemies, then he shouldn't have trouble answering our questions," Corinna seethed. "I wouldn't put an attack past them—it's been years in the making." From the corner of my eye, I saw her lean forward until she was barely perched on the edge of her seat. "We need to know if they're planning a slaughter. We need to do away with our *guest*"—she spat the word—"and send Sandire a message. We will not go down without a fight."

"I agree," Haiden said, "but I don't think we should dispose of our guest yet. As soon as he wakes, I want you to question him."

Bile rose in my throat when he caught my chin and lifted my eyes to his. I held back from swallowing until he released me, my heart stuttering. His eyes darkened as his stare lingered on us both. "Later in the morning. Use any method at your disposal."

With no other response acceptable, Corinna and I nodded our understanding. The Viking did not need to be in one piece when we finished with him.

I could practically feel Corinna's excitement. She'd always wanted the chance to repay the Vikings for their cruelty—make them suffer for those of us they had sacrificed. I couldn't agree more, but I wasn't nearly as vindictive. I couldn't imagine doing more than standing in the corner.

But I was being given an opportunity.

Not only was Haiden giving me a command, but I was set to work beside Corinna.

"Tell me you understand," he snarled, the slits of his eyes clouding with utter demand. "I want to hear you say it. Tell me you understand and you will get those answers."

"We understand," Corinna and I said in unison.

He gave a nod. "Then you are dismissed."

Without another word, we left, remaining silent well after the doors had shut behind us. My heart was fluttering faster than a hummingbird's wings—near ready to burst from my chest. I had to clench my hands to keep them steady.

It was only after we reached the waterfall that Corinna turned to me with a wicked smile. "Tomorrow morning should be fun. We haven't had the chance to deal with a Viking before."

"It's morning now," I pointed out, my stomach still in knots. "And if either of us can get the brute to talk, it's you."

"You make me sound so savage." Her smile widened before she sighed. "They say Vikings do not fear anything, but I suppose we shall test that legend soon."

I forced a smile but couldn't hold it for more than a second. I wanted to go home. My head was swimming in denial—and I was still tense from our meeting. With exhaustion trembling through me and unease chasing behind it, my body was barely holding on. It probably didn't help that I still hadn't tended to my shoulder.

She pursed her lips. "Breakfast as usual?"

"See you bright and early."

"You know what they say, don't interrogate on an empty stomach." With that, Corinna spun on her heel, leaving me alone at the end of the passage.

Slowing my steps, I touched my shoulder, the quick bite of his ax slicing across it burned into my mind. The gash stung but was shallow and had already stopped bleeding.

Feeling it didn't help the nausea rolling in my stomach, though.

With my home at the far end of the cave, built into the rock in the back, I wished I could fly. As I mindlessly passed the moss, stones, and wildflowers that decorated the ground in a seemingly organized fashion, it felt like hours before I reached my front door.

Once the door was shut behind me, my eyes adjusted to the dark after a blink. Like all homes, mine was empty of the glowing fruit. Candles were one of the only ways to light our spaces. No one could pick or eat the glowing fruit hanging from the limbs of the Great Spirit. Each and every one was meant to be savored for rituals. Though, if we were lucky enough to have one fall, it was saved by the shamans until ready to bless the young shifters set to discover their animal skin. The ritual took place every spring, and there was always just enough to congratulate them by smearing some of the fruit across each of their foreheads. It was sacred and believed to strengthen their animal skins.

I, however, was lucky enough to have eyes that adapted to the dark.

Padding away from the entrance to the kitchen, I released a sigh. Not bothering to light a candle since I planned to head straight for bed afterward, I pulled a tin from the medicine cabinet above my water basin. Pouring water from the pitcher resting beside it, I dampened a soft cloth.

The first touch of the damp cloth was soothing enough that I closed my eyes.

They only snapped open again when my thoughts drifted to what I'd been commanded to do. Disobeying was out of the question. I had to show up come sunrise and take part with Corinna. Haiden wouldn't let disrespect go unpunished in any way, shape, or form.

Shapeshifters had never encountered a Viking so close to our home—never had to perform an interrogation before.

While Corinna was ready to enact vengeance, I wasn't sure what I felt. I could decipher the anger for everything Sandire continued to do to us and felt the determination to get answers for the sake of protecting Waylria, but my stomach twisted at the thought of how far things could go.

But I was being included, not sidelined as I had been.

Perhaps that would give me the strength to do what was deemed necessary.

Discarding the towel, I twisted the top off the healing salve. My muscles were still wrung tight, adrenaline subsiding with each beat of my heart. My shoulder barked in pain as I eased the salve over the dark-pink cut.

Pushing every thought to the back of my mind, I put away the tin. With the herbs already working to mend the wound, I didn't bother bandaging it. The salve would dry over the cut, and my shoulder would be as good as new within a few hours.

I didn't remember stripping down to my undershorts before I stumbled into bed. Still, I curled under my covers and closed my eyes tighter against the thoughts of torture and death. To pretend Waylria wasn't in potential danger and my enemy wasn't sleeping on the other side of the borough.

Chapter Eight
Riker

DAMP. The earth under my cheek was damp. My wrist was raw and torn and stinging. The butchered skin throbbed with a vengeance as I slowly pushed myself from the cool ground. I clamped down on several curses, hissing a breath through clenched teeth; the air was slick with mildew and moss.

Sitting up, I tore my eyes from my mangled wrist to take in everything around me. I was surrounded by shadowed darkness but could make out the bars of the cell containing me and the bordering damp walls. I released a long, hot breath—my anger spiking when my eyes landed on the iron bars lodged in the stone floor. The other walls were thick stone that blocked out all shred of light, leaving me questioning what time of day it was.

My hand fell in search of a weapon—even though I did not feel its weight fastened to me.

My ax had been stripped from me.

Forcing my way out would prove difficult without it.

Fights always ended with me bashing in the skulls of my opponents, or plunging my weapon through them, or with my ax coming down to utterly obliterate them. I seldom lost.

I should not have underestimated the girl.

But I would not make that mistake again.

My father's voice rang in my ears. *"You should have known better to begin with."*

Legends spoke of their savagery. Our duty to hunt the monsters spoken in legend was known across our land. It was what I was built and born to do, like so many others in our village.

Hunting shifters was in our blood. Every story that told of shapeshifters destroying villages and mutilating the remaining bodies pounded through our veins. Stories that claimed shifters didn't even devour those who lived in the villages but instead fed off the sounds of their agonized screams was what fueled every hunt. Each shapeshifter sacrificed to our gods was a blessing because it meant one less beast in the realms.

Yet I was here. I had crossed their borders on my own.

What if this was the wrong way to save my family? What if Father reacted senselessly when finding out where I had gone? Lashed out at his remaining family? What if this was the wrong way to stop him?

Pressing the heels of my palms into my eye sockets, I fought against the dull ache in my chest. I had come so far. I could not abandon what I had set out to do, to save. My family would not last if Father was not stopped. He was too mad, too lost, too out of control.

Gritting my teeth as I got to my feet, I directed my focus to the bars.

I was already here. It would be at least a day before my father received word of my location. By now, it would be too late to stop communications between the men hunting me and the man who wanted me dead.

I had made it far enough to receive shelter. Now I needed to barter for my freedom—my life, and information was the only way to ensure my survival.

Before someone came for me and decided to kill me in the

same brutal way we killed them, I had to find a way to make myself invaluable.

Needing to clench the hilt of my ax, my hand wrapped around air at my hip as I stepped up to the bars of the cell.

I had heard plenty of old stories about captivity around bonfires—torture, questions, humiliation … death surely around the corner, but Vikings were always the captors; never the captured.

We had caught and abducted countless shapeshifters. Sometimes, we sacrificed their kind by burning them and ripping their chests open to throw their pounding hearts into the reaching flames. Other times, we cut them open and drained their blood.

Few gave up information, and none left Sandire alive.

After all we had done to one another, would I even be believed? Would they walk in and execute me on the spot? Why bother putting me in a cell?

I stalked along the bars, trying to find one that was loose. I would not die here. Not without speaking to someone first.

I had to try. For my family, I had to try.

I yanked on every bar, my arms quivering under the strain, but they were lodged deep in the rock. None of them so much as moved under my strength. I even shook the door at the far end, trying to bend it to my will, but it held strong with the large lock.

Clenching them hard enough to turn my knuckles white, I stared beyond the bars again, waiting, listening to see if anyone was near or coming. With each passing second, my heart sank at the realization that someone coming for me might be my only chance. I might have to fight my way to the chief.

Chapter Nine
Zyra

STANDING in the kitchen waiting for Corinna, I thrummed my fingers along the tabletop. I stared, unseeing, at the fruit bowl I'd traded Lizeth for, fruit piled high inside it, while my thoughts went in circles, stuttering and tripping over themselves.

I was following Haiden's orders—following his every whim after ridiculing Corinna and years of exclusion. The Great Spirit had to be laughing at me, but I had to stay focused on the opportunity. After being cast aside for so long, I had to prove myself.

I needed to find the strength to keep up with Corinna today —or risk being left behind forever.

I had to show I was better than they assumed. Exceed every doubt and snide comment made by my family and crawl out of the hole they had banished me to.

"Happy Torture Information Out of a Wretched Viking Day!"

The cheer in Corinna's greeting snapped me from my thoughts. My fists relaxed to grip the edge of the table instead, my claws creating small divots.

She sauntered past me to the shelves and snatched up the closest jar, not wasting a second to unscrew the lid and tip her head back as she moseyed to the table. Gulping, she sat in the seat across from me, crossed her legs and leaned back, not letting her red cloak slow her fluid motions.

I sighed, knowing only two jars of fruit syrup remained now that she was downing one for herself, and I was willing to bet apricot syrup was one of them since she harbored a special hatred toward the fruit.

"Save it for the enemy," she said when she came up for air. "You can always make more fruit syrup. No need to get all pissy."

My heart stuttered at the comment. "Think he's awake yet?"

"And contemplating his next move? Absolutely. Wouldn't expect anything less from a Sandire brute."

Trying to hide the tremors in my fisted hands, I picked up the sweet pastry I had platted for myself this morning. Her head snapped up from her syrup before I had the chance to speak. "Ever the sweet tooth. There's probably more sugar in your veins than blood at this point."

Taking a second bite, I grinned. "You say that like it's a bad thing."

"If you would choose to eat syrup rather than take a bite from the sacred fruit, then yes, I would say you need to rethink your priorities. Your sugar habits haven't changed since we were kids."

"You still think the fruit is magical, don't you?"

Her fingers tightened around the jar. "Look at the shamans. Their talents are enhanced by the fruit when they assume their duties." A smile spread across her face. "Who's to say a bite of the fruit won't enhance my own?"

"But we're not shamans; we'll never be given the chance."

"For a daughter of a shawoman, you hold a lot of skepticism—" She swallowed another gulp of her syrup. "About the sacred fruit that gave your mother her sight into the spirit world."

"You know I love our rituals—our traditions." *So long as my mother stays far away from me.* "I just believe the fruit only blesses those already gifted."

"We all are gifted by fate. We can transform our bodies from human to animal and back again by no more than pure will. Eating the fruit could make us stronger, faster. It could help us strike fear in the very hearts of the brutes who want to sneak through our territory—"

"They do not fear, and I doubt they have hearts." My own heart sank into the pit of my stomach, sending tremors through my blood. "And if we are already so blessed, why are we hunted? Why are we wanted extinct? How can the fruit aid us in an age-old conflict? Save our people from needlessly bleeding to death for their sacrifices?"

A beat of silence passed between us. Corinna swapped her crossed legs, and I took another bite of pastry.

"A warrior with sugar in her blood asks too many questions."

"Whispers will soon spread through the borough," I pointed out. "Our prisoner is no secret by now."

She downed the last of her syrup, sliding her empty jar into the collection already on my counter. "He certainly won't be a secret once I get him to scream."

"Your idea of fun is harsh."

She pushed up from her seat and started for the door, pulling up her hood. "Don't spit all over my fun before I've had the chance to have a few words with our prisoner. We need to get going. We've wasted enough godsforsaken time."

After a roll of my eyes—and one last bite of my breakfast—I followed her, snatching my cloak from the nearby hook on the way.

A bracing silence swarmed us as we walked beside each

other on the narrow path, organizing our thoughts to face a day of relentless questioning. Words did not need to be exchanged. Sharing a meaningful glance was more than enough as we made for the passage.

I, for one, felt like my pastry was going to reemerge any moment.

Chapter Ten
Riker

MY ANGER FESTERED as time passed. I wanted to lash out, punch the walls, pry the bars apart with my bare hands. Vikings were strong, but we didn't carry such inhuman strength. Adrenaline was still pouring through me, my anger fueling it like kindling to a fire, and making me crave for such things to be possible. My breathing was deep with it, ragged. I took in and released one hot breath after another.

Then I heard footsteps.

I did not know how much time had passed or how long I had been unconscious beforehand. It did not matter. Now was the time to act.

I was still in front of the bars, sneering as two figures drifted into view.

My focus went to the figure in the blood-red cloak, hood drawn up to keep their face hidden in shadow. "It looks pretty angry," a female said from under the hood, with a click of her tongue.

Turning from her, I allowed myself a moment to take in the girl who had tackled me in the forest—the one I still wanted to crush into snow-like powder. Her cloak was darker than the night sky above the dunes, but she hadn't bothered to wear her hood.

Lean but proven strong after her assault, the girl held herself casually, but by the set in her shoulders, I knew she was anything but relaxed. She crossed her arms over her chest, studying me, the cloak pushed back enough to reveal more of her almond skin. Deep-brown near-corkscrew curls cascaded just below her shoulders.

As if sensing my harsh amusement, her eyes narrowed, reminding me of the wolf that had formed from her skin, muzzle trembling with the growls snaking up her throat as she'd thought about ripping out mine. Hatred and disgust rippled through me, causing a shudder to thunder down my spine.

When the female voice came from the red cloak again, I somehow knew she was wearing a sly grin. "Ready to have a bit of fun, Viking?"

A third set of footsteps echoed down whatever passage they were coming from.

His eyes slid to me before he even halted beside the other two. While his attention was on me, mine went to what was gripped in his hand. Iron handcuffs. The very same we used to restrain the shapeshifters we caught to prevent them from shifting.

"I have information that might interest your chief," I said in a rush.

With the male shapeshifter now beside her, the shifter in the red cloak turned back to me. "Hope you're ready to beg your gods for mercy."

Further ignoring me, the male threw the cuffs into my cell, and they clinked against the ground, landing at my feet. My jaw locked. I clenched my fists so hard they twitched at my sides. I no longer felt the throbbing of my wrist. It had been replaced by pulsing rage. I let it surge to the surface as I kept my eyes on the three shapeshifters in front of me.

I would spill their blood in Odin's name before I begged the chief Viking god.

"I am here," I bit out, "because the Viking King of Sandire is losing his mind to power, and your kind, above all others, needs to know. If you let me speak to Haiden—"

"The likes of you will not speak to *our chief*," the red-cloaked shifter seethed through clenched teeth.

"Put them on," said the male, nodding to the cuffs. My gaze snapped to him, fixating. His hair was collected into a ponytail that rested over his shoulder, but it was the structure of his face that struck me. The shape wasn't completely Waylrian. His sharp chin and cheekbones—the slight way his ears were pointed—belonged to the Fey.

Urute was the closest realm to Sandire. They lived in private tranquility beneath our lands, hardly leaving their domain. The Fey did anything and everything they desired, never challenged by consequences. Even so, I had never imagined our allies to lay with filth.

"Put on the cuffs. I'm ready to have some fun," said the female hidden under the hood of red, her tone dripping with boredom. "Don't make me secure them myself. I'll be sure to hurt more than just your pride if I have to come in there."

Repulsed at the thought of having their hands on me, I grabbed the restraints. I still had a chance to get them to listen to me. I would just have to be intentional with the information I shared.

My stomach felt like an endless pit.

There was no reasoning with such beasts.

I was moving closer to the door before I had both wrists restrained. Red Cloak was the one who stepped up to the door, her posture stiff, ready to assault me. Running, though, would only worsen my chances of being heard.

She waited until both my hands were bound before moving to open the door. "Don't make us do this here, Viking," she warned. "It will not be pretty."

Snatching the chains of my cuffs, she spun around me and pressed a dagger to the back of my neck, forcing me forward, deeper into the chamber—where the cells became smaller—until we reached thick metal doors.

Inside, the space was completely isolated, blocking all outside noise and keeping all sounds from escaping. The walls were constructed of stone like the rest of the cells, except it wasn't damp. The air wasn't even humid. Far from it, the room was much cooler and much quieter without the waterfall.

In the center of the room, a wood brace hung from the ceiling, two metal cuffs affixed to it.

Torture devices hung from the left wall.

The door echoed shut.

She wrenched me toward the dangling cuffs, blood trailing down my neck. Questions and plans on how to make it out of here alive, believed, and not in the hands of my father consumed my thoughts.

I had to get them on my side—and before they decided it was pointless to keep a prisoner who did not benefit them.

"I'll tell you anything you want," I said, my voice hoarse. I hated how they likely determined I was weak—pleading to not be tortured.

But my words were true. I had come too far to speak anything less, so I was ready to withstand their torture.

The wolf shifter came forward to undo my cuffs while her friend restrained me A heaviness settled in my stomach as I watched her work, then suppressed a wince when she pulled the iron from the wrist she had destroyed with her canines.

Once it was free, she yanked my hand over my head, securing it to the board dangling from the ceiling above me. I ignored the bite of metal against the tears of my skin. She let the handcuffs fall to the ground once my hands were locked in the dangling cuffs. The dagger fell from my neck now that I was chained, and they fastened my ankles in the irons fixed to the floor.

It wasn't until then that I noticed we were the only ones in the room. The hybrid hadn't come to join in on the fun.

Red Cloak had gone to the torture devices and snatched a whip from the wall before storming back to me.

After a beat of silence, and swallowing back my disdain, I said, "I can give you information. It just might not be the information you expect." Refusing to look directly at them, I took steadying breaths, readying my body for what was about to take place.

She finally pulled back the hood of her cloak.

Dark hair framed a pale form. Sharp, red tattoos spiraled and slashed across her skin, matching her red cloak. Her voice matched the savagery of her features. She was pure Waylrian. A shapeshifter that prowled the nightmares of Viking children.

Her smirked mouth held a glint that would have been unsettling if I wasn't working to disconnect myself. "I would get comfortable. You're mine for the next few hours."

She slithered around me, dragging the whip across the floor, taunting, her petite but sharp teeth gleaming.

The wolf shapeshifter drew closer, her head tilting as her glower ping-ponged, taking in everything she could before speaking to me for the first time since entering the room. "Your wrist will have felt like a scratch before this is over." The way she spoke forced me to focus on her rather than look elsewhere.

The other shifter growled before taking the lead. I kept perfectly still as she neared, slashing the whip against the ground with a *crack*!

"What is your name?" she demanded, voice bouncing off the walls.

I clenched my jaw. A simple question with a simple answer. One I could not give up. One that might be necessary for them to believe my warning about my father. One that might get me killed if revealed. Or worse, sent back to Sandire.

My hesitation was enough to make them act.

The whip barely made a sound when raised, but it cracked against my torso with the same loud force it had thrashed the ground.

Fire flared through me. Ruthless and quick yet brutal.

I locked my jaw to keep my shout restrained behind my teeth.

Letting the blaze wash over me, I focused on a crack in the stone wall across the room, clenching my hands as the metal bit into my wrists.

It was a pain both familiar and foreign. I had dealt enough injuries to know what to expect, but I hadn't been able to prepare myself enough.

And this—this was intense as it spread.

Fever consumed my blood and skin before seeping into the marrow of my bones.

It was excruciating fire, eating away my flesh—burning hotter than the Sandire sun.

The blaze was almost impossible to work through, and I struggled to think clearly around it. Most knife wounds were quick. The pain was usually delayed, and even then, I endured. I had learned how to swallow that kind of pain and push past it to make it through a fight. To see it to the end. Lashings were like a burn. The flaming sting of it was so much worse than the sound that came with raising it and the sound it made when it walloped against flesh.

"I merely asked for your name, Viking. It's a simple answer." The tattooed shifter practically spat. "Are you going to submit?" she asked, her voice chasing the echo of her whip.

"*Ek mun ekki nafn mitt þik gefa.*" I managed to bite out through gritted teeth. My muscles clenched as I waited for the next slash.

But she didn't raise it. She was dragging it out, waiting until I wasn't expecting it.

Without looking at the other girl—without breaking her

fierce stare from me, she said a name in the form of a command. "Zyra."

I did not back down from the tattooed beast in front of me. Did not break our gaze to look at the shifter who had brought me here to begin with.

"I have something else I can tell you—something I need to tell your chief about," I tell them, struggling not to pant at each word.

I could not tell them my name without being gutted, but I might be able to convince them of my father's intentions without revealing too much.

From the corner of my eye, I saw her move. The girl—Zyra—hesitated to push off from the wall to cross the room to the torture devices. However, she didn't reach for anything that hung there. Instead, she crouched in front of the brazier resting in the corner.

Then the nameless beast struck with her whip again.

My knees buckled, but the cuffs made sure I stayed standing.

I barely swallowed my shout. My entire body was burning with pain. The heat spread farther and lasted longer.

With my fists loosening, I slouched against it and slowly released the breath I'd been holding.

The pain rose—until my ears were ringing.

Sweat dripped into my eyes, and I blinked against the blur bordering my vision.

Question. Silence. *Crack.* Question. Silence. *Crack.*

Again, and again, and again.

Chapter Eleven
Zyra

THE WHIP CAME DOWN on the Viking with such harsh quickness that its crack echoed through the room like lightning. The sound was infinite with the way it reverberated off the stone walls around us—and then there was the hiss that escaped his gritted teeth. Though, despite the endless crack that came with that pain, his eyes were still bright with the same fervent challenge when he lifted his head to stare Corinna down. A stare that longed to curse us.

I turned my back on the whipping and stirred the coals with an iron rod.

When Corinna simply said my name, I knew what she wanted.

We had grown up together. Years connected us. Saying my name a certain way—without breaking her gaze from her trapped prey—had been enough to send my feet in the direction of the brazier. Enough to direct me to light the coals and set the tip of the rod in the center of them.

Corinna's whip came down fast again and again, barely giving him time to recover or brace himself for the next lash. Yet the Viking still didn't cry out.

"Why are you here?"

Another slash.

"Are there more of you?"

Another.

"Answer me!"

Every slight noise echoed through the room, the sounds crashing together in the large chamber. All imprisoned within the four walls surrounding us.

I stirred the coals one last time before rising to my feet.

She was building—not giving him enough time to answer before bringing the whip down. Not yet.

My attention going straight to her, I didn't have to imagine where Corinna's mind was. Focused, tightening her grip on the whip—she had accepted her role. With Nabil on the other side of the door, incapable of helping with the interrogation due to it being too up close and personal—because he believed no one deserved to suffer for a past they might come to regret—she was taking over. She had already pushed all her thoughts and feelings to the back of her mind to focus on getting answers for Haiden. For Waylria. She was unreachable—nonnegotiable— once she disappeared into herself.

Hard as stone, she took on someone ferocious, unrelenting. The Corinna I joked with, relied on, and hunted beside was no longer with us. She was someone else entirely; someone without an ounce of kindness or happiness in her eyes— vacant.

"Tell us your name," she seethed. "Tell us *why you are here.*"

"You are exactly what the legends say," the Viking spat. "I told you why I'm here."

She dropped her whip, only to pick up the iron rod that had been stoking in the fire of the brazier.

While I swallowed back against everything I was about to observe, his words also gave me pause.

Vikings were the cruel barbarians. They hunted shapeshifters; sacrificed us to their gods. They wanted to kill every last one of us since they thought we were monsters that did not belong on this earth. And thus, to appease their gods, we were to be hunted into extinction.

While Corinna could stand here and demand to know what more they could want with us, we all knew Vikings felt a need to massacre our entire being.

We had been waiting for the moment they had the numbers and guts to invade our lands for such a slaughter.

My anger rose. It was sickening, and I found myself wanting to take a whip to the Viking myself.

We needed to know why he was here—if his presence would turn into a bloodbath.

"Why do you need to speak to our chief when you can tell us what you have to share?" Corinna asked, grasping the iron tight, her face set in a hard expression as she stalked back to the Viking. "Tell us your intentions."

I snapped when I found his eyes searing, his jaw clenched. He was about to play with a dangerous fire—a fire that would leave him as mere ash at Corinna's feet before she was even finished with him. Yet, there was no fear in his eyes, only a challenge.

Eyeing the tip of the iron as it glowed orange, the Viking pulled against his restraints as if he couldn't help himself, stressing against the cuffs around his wrists and ankles in an attempt to put some distance between him and the rod intended for his waiting skin.

There was no way he could get out. No way he could hurt us. But we were free to hurt him to get the answers we desperately needed.

"The Viking King is hungry for more—more power, more land, just ... more."

"Why should we believe you?" I asked. "Not giving us your name is concerning enough. Why should we trust a word you say? What are you hiding?"

I ignored the chills that erupted across my skin, not turning away as Corinna pressed the glowing iron against his arm. At first, he bit down on his lip to keep from making a sound, nearly drawing blood, and his arms strained under his sweat- and blood-soaked shirt, but eventually, he started shouting against the pain.

Corinna had to yell her questions.

"We know there's more. What are you planning?"

"What is your name?"

"Are there more of you coming?"

She moved the iron a little ways down his side, giving him a fresh burn.

"No!" he bit out. "There aren't more coming. Not yet, at least."

He gasped. Anger and the stinging pain rolled off him, creeping through the room like a storm about to unleash its entirety.

"What does that mean?" I demanded, focused on the last part of what he'd said. At the same time, Corinna asked, "Does that mean Slate is coming with an army?"

"A group of them were following me," he admits, "but I lost them when I crossed into Waylria. But *I told you*, the king is hungry for more."

"Your kind, above all others, needs to know."

I couldn't push the thoughts away of how they hunted and butchered us as if we were nothing. They would kill us without a fraction of a thought. They murdered the innocent, the defenseless, the young and the old. So long as shapeshifters eventually went extinct, they did not care what they had to do.

And they slept in good conscious with such blood coating their hands.

They claimed falsehoods, spreading fabricated legends about us to justify their actions — our murders.

Desperation and fear spread through my veins, urging me forward.

His anger was like a clinging shadow. I wanted to stifle it. Replace it with punishing agony.

There was no room for fear or hesitancy in this moment … in this room … in this fight.

We had to know who this Viking was, why he was on our lands, and if war was about to finally break out between our realms.

"None of you have been this far," I finally said. "You're scouting our land to report back for an attack."

Gritting my teeth, I picked up Corinna's discarded whip and brought it down across the very arm being burned. We needed to know if our people were about to be snared in a massacre. We needed to know—to decide if we would stand and fight for our future or flee to protect our people and children. After all the Vikings had done to us over the generations, we deserved far more.

I brought the whip down again, lashing him in the same place over and over. His yells were not enough to lessen the rage howling in my ears.

"Tell us everything! Tell us now!" My voice echoed, but it wasn't as rageful as I felt.

Corinna paused, watching me. She could feel the sadness rolling off me at how we had been hunted and would be hunted if nothing was done against it while we had the chance to prepare. I swallowed against the lump in my throat and ignored the burning pit in my stomach that flared every time I raised the whip.

I might not be seen as anything more than a wolf to everyone else in Waylria, but I knew—after all I had endured —I could withstand more and be more than their expectations.

I was here, and I could help stop this.

The smell of burning skin and sweat filled the room. The Viking's heavy breaths and the sizzle of the hot iron rod were the only sounds echoing off the walls. His charred skin was feverish and red, the pain evident. Bubbled skin caused by refusing to give in to our questions.

My rage flared once more, so I brought the whip down again, again, and again.

They were the only sounds—until Corinna stepped forward again.

Until the Viking shouted.

"I'm telling the truth!" he finally bellowed in the same moment Corinna pulled the iron away from his chest. His shoulder, arm, and side were blistered and oozing, with several more traveling across his stomach. The burns stretched with each breath he took.

There was no way the burns wouldn't scar.

He sagged when the poker was finally pulled away, sweat beaded across his forehead and clung to his beard. "Slate plans to overtake the realms. It's only a matter of time before he crosses into Waylria; I couldn't imagine him not coming here first. That is all I know," he said, his voice thick and dry.

Corinna stepped forward. "And why give us this information? How do you know it? Why bother sharing it?"

Something flashed across his eyes before he answered. Some emotion or thought I could not decipher. *"Nei."*

"And what is your name?" I pressed.

Looking to me, he didn't answer. His lips were pressed into a thin line, and I could tell they contained his pain by the way his face strained. His eyes stood out against his pale features. Golden eyes which burned the same color as the cooling iron tip. Eyes that could pin someone with a mere glance. I stared at him, wondering how they hadn't stood out to me in the dark hours of this morning. As I questioned why he was here if there was no imminent threat.

"Your name?" I asked again, flashing my canines.

He looked away and said, "I've told you enough."

I stopped breathing. He hadn't. He hadn't told us anything. Admitting that Slate was plotting against us more than ever wasn't enough. It wasn't enough. What was Sandire planning? How much time did we have? Were there men waiting in the shadows of the forest? My mind spiraled as everything gnawed to the surface. What were we in danger of? What did we need to expect? We needed to prepare —

Corinna quieted my thoughts with a hand on my shoulder, signaling we were done for the day.

Chapter Twelve
Riker

Legs trembling under my weight, I'd have collapsed if my wrists weren't still bound to the board above my head, keeping me upright. Panting, each breath harsh, I struggled to gather what little strength I had. Once I wasn't hanging from the ceiling, I needed a plan for them to heed my warnings without me giving up my name. That or leave this worthless land and head northeast along the ocean to disappear deep into the mountains until I could come up with something else.

Before they decided to kill me. Before my father's men found me. I could not let either get close enough for execution.

They wouldn't expect me to try anything in my state. After inflicting burn after burn on top of each lashing, the shapeshifters would assume me too weak for an assault.

I forced my eyes to rise — to spare a glance where they were huddled at the wall of torture devices. Their gazes flicked to me often. I tried to pick up on what they were saying to each other but couldn't get my mind to focus. Their voices were muffled, their words inaudible.

My eyes straining to stay open, I let the cuffs bear some of my weight.

Even with my wrist still trapped by the biting metal, it

wasn't the leading source of my pain despite how it rubbed the tears in my skin. I barely felt the sting where Zyra had mauled me with her canines. However, I couldn't deny the scorch of the burn on my left side.

My breaths were coming in quick, heavy shudders. Each intake caused the burns across my stomach and chest to erupt in a blaze that spread through my entire body. Somehow, I was sweating and shivering at the same time and found it nearly impossible to concentrate on any one thing for more than a few seconds. My vision rimmed with darkness.

Despite my shirt being in tatters, slashed by the shapeshifter in the red cloak, to ensure nothing prevented her from pressing the rod to my exposed skin, fevered shivers racked through me.

The fire roaring through my veins was more intense than the beating sun on the dunes of Sandire. There was no way to quench it.

I tried not to examine too closely what they had done, but with the smell and sight of blood and sweat, I struggled to keep thoughts of *that night* confined in the dark corner of my mind.

I couldn't stomach seeing those haunting images now.

Or ever again.

Finally, breaking into my focus and freeing me from the images driving their way to the forefront, the girl in the red cloak—whose name was still unknown to me—broke away from Zyra to prowl toward me. She quickly followed, though, and while Red Cloak positioned herself beneath my raised arms, Zyra went to release my wrists from the cuffs.

I wanted to snap at the tattooed beast beside me, lash out like her whip and tell her I could walk on my own.

But I couldn't manage bitter words. I was too weak—in too much pain. My own rage took too much energy. I needed to save it—gather my strength and use it when the right moment arose. Just in case.

My wrists barely had the chance to feel the brush of cool

air before they were buckled back into the iron handcuffs from before. Then they went on to remove the chains around my ankles.

Despite the tremors of singed pain, I drew away from the shapeshifter beside me until I wasn't leaning on her for support. She still kept a firm hand on me, though, and a bitter laugh rose to my throat.

I was weak, but I would gather my strength — seize my anger — before we reached my cell, and a firm grip would not be able to stop me.

As if she could read my intentions, Zyra walked ahead of us to open the door, never fully turning her back to me. Her eyes stayed trained on me the entire time.

My eyes fell from her. I struggled to focus on staying upright and keeping my steps steady. My mind fought to grasp how it all had come to this — how I had gone from loss after loss to becoming a prisoner of my greatest enemy. I couldn't help but feel weak and a little confused. That never happened — it wasn't in my blood, but I had felt helpless once.

I sucked in a breath through clenched teeth when I took too quick a step.

Outside the interrogation room, the male shapeshifter pushed away from the wall, his hands falling to his sides as I was shoved forward into the passage. I bit down on my tongue to keep from groaning at the sudden movement, not wanting Red Cloak to flash another arrogant smirk. She would take joy in the pain she had caused.

I barely looked at the male shapeshifter before I was forced to move again, Zyra not far behind, tracking my every move with piqued wariness.

With each step, I reached for my strength, using my anger to pound through adrenaline. My lungs burned from the effort, and my ears rang while I pushed through the fevered fog of my mind.

I would not go down without a fight, even if I was battling against myself.

At my cell, Zyra stepped out from behind me to open the door—where I wouldn't be able to tend to my burns. Where I would be trapped with this pain for days. They would only return to inflict more burns overtop the ones already seething.

Staying might mean my death. At least on foot I had a chance of avoiding execution—from both Waylria and Sandire.

My movements were swift, faster than what should have been possible as I wrapped my fingers—sore from digging my nails into my palms while I'd braced for the iron and whip— around the hilt of the dagger resting on the girl's hip.

I denied letting the pain take over, focusing on my objective instead.

Zyra inhaled a sharp breath when she realized what was happening and moved like lightning against my fevered movements, grabbing my wrist before shoving me up against the bars of the cell.

I bit back a shout as my fresh burns burst with pain. The bars dug into my back—the only part of my body that remained unharmed. Despite that, she was not touching any of my wounds. She knew where all of them were, yet she wasn't digging into them to get me to submit—like her red-cloaked companion surely would have if their places had been reversed.

However, her avoiding them didn't make me any less angry.

"You have to listen to me." I wished I could growl with the same velocity she did. "You need to tell Chief Haiden."

"You don't want to do this. You're too weak to fight me," she said, but her hold loosened slightly. She pulled me away from the bars and shoved me into the cell, slamming the door shut so hard it rattled through the passage. As she twisted the key to lock me inside, I turned to meet her scowl one last time.

The fierceness that seemed to constantly swim in her eyes

flashed, but there was something else, too. Something I couldn't quite place.

Then she broke our stare and stalked down the passage, her cloak flowing behind her. Her companions trailed after her. Though, not without glaring in disgust first.

They would be back.

Chapter Thirteen

Zyra

When I had taken the whip to the Viking, my mind had clouded. Anger had corrupted my thoughts—claimed my body and mind. Losing myself to the harsh emotion had scared me. I felt like the bloodthirsty beast the Viking saw whenever he looked at me, and I never wanted to be that.

Anger was a powerful emotion. Safety was a powerful motivator.

But a large part of me regretted it once we were out of that room.

I felt dirty for stooping to his level.

I should be better than them—than *him*.

Torturing him did nothing but prove to him that shifters were everything Viking legends claimed.

All those burns.

And barely anything more than a warning.

He was hiding his name, putting up a wall of cruel rage to keep it sealed inside him. I had a feeling his anger was the only thing that had kept him conscious as Corinna burned him and while I had brought my whip down upon them.

His rage.

Those burns.

We could not relax until we knew of the dangers.

For our survival, we had to know. The risks were too great. Our entire existence was at risk unless we got the Viking to talk.

No matter how much I tossed and turned, I couldn't think around the possibility of our slaughter. It loomed over me like a dagger waiting to plunge. Every time I closed my eyes, I saw a leather-clad army waiting in the depths of a snowy forest to butcher shifters to extinction.

I jolted at the image, giving up on the possibility of sleep as I threw the covers back from my sweat-soaked body.

Yes, we needed answers, but I couldn't shake the image of those burns. Maybe I was weak like Haiden thought, but I certainly didn't care as I stormed into the kitchen to pull jars from my shelves.

Herbs and oils in hand, I sparked a small fire, then moved to my mortar and pestle to make a salve.

A LOUD CRASH exploded through my dream, snapping me awake. My gut knew the sound didn't belong—that it hadn't been part of the dream—and yet, I could remember none of it now that my eyes were open.

My gut twisted as I jumped from my bed, my canines bared, claws ready to defend. "What is going on?" I shouted, storming for the kitchen.

Nabil's voice floated from around the corner. "You can retract those—"

"Unless you want to cut him into itty-bitty pieces for making a mess of your kitchen," Corinna finished, her voice containing her wicked smile.

I drifted around the corner, letting my claws disappear.

Corinna was casually leaning against the wall next to the shelves, her arms crossed over her chest as a large devious smile spread across her face. She nodded, and, as I stepped farther into the room, I spotted Nabil standing in the middle of a bunch of fallen-over pots and pans. He looked up, flashing a bashful grin, his dark hair falling in his eyes.

"I made a mess, but I'm making flapjacks if that makes up for it," he told me sheepishly. He already had a few stacked on a plate.

"How long have you been here?" I asked, rubbing the remnants of sleep from my eyes.

"About two minutes," Corinna answered.

"You wrecked my kitchen in two minutes?"

Nabil handed me the plate of perfectly cooked flapjacks as a peace offering.

I eyed the messy bowl of batter. Every ingredient—from the flour to the sugar—had come from our tradings with Nedfin, as they were the only realms that had mastered such things. Between their ingredients and Nabil's impressive cooking skills—compared to the poor attempts Corinna and I usually executed—I knew they would taste as perfect as they looked.

"They look amazing," I said, my mouth watering.

"I bet they taste even better, but someone"—Corinna sent a sharp look toward Nabil—"wouldn't let me sneak a bite before you woke up."

"I bet you can't guess who's truly behind this mess," Nabil mumbled to me.

He turned his attention back to prepping flapjacks, and by the time he set them on the table, Corinna was already perched in a chair, fork poised and ready. Nabil looked back at me with wide eyes. I had to bite my lip to hold in my laugh. Corinna somehow always managed to eat enough for the both of us combined despite her size.

Her massive bites made the tattoos engraving her face

bulge. The piercings lacing up her ears jangled as she nodded to herself in pleased approval. Another flapjack was added to the pile already on her plate.

Nabil openly watched as she chowed down, practically inhaling her flapjacks.

"I see you hate my flapjacks," he said as he picked up his first while she was on her third.

"I hate the way she eats your flapjacks," I quietly grumbled.

"I was up late with Haiden last night," she said around a mouthful, pretending she hadn't heard our comments. "He's ready to end this if Sandire invades. He won't even attempt to make a deal with them. He knows every shifter in our realm would rather keep our honor and fight for our home. But he wants to make an example of the Viking, carry out a public execution before his people siege a war on us."

Silence seeped through the room.

"What does he even *want*?" I mumbled. "There's something missing. He's not telling us everything." I was on edge, my skin beginning to itch. "He won't even tell us his damn name."

"None of it makes a lick of sense, and I'm sick of being on edge all the time," Corinna growled as she stabbed another bite. "They've gone this long without assassinating shifters. No Viking has ever made it this far before. Why now?"

I had felt how close Corinna had been to snapping when she was around the Viking, ready to slip into that cold, vicious calm that sometimes swept her away. She wanted him to suffer for holding back information, and punish him for whatever he'd done before coming here.

I had a difficult time bringing her back from that scary place she slipped into.

She would do anything for Waylria and those she cared for. With her ambition to protect, there was no one more devoted.

But also no one more lethal.

At her core, Corinna was *loyal*. True, loyal, and beautiful on the inside and out, even if she sometimes did or said horrible things. She was nothing short of what she wanted to be and had the strength to do what most couldn't because she wanted what was best for our people. While doing everything she could, she still felt like it wasn't enough, and it was eating at her. She wouldn't stop without answers. Not while we all held our breath and waited for danger to present itself.

"We can't know everything," Nabil said. "But the truth will come eventually, Corinna. We just have to wait it out. Don't wish for something to happen—you might come to regret it."

I looked away when I glimpsed the admiration as he watched her.

More silence.

I was the first to break it. "I heard the baker's son shifted for the first time. His father had no idea until he found a ferret in his cookie jar munching on an almond biscuit."

Silence, followed by a burst of laughter that began with Nabil before Corinna finally cracked a smile, her own laughter ultimately blending with ours. Our cackling died away as we made to dig into our flapjacks again.

Once we were all finished, we gathered ourselves to head down the path. My gut was in knots before we even stepped out the door. And it was not because of the flapjacks.

Nabil and Corinna were chatting ahead of me, my steps having slowed when we neared the stalls. I glanced at mine, wishing I could return to my preserves instead of torture when Lizeth stepped out from her stall. Seeing her gave me pause, and Corinna seemed to sense the hesitation in my steps because she stopped in time to watch Lizeth run up to me.

Lizeth barely seemed to notice Corinna as she reached me. "Did you get anything on the Viking?"

I froze, words stuck in my throat. I could feel Corinna's stare on Lizeth like a brand, but she seemed oblivious to the seething. With the uncertainty of how much Haiden would want me to share, I felt like a fish gasping for water.

"I-I'm not sure how much I'm allowed to say right now, Lizeth."

She nodded, then side-eyed Corinna. "I understand."

My heart dropped to the pit of my stomach. "I'm sorry. I think I'm only involved because I found him."

Lizeth shook her head, returning her focus to me. "You have nothing to apologize for. I understand. This is what you wanted, and I'm glad they're finally recognizing you."

I nearly flinched at the underlying meaning of her words.

"We have an enemy to interrogate," Corinna called.

"Be careful, Zyra," Lizeth said before walking back to her stall.

I was involved. Finally. After all this time. But I needed to be careful of how quickly that could be stripped away again. I could be thrown back in the dark at any given time. With that in mind, my heart sank even further when I thought about what I had done the night before. My skin itched; the wolf inside me restless. The desire to flee to the woods was undeniable.

Still, I forced my feet to carry me toward the passage behind the waterfall.

Corinna whispered something to Nabil, who then disappeared to walk ahead of us, presumably to Haiden's chambers. I practically gulped when she turned to me.

The moment I reached the entrance to the passage, I felt a shadow at my heels. Corinna said nothing as she waited for me. I could barely lift my head to look at her.

Corinna crossed her arms over her chest. "You went to visit him." It wasn't a question, and though it didn't sound like an accusation either, she wasn't mentioning it out of curiosity.

The wolf inside me was writhing.

"I only went to give him some salve —"

"I know you gave him salve," she bit out. "I went to check on the bastard and caught him using it. You do realize the point of interrogation, don't you?"

My steps halted. "Yes, I realize the point."

After making him something to help ease the sting that came with his wounds, I placed it into a tin can I could toss into his cell without getting too close. I went straight home afterward. No lingering, no questions, no harm.

Corinna said nothing, glaring as she waited for an explanation. It didn't take long for me to snap under her gaze. "I felt sick at the thought of being no better than him."

"We still need answers, Zyra."

"And we will get those answers, Corinna," I shot back, wringing my hands together. "We're not what they think we are, and I know a bit of salve can't undo that, but I thought it would at least make me feel less disgusting."

Corinna sighed and crossed her arms over her chest, stretching the tattoos on her arm. "You shouldn't feel disgusting. You're doing what you need to for us and yourself. You're doing everything you can to keep Waylria *safe*."

I knew that. I *knew* I was doing the right thing. But the revulsion was hard to shake, especially as it denied her words. How the Viking had looked at me with sharp disdain … I felt it as if he were looking at me now, burning through me with a sneer. Taking the whip to him, though for the betterment of Waylria, left me full of regret.

I would not fall to what he thought I was. Shifters were not awful creatures undeserving to live. We were not savage killers that couldn't deny the desires of our animal forms as their legends claimed.

As I watched her, I wondered if my friend regretted the harsh measures we had to take. I wondered how she was able to put the hot iron to his skin without flinching from herself—without thinking of the torment her father had endured.

She must have buried herself deep enough to block it all out.

But I did not need her questioning my loyalty because I couldn't cut off my emotions the same way.

"I'll do whatever needs to be done," I reassured her. "To protect the borough. I won't jeopardize our safety."

"Zyra," Corinna began, "we are better than them. They can't see beyond the stories they've created—that have been handed down to them through the generations. Seeing us as anything else—it's laughable to them."

"You act like you enjoy it," I grumbled.

"I do what I have to so I can get the job done. And even then, I have to think about the shifters they've snatched."

She has to think about her father, who had been caught just inside our borders, then tortured until death before she had even left her mother's womb.

"I lost control," I admit. "I was thinking about everything we'd ever heard about Sandire's sacrifices, and I-I lost it. Bringing down that whip became easy."

"I understand, Zyra. You lost yourself in there, but giving into our anger is the only way."

Silence plagued the air around us.

"There will be no convincing them not to hunt and sacrifice us," Corinna went on. "It has been engrained in them for generations. We cannot prove them otherwise. It's what they claim their gods demand. It's what they do."

She turned to walk down the passageway, then paused when she spotted Nabil standing outside Haiden's chambers waiting for us.

That could not be good.

Corinna stared at Nabil, seeming to be thinking the same thing because her hand gripped the blade at her hip. "Vikings are hard to break. They're strong—not meant to crumble under torture. We have to figure out what he's hiding. Soon. It could mean our end if we fail."

Chapter Fourteen
Riker

SITTING with my back straight against the wall, I fought the bite of complaint my burns sent raging through me whenever I moved too suddenly or forcefully. I would not allow myself to show even the slightest discomfort. Despite the salve's best efforts to dull the blaze of my wounds, it still singed if I made a wrong move. Breathing too heavily tore at them, too.

It no longer felt like I was burning from the inside out, but my skin was still hot to the touch, and I was surviving on minimal sleep. Not because of the pain, but because I wanted to be aware if anyone came down the passage. I wanted to be awake if they came to drag me from my cell. So I forced myself to stay awake through most of the night, only falling asleep once I felt that it was too damn early in the morning for an execution and I convinced myself the cell door would make enough noise to pierce through my dreams.

Though, I had awoken when the figure of the wolf shifter threw a tin can between the bars.

It was late morning now, so I was listening for the echoed steps coming down the passage.

"Well, Viking," a voice drawled, "I think it's time we talk again."

I was sitting still in the corner of my cell when the red-cloaked shifter came for me. With a sword in one hand and the infamous iron handcuffs in the other, she entered my cell with a grim expression. I forced a snide smile. "A little early to be playing this game, don't you think?"

She threw the cuffs at me, her expression never losing its hardness. "Put these on and keep quiet. It's too early to listen to your bullshit."

I stayed silent as I worked to buckle one cuff around my damaged wrist and she secured the other, then she tugged on the restraints to make sure they were secure.

She leaned back on her heels, a snide grin playing on her lips. "I could give you one last chance before we head off. Tell me your name."

I grinned up at her before saying the words I knew she wanted to hear. "Over my dead body."

She matched my grin. "We shall know soon enough."

"Are you finally going to let me talk to your chief?"

With a quick look that promised a slow death by whatever creature she could shift into, she said, "My friend accidentally gave you some salve for your burns last night. I'd like it back so we can continue our fun."

I pretended to think about her request for a moment before dragging out, "No. I think you need to brush up on the word 'accident' so you can get a better understanding of what it means."

Her promising look darkened. "I would watch that mouth of yours before I melt it off."

I tilted my head, matching the grin she had given me earlier —before she'd burned me.

She hissed in warning, then her voice echoed off the stone walls. "Why won't you tell me your name?" she asked— demanded, more like.

I shrugged, knowing I was driving her mad. "Sharing names has consequences."

With a bored eye roll, she said, "I don't want riddles, *Viking*. I want answers, and I asked why you won't reveal your name."

"Maybe because I don't know yours."

She smiled grimly, keeping her dainty teeth visible. "We both know you still won't give it up." A shrug. "But my name is Corinna."

"Where are your friends, *Corinna*?"

"Waiting for us. We're ready to find out what you are here for."

She pulled me to my feet by the chains. I had to bite back against the pain that rushed through me. I struggled to drown out the throbbing as she led me from the cell. However, I didn't let my feet falter; I kept upright with my shoulders back, head high, even as my jaw worked to contain every vulgar word I wanted to shout. I had to force my legs to move properly when they bowed into a limp.

Instead of leading me down the left side of the passage, she hauled me the opposite direction.

My muscles tensed, sending another wave of searing pain across my burned skin. They'd finally decided I wasn't useful to them. I was either being led to my awaiting death, or my father's puppets had found me. My stomach sank at the possibility of who could be waiting.

Corinna dragged me farther down the passage until we reached large double doors lodged into the stone walls that seemed to surround this place.

Two expressionless guards stood on either side, white-knuckling the handles as they readied to open the doors.

I tried to breathe as evenly as I could, but between the burns covering my stomach, arms, and chest and the anxious fury building, it was damn near impossible.

"Wishing I was torturing you now?"

A cold smile spread across my face to let her know every word I spoke was nothing but truth. "You can do whatever you want. I'll just laugh it off—spit at your feet. You might as well do your best to kill me or listen to what I have to—"

I heard her teeth snap together. "Tongue, Viking. Watch that tongue, or you'll find yourself without it." She shook her head. "How no one's already cut that filthy thing out of your mouth is a mystery to me."

The double doors opened to reveal a large office-like room.

I narrowed my eyes at her. "Cutting my tongue out is not the way to get me to talk."

She narrowed her eyes, the left corner of her mouth twitching ever so slightly.

As she shoved me into the room, I examined everything I could. I took in the three stone walls slick with trickling water, stared at the patches of moss, and analyzed the books and jars stuffed in the alcoves of stone. The jars could be used as a weapon, but I would have to jump to reach them, and my burns would split open all over again if I tried.

The guards stepping into the room behind us did not go unnoticed either.

When Corinna pushed me away from the doors, the male shifter guards placed themselves in front of them, clasping their hands behind their backs with blank stares, but I wasn't a fool. I knew they were watching me out of the corner of their eyes. The male shifter who had helped Zyra and Corinna escort me to be tortured also stood on the other side.

In the center of the room sat a large oak desk. A man stood behind it, but he wasn't sitting in the chair, nor was he moving. He was carefully watching me.

Chief Haiden.

I hoped my sneer sent chills down his back.

Standing a little ways from the desk was Zyra. Her eyes were ablaze as she studied me from across the small space.

Her stare followed me when Corinna moved to the side, shoving me in the corner but keeping her eyes on the man standing behind the desk all the while. Her hold on me was firm. Though not in the same way as Zyra's stare. Something else resided in her eyes. Almost as if she was worried—waiting for something.

I straightened, setting my shoulders back. Pushing down the pain, I reached deep to draw on the very depths of my anger. I would need the adrenaline. In case things went south, I would need rage to get me out of here. The burning pain would have to be ignored to fight my way out.

"I've been hoping to speak with you," I said.

All eyes were on me, but mine were on the man behind the desk. Chief Haiden Asdire—The Great Tiger of Waylria. The man every Sandire Viking hated, especially my father. Their rivalry went back decades and would burn long after their deaths.

Yet, here I was, asking for him to heed my warnings before things went too far.

For a moment, no one spoke.

If this was the end—I would not go down easily. Not after barely escaping my father's clutches. I would survive this as I had survived that. I would make it out of here. If my father's puppets were standing behind the very doors I'd just entered, I would take them down, too.

"What could you possibly have to say?" Haiden finally spoke, his eyes narrowing to slits. "Evidently, Sandire has recently experienced a great treason and sent notice to all the realms. Though, because of the relationship between our two realms, Waylria did not receive one of these notices. Nevertheless, Nedfin was gracious enough to send me a letter to catch me up on the contents in regard to this notice."

He glanced at something on his desk, knowing I would track his gaze. A letter laid open in front of him, and he cleared his throat to go on.

My stomach plummeted, and I had to force my words to come out steady when I spoke next. I had endured hours of interrogation—held my name back with clenched teeth—and still, my father's words had beaten mine. "I need to explain first."

Haiden shook his head. "It seems that Sandire's own prince is the cause of such betrayal."

I released a hot breath that sent a storm of rage trembling through my body.

I would get out of here.

I didn't care what I had to do. I *would* get out.

Haiden, with his hands clasped behind his back, walked toward me as he continued. "This prince escaped and is now a wanted man. Wanted *alive*, specifically. Sandire's king is persistent about his son being handed hand over so he can be dealt with accordingly." He stopped not even three feet from me, and Corinna's grip on me tightened. Haiden's eyes bore into mine, unafraid, containing decades of fierce loathing. He didn't blink as his pupils became slits, as he challenged me to look away from his tiger eyes. "Welcome to Waylria, Riker, Viking Prince of Sandire."

Chapter Fifteen
Zyra

I CLENCHED my hands into fists, mindful not to puncture my palms with my claws. Prince of Sandire. The Viking Prince of Sandire had trespassed onto our lands and attacked me, and now he was standing in this room with us. And he would have to be returned to his kingdom. Hearing those words changed everything.

The pit in my stomach grew wider; my body hollow.

He deserved more marks than we had given him. The burns, the whippings—it wasn't enough. Death wouldn't be enough. Not unless it was excruciatingly slow. I hated myself for the guilt I'd felt. I hated myself for giving him salve for his burns and lashings. In that moment, I wanted to take it all back.

The night I had discovered him in the trees, he'd been running. He had escaped Sandire and likely headed straight for Waylria knowing his father couldn't reach him without walking into enemy territory. Cutting through our territory was a smart way to get out from under his father, but trespassing on the lands of his enemies was a critical mistake.

I growled. I should have killed him.

My teeth should have sunk into the Viking Prince.

His body should be on the way to Sandire now—to send a message to his family and all of Sandire.

Another mistake I would surely pay for once Haiden and I had a moment alone.

"You don't understand," the Viking Prince said before anyone could continue. "My father is plotting against the realms. He is looking to eradicate it all to take it all for himself. I'm wanted, yes, but that is why I'm here—I had to get away to warn others."

"Why go to the trouble?" Haiden asked. "Your lies are worth nothing here. You're wanted for treason."

I was frozen in place.

"I just threatened him; he'll do anything to get out of a thrashing," Corinna seethed from the corner of the room, where she still held the Viking in a tight grasp that probably meant nothing to him. "What's our next move?"

"We no longer believe it's a trap," Haiden said. "We will still need to protect the borough in case there are further surprises, however. With this in mind, we can spare Zyra to be the one to return the traitorous brute home. We need all the capable warriors possible in the meantime."

"Me?" My chest hollowed out. I wanted to sink into myself —disappear into the wall as if I had never existed.

"With you taking the immediate threat, I'm sending my guard William with you."

Haiden was casting me aside. Expendable but not trustworthy enough to send out alone. That was all I was good for. Haiden's own sacrifice. Even after being the one who discovered a Viking—the Viking *Prince* of Sandire, no less—I was not capable enough to protect the borough.

Whether I came back did not affect them.

I swallowed the bile in my throat but nodded.

When I looked over at the black bear shifter, he gave me a curt nod, his black hair skimming his shoulders. I turned away once Haiden went on, trying not to crack a tooth or bite my tongue off.

"If we don't get his son to him soon enough, Slate will purge our lands out of spite. I cannot rely on any one person to return him to his father before he sends an army to march onto our lands."

He cannot rely on *me*.

"It's already too late! That is what I'm trying to tell you," the Viking said. "Whether you give me back or not, my father still plans to overthrow the realms for himself. I'm trying to—"

"I highly doubt a word you're saying is truth. Even if he so plans to overtake the realms, perhaps this will have your father consider leaving us as we are."

I swallowed back a scoff. There was no negotiating with Slate to spare shifters in any capacity. For Haiden to think such a thing …

"Even if he only wants you back so he can kill you himself, there will be no negotiation." Haiden turned to me then. "First thing tomorrow morning, I expect Riker to be restrained"—he spared a glance in his direction before his eyes were back on me—"and you are to lead him back to Sandire so his father can deal with him however he so chooses."

I could hear the unspoken words underneath. *I expect Riker to be returned to Sandire alive. Don't fuck this up.* I gave a slow nod. "Yes, sir."

He feels he cannot rely on me was all my mind echoed back. Haiden was forcing me to escort the Viking Prince back to his realm. I was to enter enemy territory, where I could be captured. Sacrificed. Or even killed by the prince on the way there. Even if he was sending me with a personal guard he trusted, so much was at risk.

Perhaps we were both expendable.

Most shifters never wandered too close to Waylria's borders since some never made it back to the borough. The mere thought made children cower and clutch their mother's skirts. And I was going to cross that border, risking my life every moment.

"Good." He turned to Riker, who was no longer smirking, but Haiden still wore his tiger eyes as he took in the Viking. "I would say it was nice to meet you, Viking Prince, but I can honestly say it was not. You're lucky your father wants your head for himself. Otherwise, you would not be walking out of here." Haiden turned away, adding, "Now leave."

Corinna pivoted, throwing open the doors to haul the Viking away. I followed, securing the doors behind me. The guards watched to ensure we left.

No one spoke as we walked down the passage back to the cells. The only sound audible over the waterfall was the occasional flap of her cloak.

My skin itched. The wolf growled within my chest, trembling to the tips of my fingers. While I still held disbelief, the wolf in me wanted to sink its teeth into the filthy Viking.

Not just a normal Viking. Far more horrendous and cold. Royalty. His father was responsible for sacrificing shifters: our deaths and our missing. And this Viking Prince would be the one to take up those responsibilities once his father passed. At the least, he would have grown to rule like his father if he hadn't committed treason.

We reached Riker's cell, and Corinna used more force than necessary to shove him inside, and he didn't stumble, but he clenched his teeth against the sharp pull of his burns. Coming up behind her, I slammed the door hard enough to make the bars rattle. I glared at Riker through the bars, my fingers twitching.

I locked the door before meeting his eyes once again. "I will see you in the morning."

Before he could respond, I turned and walked out with Corinna at my heels.

It was going to be a very long journey. A long journey where I would be responsible for the prince getting to Sandire alive. Because I was disposable here. I was disposable enough to be sent to the land of the enemy. Haiden lacked confidence in my abilities enough to send me with one of his stupid yes-men. And Corinna had said nothing.

My mind spiraled, seeking how true it was.

Was I truly that useless in the eyes of Haiden? Even Corinna? After being included in getting information from the enemy … after all the lashings I had given for Waylria …

I clamped my teeth together. Why trust me with this if they did not trust me at the frontlines? To send me to my death?

Chapter Sixteen
Riker

I JUMPED up when I woke to realize I'd slept through the night. Then winced at the sharp movement, releasing a breath through clenched teeth. Every inch of me was stiff from lying on the floor.

I hadn't slept through the night since fleeing Sandire.

Evading sleep in case someone approached was likely the only reason I had made it this far, because on more than one occasion, I had woken and kept moving.

I had grown disoriented from the constant running and lack of sleep, and it had taken me around a week to get to the border of Waylria. That much, I knew. How long it had been since Zyra had come across me was impossible for me to determine.

And now I was getting out of Waylria.

Out of my cell.

Only to be taken back to Sandire.

Escorted to my death under the sweltering sun.

It would not be a fast death either. My father would be sure to take his time.

Even if more death was the last thing my family needed.

I could not go back. Once I was out of this damned cell, I

had to find a way to save my family and stop my father—all while keeping my distance, for now.

I would find a way to stop him. Only, my options now were limited. I was cornered by death and faced with not knowing what to do next. I had gone this far, but aside from warning Waylria and them not believing me, I was certain my father had spread falsehoods across the realms.

I needed someone on my side.

Maybe the girl—Zyra—could guide me on what to do next.

The thought of asking a shifter for help had me grinding my teeth. I had to remind myself my options were limited. But if not her, then ... *seiðr*.

When Haiden had initially given Zyra the duty of escorting me, I had hoped she would do so alone. Because then escaping would be easy. I would have waited, caught her off guard, and started for the mountains of Nedfin.

Seiðr magic and those who practiced it were unwelcome in Sandire out of fear of their ability to tell and shape the future. The women associated with Freyja—the goddess of love, fertility, beauty, war, gold, and magic—were only called upon during inherent crisis. They terrified most people who did not want to know daily predictions. Kings did not want their decisions challenged, nor did they want the average person to shape the future, so *seiðr* practitioners were an unwanted presence in Sandire.

Now they were the key to stopping my father.

I propped my back against the wall, my burns protesting now that they were beginning to heal. First, I had to get out from under the shapeshifters. Maybe I would hack and tear until they lay on the ground in pieces. Maybe I would smash her head against a rock. Maybe I would cut him open and sink a dagger into his exposed heart. Maybe I would take her pelt to keep me warm.

The possibilities were endless, and not only would I enjoy any of them but I'd also savor every minute.

Footsteps echoed down the passage. Steady with a purpose and heading straight for me. I pushed myself from the ground, using the wall for support. Once I was on my feet, I leaned against it with my arms crossed over my filthy shirt, careful not to brush against my bubbled skin. Dirt, sweat, and blood covered my once-white shirt. My pants had some of the same stains, but they weren't covered to the same degree as my shirt.

Zyra was the first to appear, stopping in front of my cell door. She already had her arms crossed over her chest in the same way mine were and stared at me without saying a word. My lips pressed in a thin line, I stared right back.

Maybe I would get the chance to kill her before we even left.

She tossed something into my cell, but I didn't break eye contact to see what it was. I matched her hate as I always did, though it was impossible for her to hate me more than I hated her. She would find that out once I bashed her skull.

"You're going to have to come in and get me," I told her.

One of her eyebrows quirked up. Her arms tightened, like she was holding herself back from clawing her way to me. I couldn't help but smirk. She wouldn't catch me off guard again. I knew what she was capable of now and wouldn't pretend she wasn't a good fighter. I would only fight harder; show no mercy.

"You sound like a whining child that doesn't want to go somewhere with his mother," she spat back. "Change your shirt —it's filthy—and put on the cuffs so we can get out of here. The sooner we leave, the sooner I can return."

And the sooner I die. She didn't say it, but I knew the thought crossed her feral mind.

I finally looked down at what she'd thrown into my cell, and sure enough, a shirt laid on the floor, along with iron cuffs.

"At least put on the cuffs so we can go," she said when I didn't respond. "I'm not coming in there until you do."

The sooner we left this cave, the sooner I could halt her beating heart.

I pushed away from the wall, my burns giving a small protest as I bent to retrieve the items. The clean tunic was soothing after being in the stiff fabric caked in dirt and dried blood for so long.

Once I was dressed and finished binding my wrists, Zyra straightened and crossed the distance to yank open the door. I waited, watching her as she checked over the bindings and even pulled against the chains to ensure they were secure.

That was when the other shifter, William, chose to appear.

"What are you doing? You shouldn't be in there when the prisoner isn't fully secured."

She didn't glance away from me as she responded to him. "I was ensuring our prisoner was fully secured so there aren't any surprises."

Scowling at me with narrowed eyes, she grabbed the dangling chains and yanked me forward.

"We need to do more than cuff him," the male shifter said to Zyra. "We can't let him see inside the borough, even if his father intends to kill him."

He tossed her a piece of cloth, then watched her tie it around my head. I ground my teeth but knew arguing or fighting was futile.

I had to bide my time.

Zyra stepped up behind me. The male shifter, on the other hand, had a stiff posture, glowering at me as he waited for her to finish. His claws—resembling that of a bear—were elongated while he awkwardly clutched the hilt of a dagger sheathed at his side. Over his tunic was a pointless piece of chest armor.

Too bad it wouldn't save him.

The male shifter disappeared once my vision was cloaked

in darkness. Moments later, I was being wrenched forward by a force stronger than Zyra. Our footsteps echoed through the passageway. I felt Zyra on one side of me while the male flanked the other. The crashing of the waterfall grew louder, but I wouldn't get the chance to see it or anything else within the cave.

We hadn't made it far before I was halted again.

A third presence had stopped us.

"Haiden won't let me come with you no matter how much I try to reason with him" came Corinna's voice. "He wants me here in case some of the Viking's friends come looking for him. Nabil is under the same orders."

"I—We can handle him," assured Zyra. Though her tone was far from certain. It nearly brought a smile to my face.

"Just remember that his daddy is going to do the chopping when you get there. Don't waste your energy killing him."

"We don't have time for this nonsense," the male shifter barked, shoving me to walk in front of him. Under his breath, he said, "If this bitch doesn't focus, I'll leave her at the border myself. Or maybe even with your kind."

I didn't try to push back my anger.

Filth. Abominations. Leeches. Killers. Hunters. Savage destroyers. Barbarians. Sacrifices.

They all deserved to die.

They needed to be hunted to extinction.

Including the wolf girl pulling me.

Corinna called after Zyra, "Watch your surroundings. Don't fall close to Annarr, and watch for rogue shifters. Be careful!"

And then we were out of the passage, wet stone being replaced with dirt. We walked a few winding paths, and even with two beasts flanking me, I struggled not to trip.

Stone soon replaced dirt again, my boots scuffing against the surface. The stones made steps that went up and up, never seeming to end. Not a single one wobbled under our weight as we ascended. I forced myself to breathe through the pain, even when we reached the top.

Fresh morning air cooled my cheeks. I couldn't help but wonder if they put the mountain of steps at the entrance to deter attacks. I was fit, but I didn't want to climb or descend the steps again. Once had been more than enough.

I couldn't pinpoint how the wolf managed to get me down such steep steps while I'd been unconscious.

Zyra hesitated for just a moment while the male pushed forward. She had to be looking at something. Perhaps back at the borough. Just in case she never returned.

She was right to feel apprehensive.

She would never see her home again if I had anything to do with it.

Chapter Seventeen
Zyra

I WALKED out of the mouth of the borough, my breath immediately clouded in front of my face. Snow crunched underfoot as I looked up through the branches of the evergreens. The sky was bright blue without the sun. Winter was almost over, but there would be another snowfall or two before the sun would be ready to replace the white powder with green life.

I didn't care how long I would be gone, I was going to miss my small warm haven.

I refused to linger on the chance I might not return. The thought made me feel like the ground had fallen out from under my feet, like I was about to be sucked into a dark mist. And when I thought about how I could become one of their sacrifices …

No one would miss me anyway.

William had no patience for me as it was.

Exhaling a breath to release the tension coiled in my shoulders, a cloud of air floated around me.

William tugged on Riker's restraints to get us both to move. As I tried to ignore the tether I felt to what little I was leaving behind, my eyes snagged on the key gleaming around William's neck.

The Viking pulled away but followed without speaking. Likely thinking better of running when he was blindfolded. Regardless, William kept one hand on the dagger at his belt while the other kept a tight grip on the chains connecting to the cuffs restraining the Viking.

Riker wasn't going anywhere the bear shifter didn't want him to. Even the dagger was a precaution in case our prisoner decided to make a run for it.

I kept pace, with my claws extended.

We had a lot of ground to cover, and I wouldn't let either of them slow me down. The sooner I returned the Viking, the sooner I could return to the soil of my home.

The sooner I could prove myself worthy.

Before I left, Haiden had shared his intentions to send Corinna to fly ahead to deliver a letter to Slate about the return of his prince. Corinna had argued that Nabil could fulfill the job in order for her to go with me, but Haiden refused at every turn. It came down to Haiden wanting to rub it in the Sandire king's face—to be able to say a shapeshifter had trapped a Viking and was now leading him across the realms to deliver him back to his father, and he wanted his best warrior to deliver such a message.

"You must be pissed to have to drag me back to Sandire." Riker interrupted my thoughts. "You both must want to slit my throat pretty badly right now."

I nearly jerked to a stop. His voice disturbed the morning silence.

Birds had to be pissed to have such a wretched thing waking them up.

He wanted a reaction, to get a rise out of us both. He wanted to see what we could take. Perhaps tempt us to kill him? Either way, we could not let him see anything but strong shifters. If he snuffed out the smallest bit of vulnerability, he would strike.

"I don't want to slit your throat." I bared my teeth with a murderous grin, momentarily forgetting he couldn't see me. "I want to bury my teeth in your throat until I hear a snap."

Was this what William wanted to hear?

He gave away nothing. "Well, aren't you a delight to be around."

"I wasn't aware Vikings knew such words. 'Delight' is in your vocabulary?"

"*Enough*," William bit out. "You're going to make this trip more difficult than it's worth." He got in my face, and I stood frozen, planting my feet so not to flinch back. "Don't get any ideas that you're essential here. Know your place."

I bit the inside of my cheek, struggling to breathe evenly as my heart pounded wildly. I suppose that wasn't what he wanted ...

I didn't have to look to know the Viking was wearing a sly smile as he said, "More difficult than you realize."

The threat of him killing a shifter made my blood run cold. I spoke before I could think twice about it. "Don't make me kill you."

It had become impossible for me to fathom how I had felt such regret after torturing him. Still, killing the Viking Prince of Sandire was not at the top of my priority list. Getting home in one piece was. Perhaps then, I would become an asset. Perhaps then, my family would do well not to ignore me.

"We'll see who's left standing when this is over."

Swallowing a gulp, I narrowed my eyes. "It won't be you," I told him in feigned confidence. "I'll either end up killing you before we get there, or your father will do the job for me if I can control myself long enough. But one way or another, I'll be the one left standing, Viking. Remember that."

Chapter Eighteen
Riker

Her words would not stop echoing over the pain.

With heavy feet, my legs wavered with every step. Each deep breath sent fire blazing through my lungs. I was almost convinced Hel was using my very flesh to tear her way from Helheim, the realm of the dead, to punish me. Perhaps she believed the lies, too. Perhaps Loki's daughter felt I deserved her wrath for failing to shield against the events of the night that tore through my mind like a sandstorm.

The rise and fall of my chest was excruciating as I forced my feet to move. Raw heat rose with each open wound. Sweat coated my body.

Beads of sweat collected on my forehead, tempting me to beg for night to fall as the day moved with agonizing slowness.

I had to think through my escape. And soon.

We had gone the entire day without speaking, so I only broke the silence after enough time had passed. I steadied my voice, willing it to be normal as I said, "Are you planning on stopping any time soon? I can't see a damn thing. I'm eating branches back here."

The wretched male growled out, "Stop talking, then."

I gritted my teeth. The gnawing feeling in my stomach was nearly impossible to ignore until I imagined how these predators would eat on the way.

We continued for a few more yards before the female withdrew from me. She threw her satchel to the ground, seemingly barely holding back her irritation.

I snickered. "I didn't know a wolf's fur could stand on end like a cat's."

It didn't matter that I couldn't see her. I still got under her skin. While she released a long sigh, the beast on the other side of me tightened his grip on the chains of my cuffs.

"Corinna's right about that tongue of yours," she said.

I heard her dig around in her bag for something and held my bland expression in place as I geared up for another night of little sleep and plenty of discomfort.

She returned to my other side, then I was pulled until my back was against the rough bark of a tree trunk. I bit back a yell when the male on my left forced me to sit. Rope dug into my torso as they both worked to wind it around me and the tree.

The knots they tied were tight, nearly cutting off my circulation while the bark dug into my back. Sleep would be difficult, but I suddenly felt drained enough that I thought I could manage the discomfort. As long as my burns didn't sting.

Bound to the tree, I listened to the girl pace, likely surveying everything around us. Then she paused. The male braced in the snow alongside her.

I expected something—sound, movement, a scuffle. Only after a few beats did they both move again. I heard her slide to the ground. The other male did the same, but with some distance from her. I couldn't tell where he was; he was too still.

I fought back the sigh building in my chest. I was exhausted, still damp with sweat, but I wasn't about to fall asleep. I wasn't sure *she* would do anything, but I wouldn't give *him* the chance to seize an opportunity. My mind raced through the possibilities of who I could find and how.

I needed them to let their guard down. Even if only a little. Allow her to get comfortable enough to slip up. Maybe he would sleep too soundly; maybe they wouldn't tighten the ropes enough; maybe she would feel bad for me again. They would screw up somehow at some point. And it would be enough for me to walk away. With their bodies lying limp behind me.

I JOLTED awake every time the rope rubbed against my burns, which was more often than I would have liked. Each flare of discomfort sent my eyes widening, yanking me from uneasy sleep. Aside from the burns, restlessness also pulled me from sleep. I woke with numb fingers and shivers that tumbled through my body in waves. I woke to make sure no one was approaching.

Sometimes, I woke to one of the shifters walking around me. It had me on high alert, thinking one of them was moments away from strangling me. They would sniff. They would ensure I was still tied up. Then they returned to their claimed spot. Only to get up and repeat it all a few hours later.

When dawn broke, all of us were awake.

"Hope you're ready for a long walk," she said in a half-hearted cheer.

I was growing tired of the back and forth. There were bigger concerns.

"I can't tell you how much it pisses me off that I've come this far, only for you to make me trek all the way back."

The male growled. "That's enough. If we could make it through the day without either of you talking, it would be a blessing from the Great Spirit itself. Truly. And I didn't know they even let you speak anymore."

The silence was palpable. I didn't care who he was speaking to; the words set me on edge. She said nothing, however, but she had to be furious about the comment.

Disgusting hands untied me from the tree. One of them snatched me up by my cuffs. With my lips pressed together tightly, I wished I could stare daggers at them. Enough time had been wasted on Haiden. I refused to let more time slip through my fingers without answers—a direction.

I could do nothing more than put my life in the hands of the gods. No matter which had helped me get this far, I was still here.

I yanked the cuffs, pulling whoever held them closer to me. Blind, I reached for that figure, winding the chains around their neck the same way they had tied me to the tree. Only tighter. Without a moment of hesitation, I jerked to tighten the iron.

I released a long hiss through clenched teeth as my burns flared. They had been rubbed sore last night, thanks to the rope wound around my chest and stomach.

I bit back against the pain that struck me with each step.

My burns had opened up again, but that didn't stop me from stopping that final gasp of air from her throat.

A head of wild curls brushed along my arm. Leaving her hair down was a mistake.

I kept focused.

Until her fight nearly left her. Until a force struck into me hard enough to knock me off my feet.

My blindfold fell slightly, allowing me to take in my surroundings. And the male shifter was racing for me. A key resting against his chest snatched my attention.

I barely managed a sneer as I got back on my feet, fighting to pull air into my lungs. I planted myself in the same moment I realized I had nothing to defend myself with.

I had helped my father hunt and sacrifice dozens of their kind ever since he appointed me as one of his top brutal and most-loyal warriors. Since I was a child. When my *Illska Sanðr* men and I set our minds to it, we rarely returned without a sacrifice.

Even without my weapons, I was confident I could crush him with my rage alone. It had happened once before when my men and I were out; I had my ax knocked from my grasp and my hand nearly bitten off.

I had walked away then. I would walk away now.

My sneer turned into a grin—one I hoped reminded the shapeshifter of death. The iron cuffs had a newfound use when I heaved them at his face. He went down long enough for me to grasp the key from his neck. I yanked it from his neck to break the chain.

I backed away, but there wasn't enough time to undo the restraints before he was up again.

One moment, snow was being kicked up by human feet. The next, the massive paws of a bear were sending it everywhere.

I planted my feet again, keeping the key clutched in my fist.

He met me with the same unyielding force.

PART II

PREDATORY RIVALS

Chapter Nineteen
Zyra

His arms reached around me from behind, sending my heart plummeting through my body. Once he'd yanked the chains from my grasp, his hands were on me. The Viking's strength would undoubtedly snap my neck—leave me in a heap in the snow. And in the moment he took me to the ground, all I could think was that they were right. Haiden was right not to trust me at the frontlines. To not send me alone. To send me to enemy territory. After I'd wanted nothing more than to remove all doubt about my abilities. I *was* disposable.

I couldn't even be trusted to get the prince to Sandire to face his treason.

Still, I refused to cry out. I let my claws lengthen to swipe at him. If it came down to my life or his, I would not lose without tearing him open. If I was doomed to be found as a corpse, I would leave evidence that I fought back. If for no one else but Lizeth—my only family.

I would not be useless. I would not submit. I would not let the enemy take me down without scarring him.

But before I could do any of what I'd imagined, air was cut from my throat.

It lasted long enough for my vision to blur and my eyes to shut but not long enough to kill.

Muffled fighting met my ears. My mind was too hazy to focus on identifying the sounds. There was a crunch before my vision blurred and blackened.

GRINDING MY TEETH, I clenched my jaw, keeping my eyes closed. I inhaled, careful not to move too much as I tested the air for what was nearby. Wet snow, evergreen, herbs—the stench of the Viking. He's still here. I wanted to move, to see if I was restrained or if every bone in my body was broken and I just didn't know it yet, but even the slightest movement would give away that I was conscious.

"I know you are awake."

The Viking's voice was deep but quiet, as if he were cautious of others hearing. I sniffed the air again, the sensation burning my throat, and cracked my eyes open. Nothing but forest stood out to me.

As my eyes locked with his, I dared not ask how long I'd been unconscious. I dared not ask his intentions.

If anything, I gulped as I took in how he watched me. My muscles locked up with the effort I used to keep myself from wincing at the searing pain around my neck.

He was crouched across from me. His intense, amber gaze was focused on me, unblinking, without a blindfold to hide them. The iron cuffs that had bound his hands were gone. I went to move my hands, only to find them fastened around my wrists now. My jaw locked at the sight. Not only had he cuffed me, but he had woven the rope overtop as well, and the rope wrapped around, digging into my back.

My head snapped up. I tried not to show my fear, but my heart echoed in my ears. I worried he could hear it.

"Do you know of *seiðr*?"

"I do not speak your filthy language." I wanted to spit the words at him, but they came out weak. My throat and neck hurt too fiercely. Then I realized. William — he was nowhere in sight. "Where is William?"

He narrowed his eyes at me, almost in annoyance more so than anger. "That has always been the difference between our kinds — we put in more effort."

"At killing us!" My voice squeaked and broke, my raw throat preventing me from yelling. "Sorry we don't go around sacrificing innocents like barbarians." I bit down on my tongue for more saliva. "The other shifter, where is he?"

"No, your kind just likes to kill for fun."

I scoffed. "That's you, *Prince*."

I was tired of him avoiding the question about William. He very well knew who I was asking about. The thought of being alone with this beast of a man …

Riker shook his head, launching to his feet. He crossed the distance to me before my heart could fully sink. I gasped when he grabbed a fistful of my hair and yanked my head back.

"I don't have the time, nor the patience for this," he seethed. "*Seiðr* — magic. *Völva*, a magic wielder, would know how to perform *seiðr*."

My scalp was screaming. Tears swam in my eyes. Still, my thoughts raced to understand what he was asking.

"They travel other worlds, gain information — to predict the future or even change it."

"Do you mean an oracle?"

Why did he need to know about oracles? Why did he need to see into the future?

He let go of my hair and took a step back. "What can you tell me about them?"

I swallowed a groan as the pain spread through my skull

and pulsed behind my eyes. "Why do you need to know? And why would I tell you? If I answer you, you will just kill me."

"I could kill you regardless."

I couldn't ignore the fear trickling down my spine.

He walked back to where he'd been sitting before and pulled my satchel closer to rummage inside.

As much as it made my blood boil and hands clench, he was right. I was the vulnerable one now. I was lucky he hadn't blindfolded me in the same way we had him, but even more lucky he hadn't strangled me when he wound the chains around my neck.

The Viking looked ready to end me on the spot. "He's dead. You can stop thinking about him now. Stop wondering where he is because he isn't coming to save you. Now tell me what I want to know before my patience runs thin and you end up next to him."

I tried to keep myself from gulping, but my throat *burned*. My heart felt removed from my body with how quickly it beat. A hummingbird's wings could not compare to fear. "Oracles do not stay in one place for long. They used to be accessible to anyone and everyone across the land until the realms split off—"

"I know the history of the realms"—he pulled a round tin from my bag—"and we did not just split off."

Dead. William was dead. I was alone with my natural enemy. Haiden had sent me with a guard who could not even fight off an attack. As a bear, no less. Had he known this would happen? Had Haiden sent the two shifters he found expendable? Had he truly sent me to die?

My heart nearly froze with hope then, because if the Viking was free, he must have used the key from William. Which meant it was on his person somewhere.

Riker had the tin unscrewed and was examining the salve inside until his attention snapped to me, his eyes piercing.

"Stop spiraling as if you cared about the bastard, and answer the damned question."

I blinked back my surprise. I should not expect anything less harsh from a brute.

That was when I noticed the deep gashes along his arms. Swipes from William's claws. He even lifted his shirt to coat a wound at his side.

"Or what?" My question might not have come off as the challenge I intended, but my eyes were just as piercing as his. "Why did you kill him instead of me?"

"I thought I had killed you," he answered. "I attacked you first, but then your bear got in the way. When I realized you were still alive, I thought I would make the most of it."

He was my enemy. At his mercy, I had no choice but to focus my efforts on keeping myself alive. Not giving up too much information would ensure that.

Not that I knew much about how to find an oracle—or *völva*—because they were difficult to retrieve answers from. From the little I knew from my mother, their somewhat-nomadic lifestyle typically led them to choosing natural space where they could avoid all law but that of nature. With Nedfin being the most peaceful realm, they likely had an understanding with oracles and allowed them to wander nearby. Nedfin would also be a likely resource for herbs and other necessities that came with truth-telling.

He gritted his teeth against the sting of the salve on his burns.

"I don't have time to wander the realms in search of an oracle, *völva*, whatever you so choose to call them," he said. "How can you not understand that I'm trying to stop something catastrophic from happening?"

"What reason do I have to trust you?" I snapped before I could stop myself, then pressed my lips together, but it was already too late. The words were in the air between us. "You've captured more shifters than we likely know of, thanks to rogues. You sacrifice us to some sick deity of yours. Now you have me tied up, and I doubt you won't kill me the moment I give you what you want because you have no reason or loyalty or conscience to keep me alive. You killed the other shifter with us, even." I sucked in a breath. For the first time since waking to find myself bound, tears strangled my words as I realized I would be one of the many to die by the Viking Prince of Sandire's ax.

"Waylria will cease to exist."

I fought to swallow back my emotion. I would not cry or beg for my life. "Why do you care?"

"I don't." His answer was sincere; his tone left no room for uncertainty. He jumped to his feet. "Having you realize the severity of this is the only way I can get you to help me. We are all at stake if we don't figure this out. I have nothing left to lose; why would I lie about my father's intentions?"

He had a point.

He yanked me to my feet, and I exhaled when my hands didn't shake.

"If I have to drag you across the lands to an oracle to prove I am telling the truth, so be it. It will help me prove it to the other realms before it is too late." He grinned blankly then. "Keeping you with me might also be a fair trade to anyone who passes us by."

Chapter Twenty
Riker

KILLING her would likely be the less infuriating option. Especially in the long run. She was my way out of Waylria if we ran into other shifters. I did not know how likely that was, but it wasn't a risk I was willing to take. Not only that, but I could act as though I was her prisoner and she was trekking me across the realms to return me to my father, or I could trade her for my freedom if the right person came along.

For now, I was convinced she was the key to some future confrontation.

I just had to spend the remainder of the journey with her filth.

And I wasn't even sure what my journey was. I couldn't think around saving my family. Even if I couldn't put a stop to my father's intentions, I would find a way to save them from him.

From their own blood and king.

For now, we would walk until we could figure out where we needed to go or who we needed to talk to in order to find a *völva*.

Looking over my shoulder at Zyra and her bound wrists, I knew there would be no stopping her if she wanted to hurt me.

Even on the rare occasion when a shifter misstepped enough to fall victim to *Illska Sanðr* for sacrifice, we were cautious not to let our guard down around them, for fear of them somehow being immune to the iron that trapped them in their human form.

Afternoon light already streaked the sky. Blue, yellow, and orange melded together to warn of how half the day was gone and that night would soon follow.

I had no idea where we were going, just that it was in the opposite direction of Sandire.

We had started toward Sandire at the start but were now traveling up from the borough. I did not know what was next. Not when I didn't know where my father's men were. Leaving Waylria was a risk. My life was bound to be a short one if I did not play my cards right. But I had to imagine a *völva* could not be far.

My mother and Annora, and most women in our village really, considered *völva* to be wise by way of their connection to the gods. My father, however, had cast them from Sandire out of fear of their seer abilities. Not a single one had been on our land since I was young. With their lifestyle, it seemed no one knew where—

"Why all the questions?" the shifter's voice broke through my thoughts. "You ask me about—about *seiðr*—oracles—whatever. What are you seeking?"

I refused to look back at her, pulling her along. I had not expected her own questions. "You don't get to be the one asking questions."

"You have no idea how to find an oracle. I do."

I whirled on her, yanking her restraints hard enough to put her on her knees. Her eyes shot up to me, wide.

"Stop fucking around, *shifter*, and tell me what you know." I did not have time to play games when the lives of my family were in the balance. "I am not the one with my head on the chopping block right now. I am no longer your prisoner. Your life is in my hands, and we are doing everything by my word now."

"You kill me, and that information—your proof—is gone," she scrambled to say. "And you will have nothing to barter with if your father catches up to you. You said so yourself—"

"None of that matters if I can't get what I need. Right now, you are useless to me. Dead weight." My chest heaved. "What do you have to lose?"

All thoughts of how *völva* being banished from Sandire had vanished, leaving the faces of my family in their wake.

The shifter blinked as if she had not contemplated my threat. "My mother is a shaman. It's different from an oracle, but she knew one—a shifter she had grown up with, who left Waylria. I don't know if she's alive or if she fell as one of your sacrifices. They cut all contact once they leave their birthplace, but my mother and her friend had talked before she left to find other oracles. I-I don't know for sure, but with the seclusion and their nomadic lifestyle, I think it's likely they would choose a place like the Nedfin Mountains."

The Nedfin Mountains. It made sense with Nedfin being a realm of peace. If I was to leave my life, name, and everything I knew behind, disappearing into the Nedfin Mountains would be my first choice.

Now I had an idea of where to go. An idea of who to ask about the future and what my next steps should look like. A way to end what was ahead.

"Now, was that so hard?" She pulled against the restraints, her knees sliding through the snow. I yanked her to her feet. "You're still my prisoner. Don't make me question your usefulness by getting ideas. We have a lot of ground to cover."

She stared at me with her big green *djøfull* eyes. Her eyes were piercing, like a forest aflame. I pulled a dagger from her satchel.

I wasn't going to question her reason for packing such a

thing when she was already a repulsive weapon herself. I didn't waste time to press the tip against her bruised throat.

I could not show weakness.

She swallowed against it, her next breath heavy.

"What did I say about getting ideas?"

I forced her closer by the chains. I held all control here. The shifter had no choice but to follow me as I gritted my teeth and tugged her in the direction of Nedfin.

Chapter Twenty-One
Zyra

"BUILDING A FIRE IS A MISTAKE."

The sun was setting, and we had stopped walking for the night. Riker was bent forward, collecting sticks and stuffing them under his arm. The trees were spread farther apart now, letting in splotches of sunlight. Its rays were melting the snow, so the ground was sloshy in this part of the forest.

He glanced back at my words. Every muscle in my body tensed, my instincts screaming with caution. My mind raced, pressured to understand what he could do with such information, trying to determine what he could gain if I pressed further.

One second, he looked like he wanted to slit my throat, then the next, he had crossed the distance between us.

"Save your breath," he told me. "We will be fine. If anything, I will pass you off to my father's men." Then he mumbled, "Won't be as good as being able to blood eagle me, but sending a shapeshifter to take it out on might be good."

"It's not that," I said tersely. "I don't want to get butchered over a fire. Drop the wood."

He snapped to his full height, his amber eyes blazing with fire. I forced myself to sit still and not shrink into myself.

Before I spoke again, I cleared my throat low as to not trigger the burn but to rid my voice of weakness. "Some shifters attack other shifters. Blood calls to those who crave violence. We're usually peaceful when it comes to each other, but that doesn't mean there aren't a few rogues."

"Rogues," he repeated. "Rogue shifters? Like what your friend had mentioned before we left?"

I pulled against my restraints, wishing my nails could saw through them. "Yes. Why do you think we didn't build a fire the first night?"

I pushed away the thought of William. While I had not seen a body, there was not a doubt in my mind that he was dead.

"Because you have a fur coat and don't need one and you wanted me to freeze."

Insufferable bastard!

Thankfully, the Viking spoke up before I could say something I would regret.

"You think that is who we sacrifice?" he went on, piling sticks. "Before, you said we mostly catch rogues."

I bit my lip to trap the lore behind my teeth. Only ... him knowing he wasn't harming the best of us couldn't hurt. If anything, perhaps it would hurt his pride. He had truly hunted monsters, doing Waylria a favor in carrying out a fate we could not.

"Rogues are shifters who have been banished from Waylria," I told him, watching his reaction carefully. "They kill for enjoyment. They are outcasts because of their unquenchable thirst—because they've killed another shifter for sport." The more information I could give him—the more useful I could be —the better chance I had of getting out of this alive.

Rogue shifters formed their own packs and wandered from place to place, never staying anywhere for long when there were other things to kill in farther lands. They banded together once exiled—shared their hatred and took it out on other beings. They could hunt and kill as they pleased, so long as it wasn't in Waylria. Banished. Remorseless. Cold-blooded killers.

Outcasts because of their crazed taste for flesh.

Breakers of the most basic rule: *Never kill one of your own. Never kill another shifter.*

They were the only true reason we had cells and iron cuffs.

"I didn't think shifters left Waylria if they could help it."

"If they could help it." I nodded. "That's the thing … rogues don't have a choice, and they think they can beat you. A pack of rogues, no matter how small, should be able to take on one of your armies."

The Viking Prince busied himself by adding bits of fallen and decaying tree trunks to the kindling, but I felt his gaze roam back to me periodically. I was almost stunned my words had given him pause.

"Why exile them when you could just kill them to begin with? Why let them be free when they might kill someone else?"

A pit opened in my chest. I wished I could wring my hands together, brush my hair back from my face, scratch my way free … something, anything. "Not all shapeshifters are savage killers. Those of us that go rogue are exiled and then are either hunted by Vikings or they gain the chance to redeem themselves. They don't have to kill. They can start somewhere else, change. They don't have to suffer for something they might come to regret."

Corinna's father had been one of those rogues caught by Vikings. She lay awake at night, wondering if things would have been different if he had lived.

"How often does it happen?"

"More often than it should," I murmured. Rogues piled up over time, and some were decent at staying undetected, for a time.

If one was found out or came back after being banished,

the cells were meant to keep everyone else safe. If they could not be controlled, Haiden would assign a guard to take them to the border or close to Annarr to ensure they wouldn't return. Some believed it was the Great Spirit's way of controlling our population.

Riker knelt over a flat piece of wood with a stick between his hands. He rubbed the sticks together, creating friction where the tip met the wood.

"Do you just behead anyone who kills another of your kind?" I asked him. If he was surprised by banishment, there could only be one other option. From how Vikings treated us and how the Viking Prince spoke, it would not be all that surprising.

"Not if done in broad daylight, and if you don't hide it. Being truthful about it is less punishable. Murdering someone and hiding it, however, is a terrible crime that leads to loss of trust."

"A loss of trust? You don't punish people for murder? I could walk into Sandire, stab someone, and walk away as long as someone saw it?"

His head snapped up, and he stopped trying to spark the fire. "*You* most certainly cannot."

I pressed my lips together. "What made you run to Waylria?"

With a grimace, he went back to working on sparking a fire. His movements became furious, almost jagged from how on edge he now seemed. Tension stalked along his frame. "I would rather be eaten by rabid rogues than taken to the death that awaits me back home."

"Why?" I couldn't help but press. At least my voice did not come out as a whisper.

Something about the expression was raw. Within a moment, though, his jaw was locked and his defenses were up again. His reaction only further triggered my curiosity.

Several long moments passed, maybe even minutes, and I

felt he was not going to answer. It was strange, as though we had traded places. And in more than a prisoner sense. The Viking had started as the one entering unknown territory and that of the enemy. Meanwhile, I could imagine we were drawing closer to Waylria's border, which was unknown to me. Now I was prisoner to my enemy. I could not help but wonder—

Riker's eyes cut back to mine. He looked at me with a challenge, as if he were daring me to look away—to dismiss his gaze. "Why not run to enemy territory for safety? It's the last place they'd look."

"It's not like your people stay off our territory. We know you must trespass to capture some of your *sacrifices*." I spat the last word, hating the taste of it on my tongue. A lie. An excuse. Murder. Cruelty. Another thing they failed to be punished for. If they had no repercussions for murder among themselves, it was no wonder they never stopped to question the moral of torturing shapeshifters.

The wood sparked to life, casting a glow along the ground before reaching the surrounding trees. Riker let the stick fall against the pile he had gathered. Suddenly, with the falling of that stick, I was reminded of how Waylria could fall. Because of me. Because I was weak enough to be overtaken by my own prisoner. If something more was coming for Waylria, as Riker said, it would be my fault.

Riker released a heavy sigh. "I spent years building and strengthening my father's army for that very reason, only for him to take it all back the second I was no longer useful to him."

My heart sank before a sense of foreboding seized it. "For that very reason? What do you mean?" Though he didn't answer, I couldn't let it go. I prodded how far I could press for answers. "What are you wanted for?" His name was on the tip of my tongue, but I swallowed it back, grimacing as if it were bile.

"Your chief told you." I opened my mouth to press further, but he snapped. "That's enough. I've had enough of your questions."

He eased closer to the fire, sticking his palms out to warm them. The glow of the fire both illuminated and shadowed his features. I could not read the darkness. Perhaps I did not want to. The crackle of the fire was the only sound between us. Inhaling a long breath, I was satisfied when I scented nothing out of the ordinary but kept my ears perked, nonetheless.

"If you're not going to feed me, could I at least move closer to the fire?" Forcing a bite in my tone when I felt like Waylria's biggest failure made my throat ache.

I tried to bury the thought to the deepest corner of my brain, but I knew it would still haunt my sleep.

SLEEP HAD EVADED me most of the night. My mind had raced, keeping me awake behind closed eyes. I couldn't dismiss the thought I was a failure or shake how I had allowed myself to get into such a situation.

In all my tossing and turning, I had figured out how to escape, but fear of making another mistake had festered hesitation. Now, with the fire extinguished, early morning loomed as a cold dark blanket. I lay in the snow, eyes closed against the tears there, with my arms cradled against my chest. The iron still encapsulated one wrist, but I had dislocated my thumb to slide one hand free.

It wasn't so much as confidence that sent me into action, but I felt it was the only way I could free myself.

Quietly panting around the collar of my shirt, I bit the hem. Swallowing back a cry, I convinced myself to dislocate the second.

It wasn't any easier to force my thumbs back into place.

This was it. This was my chance. The only way I could shift.

I needed to get the upper hand.

A desperate panic had set deep within my bones.

I had to do this.

My nails lengthened the moment the iron fell from my skin, and I cut the rope that still held me prisoner.

Shoving to my feet, I barely felt the wet snow on my hands before they formed into paws. Startled awake, Riker tensed when he laid eyes on me, but it was too late.

Chapter Twenty-Two
Riker

THE WOLF before me released a blood-curdling snarl. Her canines bared, the hair on her back standing on end. My blood ran colder than the surrounding snow. I could not have a repeat of when she encountered me in the forest. Had it really only been days since then? I had to act, and I could not have a shapeshifter getting in my way.

I forced back my exhaustion, jerked to my feet, ignoring the sting of my burns, and grabbed for the dagger I had found in her bag. I moved the blade between us, but the wolf was faster.

"No!"

Launching from her hind legs, she came for me with her mouth wide open. Without time to brace for her mouth wrapping around my arm, the bite seared up my arm and deepened a gash already there from the bear. Her jaw locked. Blood dripped down my arm, and I nearly dropped the blade. It wasn't doing me any favors.

I bit back a yell, and it took everything in my power not to wrench my arm back. Pulling like that would not only rip my skin, but it could trigger instinct to kill. Shapeshifters were nearly uncontrollable once they tasted blood. They went rabid.

I used my free hand to unhinge her jaw, to no avail. Her snout was still ridged in a snarl, her green eyes boring up at me. I tried not to let my heart sink at the look of fire in her eyes.

She bit down harder, and I couldn't hold back the yell that crawled up my throat. I pushed down with the arm in her mouth, letting her teeth bury deeper, and used my free hand to pry open her jaw.

"You kill me"—I strained against her, grinding my teeth as I wrenched her teeth from my arm—"and everyone in Waylria is dead. That's what he want—"

I caught her muzzle once my arm was free, shoving her from me.

Her paws slid in the snowy dirt as she caught herself, and she shifted back to her human form. She planted her feet, her eyes still blazing when she turned to me. "You are wanted for treason! If I don't take you back, dead or alive, we are dead."

"Let me go."

"No, I won't," she said through clenched teeth.

I took a steady step toward her, the adrenaline pumping through my body the only reason I was still holding the dagger. "Your life depends on it."

How much longer could I keep using my father's plans against her? Both of us were well aware I did not give a shit about the lives of shapeshifters. What I cared about was keeping my family safe from my father's madness and the war he was waging. And to do that, I needed someone on my side.

If the other realms already knew of my treachery, as Haiden had said, they would not listen to a word I had to say. This girl ... she was weak, intaking only enough of what I had to say to argue. She was all threat, no action.

I needed someone on my side, to find a way to stop what was to come. Even if what was by my side made my mouth taste of bitter and dry ash.

The shapeshifter shook her head. "If I don't take you back,

I'm not the only one who will suffer for it." I opened my mouth, but she didn't let me get a word out. "Haiden had a letter sent to your father before we left so that he would know I was bringing you. If I don't get you there, your father will punish Waylria for it, and Haiden will punish me in turn."

She seemed to gulp at the thought; the snarl and fire fading from her.

I took that moment of distraction, not hesitating to drop the dagger, and grabbed her by the throat with my free hand to slam her into the next tree. I kept her pinned there, even when she bared her canines at me.

"If you take me there, there will be no Waylria to return to. Not for long, at least. My father plans to start with your realm to finish what our ancestors started. There will not be a shifter or a blade of grass left of your realm once he's finished making you bleed." I searched her eyes, holding steady as understanding and pain swarmed there. "He intends to overtake Nedfin and Urute with no room for resistance. Annarr is unknown, but I imagine he will see if that is conquerable."

Her body was as rigid as the bark dug at her back. Her lips were parted slightly, brows pulled together.

"Coming with me means stopping all that—it means protecting your realm."

I tried to swallow against the dryness in my throat. What I wouldn't give for ale right now … I licked my lips, pulling back to rest against the tree. Her eyes tracked the movement with a grimace of disgust.

I had fought her and a bear—taken wounds from both— and all of it was catching up to me.

"I'm sure it's rightfully deserved," she ground out, her voice weak from the pain of her throat, "but what did you do to earn a death sentence?"

"Haiden told you. Treason."

I let my hand drop from her. She had not questioned my

father's plans. Was it enough to convince her it was really happening? That nothing I had said about it was a lie? I could not think of another reason she would ask about my execution.

"If you want me to listen to you—believe you—wouldn't you rather tell me yourself?"

I shook my head, taking another step back. My mind reeled for something to say. A solution for her—everything that stood in the way of me saving my family. "You wouldn't know which story to believe."

"What do you mean?"

With every step I took back, she took one forward.

"Fine," she relented. "Don't tell me. I'll likely find out soon enough, right?" When she looked at me in disgust, I could only imagine what she'd thought I'd done. "I can't let you go. I would never trust the lives of those I care about with another."

"Now that is something we can agree on."

She glanced at me out of the corner of her eye.

A hole already stood within my family. I could not watch them pass on. Sacrificing myself as another hole would keep us from becoming a pit.

"I'll go back with you."

The shifter snapped to her full height as if she were one of the warriors I corrected in *Illska Sandr*.

"But before going back to Sandire, you have to give me time to find an oracle to figure out a way to save my family." Once she knew the truth, she could warn others about my father's plans to conquer. Because I would likely be dead. If killing my father wasn't an option, getting my family away from him had to be the priority.

Her head tilted, and her words from before echoed in my mind.

"If nothing else, do it for the betterment of Waylria," I told her.

"You act like you want shapeshifters to survive."

Not at all. But she could be useful. I would make her useful.

It's the only way I can think of to stop my father from spreading his poisonous ideas. Even if I did not care about the lives of shifters, this went beyond them and their realm.

She opened her mouth to respond, but then went rigid, and a dark laugh sounded before she had the chance to speak.

Chapter Twenty-Three
Zyra

My HEART slowly sank as Riker and I searched the shadows of the forest for the source of the laugh. I knew we would come to regret starting a fire.

Riker was still clenching my dagger, but it wasn't meant for me. After so much violence, he stood with his back tight, arms tainted, his chest rising and falling with hot breath, staring at something beyond the tree line.

"We heard the arguing," a voice said, carrying the same rumble of darkness in speech as it had in laughter, "and thought we'd see if you wanted to join us."

I hesitated, afraid of what I would see when I finally forced my gaze to follow the trail of Riker's.

A monstrous smile went with that dark laugh. Awful things were contained in that smile. I could see a hint of the sharp teeth behind his drawn lips.

He stood directly in front of a tree, his body locked up with the same tension as Riker. The man's clothes were dark and ripped, some of the fabric barely hanging on by a few threads. He looked to be a few years younger than Haiden, but everything about him was more angular and grueling, and he didn't have nearly as much gray mixed in with his tangled brown hair. His hands were relaxed at his sides despite his stiff posture, his fingers twitching against his leg.

"We have a fire just beyond those trees. You see, we're camping for the night. Rare for us this close to that forest of Annarr's, but we figured … what more do we have to lose?"

My eyes traveled behind him to the three pairs of glowing eyes staring back at us. They stood farther back in the woods on either side of the man, keeping to the darkness so only their eyes were visible.

Rogue shifters.

My heart sank even further—the only reaction I allowed myself to have. Keeping my expression blank, I hoped my eyes and body didn't give away my distress as I assessed the situation. Smoke plumed just beyond the eyes staring at us.

"I doubt we'll sit around and exchange stories," Riker finally said, and I spared him a glance.

My stomach was in knots at the thought of how we would be slaughtered for fun. I would expect it if we ran into those after Riker, but I had not stopped to consider dying at the hands of another shifter. Their bloodlust was not exclusive to shapeshifters. Rogues killed whatever they could sink their teeth into. Their thirst came form the carnivores inside them. Everything and anything that bled—that had a pulse they could force to a halt—became a target.

And the man standing at the tree was no doubt the alpha.

He wasn't standing back to hide under the cover of the forest. He was standing between us and the three pairs of eyes, twitching with the need for violence as he spoke.

"Where're you headed?" He had clearly heard Riker but was choosing to disregard him. His eyes moved from Riker to me, then from me to Riker.

"That's none of your concern," I bit out before Riker could respond. I wanted to flash my canines in warning—show them the curse of my animal skin. But that would only escalate an attack. They would react on bitterness—without mercy—in revenge, to show Waylria what they thought of their banishment.

They wouldn't be able to sense or smell the wolf in me from this distance unless they really tasted the air.

The alpha's eyebrows shot up into his hair, eyes sparking with disturbing interest. "Isn't it, now?"

"We don't want any trouble," Riker ground out. "Back off now, and no one has to get hurt."

"Give us your supplies, and we'll consider leaving you alive."

"Not a chance," I said before I could think. There was no way they would leave without attacking us. Such a thing wasn't in their nature.

"You're going to defy everything I say," he said with narrowed eyes locked on me, "aren't you?" He shook his head, taking me in as if he were peeling me apart, attentively examining every layer before discarding it. As if I was nothing but trash. "I suppose it doesn't matter. I wasn't asking."

The shifters behind him snarled viciously in unison, one of them ending with a sinister chuckle.

I glanced at Riker as I lengthened my claws and teeth, just in case, knowing they were too focused on death to see the subtle shift. My heart pounded for escape.

Upon meeting my stare, there was a question in his eyes I couldn't answer right now. I could only give the slightest shake of my head. I couldn't shift. Not yet at least. I couldn't reveal my animal skin to them. All of them would be on top of me within seconds.

My panic hardened into something akin to dread. But that was something I could mold and use.

"Give us your supplies," the rogue leader said again, pushing away from the tree.

A single step, but it was enough to make my body stand at attention. My wolf cried out to be set free—to fight, to shift, to release my fierceness upon them.

I might not have confidence in my human form, but my wolf knew exactly what it wanted.

"We are not afraid of *Vikings*." He spat in the dirt at the last word, loathing written all over his features.

"That is your mistake," I said, barely containing my disgust at the suggestion of being a Viking. "You should fear for your lives—fear becoming sacrifices to our gods since you have been banished by the people who share your blood. No one will even realize you have been killed by your enemy. And even if they did find your cold, lifeless body, no one would care."

He already believed us both to be Vikings. I needed to wound his alpha ego—infuriate him to the point of seeing red. Attacking us would involve nothing more than lashing out then.

He laughed in the same way he'd greeted us, the ghoulish sound skittering down my spine. "Very well, then."

At that, the three rogues behind him shifted and burst forward. All predators with unbelievable strength and viciousness. With large teeth and sharp claws. A jaguar ran straight for Riker, followed by a black panther, while a lioness came charging for me.

I swallowed the snarl that rose when I ran to meet the lioness shifter halfway, my claws raised and ready to slice through skin. Her own claws swiped at me, her teeth flashing when she roared. My claws met hers when she went for my face. But my grasp on hers was too strong for that. I grabbed with one hand and cut with the other, dragging a line down her leg to her paw.

Though I thought I would have the element of surprise on my side, it didn't slow her down or cause her to hesitate a single moment. She reacted as if it were a paper cut, barely worth acknowledging. She didn't even look at the blood running through her fur. Her eyes—bronze and deadly—remained locked on me and only me. She wanted to strike again, pounce, claw into me. The way she waited and watched, her tail flicking with impatience, made me tense.

I ran, paying close attention to the sounds and movements around me. The lioness was not far behind.

This was a fight for survival. Part of surviving was being the first to take action. She had likely revealed my lie to the others through her thoughts, but I would still at least win this fight.

I swallowed against the lump in my throat, my stomach knotted tight as I turned to face her.

With her unable to stop in time, I lashed out. I didn't allow myself to think. I followed the pure scream of my instincts instead.

I raked my claws down her left side as she skidded past me. She sucked in a sharp breath, her ears pulling back before she released a wail. Lines of blood formed in my passing. Time seemed to slow as she turned to defend herself.

Using the surrounding trees to my advantage, I whirled around one to give myself the chance to dig my claws into the other side of her lean, muscular body.

With the fire reflected in her eyes, I raised my hand above my head, inhaling a long breath to steady my trembling body. She hissed as I aimed for the point right between her eyes.

When I drew my hand back, I refused to look at my stained claws.

A puddle of blood began to form. As the lioness reached out for me, her claws out in preparation to carve nails into my flesh, there was a loud gasp.

The gasp had not come from her.

I had not noticed the girl before.

She was barely clothed, adorning a flowing blue skirt that skimmed the forest floor, with a burgundy undergarment to cover the top half of her body. Every piece of clothing had jewels dangling from it but was also riddled with rips and holes. Everything looked to have been splattered in mud and dried blood. Her right arm was also covered in a variety of colorful tattoos that began at her shoulder, swirling as they traveled down to the top of her hand.

The rogue alpha appeared from the shadows, grabbing her by the neck and pulling her flush against his chest.

Her eyes held pure terror.

My breath knocked from me. The wolf inside me felt differently, though. Its heart did not sink, nor did it shy away from the predator before us. Instead, it released the fierce snarl I had been struggling to keep contained.

I didn't know who the woman was, but she looked petrified. She could not be with them of her own volition. And for that, I allowed my wolf to surface.

Digging my claws into the dirt, I shifted skins to face the alpha. Because while he was *an* alpha, he was not *my* alpha.

The rogue had shifted into his own animal skin, taking on the form of a hyena. And I would have laughed if not for how my tongue stuck to the dry roof of my mouth. A whooping hyena.

You're a shifter. Disgust overwhelmed his thoughts, and his glowing eyes told of how he wanted to feed on my corpse. *But you're not out here because you're a rogue. You're not banished.*

There was a certain scent involved with rogue shifters. We could smell the stink of their betrayal—their disgrace forever marking them.

If Corinna were here, or Nabil, they would not allow themselves to be intimidated or back down. They would show the dominance they held.

But I'd been sent here. And I wanted to walk away from this fight unscathed.

I would love nothing more than for you to carry a message back to Haiden for me, but killing you would send a stronger message. His teeth looked yellow in the light of the fire.

I spared a quick glance toward Riker at the retort, finding he was still through the trees. His back was against a tree, and the way he wielded the dagger against the black panther was brutal. He moved as if he had fought more than a hundred battles. Each movement was deliberate with precise feline swiftness. Brutal, calculating, smooth, and lithe—honed and ready for anything. Every step Riker took showed his mercilessness. He moved like the very predators he was up against.

And I—I was every inch of the warrior he was. I turned to focus back on the alpha. My blood pounded under my skin, warning me with each thump that the alpha was about to attack. *You really like hearing yourself talk, but I'm already tired of it.*

Another animalistic smile. *What are you doing out in the middle of the forest with a Viking?*

He was not the only one with questions. *What are you doing out in the middle of the forest with a human?*

Traveling makes one hungry. You walked up on us before we could dig in.

I charged toward him. Once he'd shoved the woman away, he burst into a run to meet me. We collided in a tangle of limbs and teeth, both of us snarling and fighting to tear a bite out of the other. With every bite and scratch I gave him, he gave right back. Dirt kicked up around us, our snarls as intense as the sting of our teeth.

Chapter Twenty-Four
Riker

THRUSTING the dagger into the black panther over and over, I refused to let exhaustion overtake me until he gurgled and stopped moving altogether. His chest no longer rose and fell. He was limp. Dead on top of me. His blood was seeping into the dirt, collecting in a pool beneath his massive body and staining my pants. His paws sprawled, his claws still reaching. They had been inches from mauling my face. Loosening my grip on my weapon, I took his ginormous head between my hands and threw him off me. The jaguar lay dead mere feet away.

Suddenly, there were intense snarls and clouds of dirt being kicked up. Zyra—in her wolf form—was biting, clawing, and wrestling with a hyena on the other side of the trees. She had the advantage, her jaw snapping down in the face of who I could only assume was the leader.

A little ways from them stood a woman dressed in bold clothes that hung in tatters. She gaped at the struggle, taking a hesitant step back. She gathered the courage to flee then, her blonde hair trailing behind her as she disappeared through the trees.

Pushing away from the panther's carcass, I stood, still

clutching the bloody dagger. I likely only had moments before my adrenaline wore off.

I had only taken a few running steps when a shrieked growl broke through the air.

Zyra no longer had the advantage. The leader had overtaken her; her shoulder and side bleeding. Human again, he threw her to the ground. Blood leaked from her wounds at the force, knotting her fur.

His hands went for her neck while she struggled to regain her breath. She shifted into her human form to try and pry his hands off her. With him pressing her to the ground, she flailed. He ignored every attempt, lifting her and pushing her closer to the remnants of a fire.

Struck by how hard she fought, I realized she had not been desperate enough to lose her composure in such a way when we had gone against each other. She'd kept fairly calm, even when I had power over her. She had seemed confident she would dominate once again.

But now … now she was fighting for her life and couldn't save face as she did. Because she wasn't sure she could win.

"What are you doing in the middle of nowhere with a Viking?" the leader asked, chuckling and pushing her closer. Zyra closed her eyes, as if she could will the fire not to touch her. Her teeth clenched, she fought to free his hand from her neck but eventually gasped for breath. "You've betrayed your own kind to the enemy. You deserve to suffer, to be despised for your betrayal as we have."

His grip slipped slightly, and my mind reeled, bringing images of the night I was desperate to forget but couldn't stop seeing whenever I closed my eyes. My fingers tightened around the hilt of the dagger, the pain of remembering stealing the breath from my lungs.

A flash of the endless stars above sand dunes.

Blood coating the rug at my feet.

Pale hands desperate to cover a flowing wound.

Blood gathering under long fingernails.

The images faded as I came back into myself, slowly pulling air back into my lungs. My physical wounds did not compare.

Then I was moving. I didn't know why—but I wasn't thinking. I only knew I couldn't watch the fire consume her. Something in my chest wrenched at the thought.

Maybe it was because she helped heal my burns. Maybe it was because I thought I might need her to convince others of my father's plans. Maybe I wanted to kill her myself. Maybe I didn't have a reason.

I didn't know why or what it meant, but I couldn't bring myself to walk away.

I was unsure what it would mean afterward, but I ran to her aid before she could be engulfed by the flames. The leader was laughing darkly again and didn't stop, not even after I shoved him and plunged the dagger into his abdomen. As I caught Zyra's wrist with my free hand, I yanked her toward me, catching her against me.

At her sharp intake of breath, I saw the questions swarming inside her wide green eyes.

I would find a way to use her astonished confusion later on.

Twisting away from her, I whirled on that dark laughter, but before I could do anything further, light flared from behind and a figure sped around me. Zyra's wolf form came into focus as she leaped, digging her teeth into his shoulder, cheek, and collarbone. Then she finished at the delicate skin of his neck, puncturing his airway.

He shouted, fighting to fling her off, but she held firm, keeping her teeth buried in his throat until he choked on his own blood. She remained on top of his body, blood dripping from her muzzle. Once he stilled, she released her annihilating hold.

She shifted as she climbed off him, pushing to her feet. And even though she wasn't looking at me, I knew she was uncertain of what she would see once she looked up.

Arms trembling with strain at her sides, her chest heaved. Her green eyes were large and striking when they finally rose to meet mine, and I felt like she was seeing every inch of me all at once. But blood coated her mouth and cheeks ...

"Why did you do it? Why did you save me?"

"I don't know." My voice sounded far off even to my own ears.

She released me from her gaze, walking over to where her satchel laid discarded on the ground. Fresh blood spilled from her cheek, shoulder, and side.

"You're going to come with me now," I said, and she blinked, failing to hide her surprise. "No more of this fucking fighting. We don't have time for it."

She straightened, her green eyes blazing like a forest fire. "Do you have a death wish? I told you not to start that fire—"

"I'm not talking about the fire or the rogues," I bit out. I blinked away the memory of a bloody rug, and a knot formed in my ribcage.

There was only one way to rid myself of such a feeling. The pain would never fade, but something could be done to prevent more of it.

The shifter watched me in silence for nearly a full minute before realizing I wasn't going to say anything further, then spoke again. "Why did you save me?"

I don't know. I don't know. I don't know. I didn't want to think —didn't want to look for the answer.

"Why would I wander onto your territory?"

Zyra blinked at the question, her own brewing in her eyes.

"Why would I enter the territory of my enemy?" I asked her again. "I had nothing to lose but everything to gain if your chief believed me and joined forces to stop my father. Warning you—" I stopped, swallowing against the lump in my throat.

"Warning your kind was the only way I could think of to save my family."

My grip on the dagger was one of death.

I had to bite down my hatred—for their sake. Showing the shifter the truth through an oracle would spread word of my father's plans. I could race home; she could return to Waylria to alert others. From there, word would spread, and I would be home in time to stop the retaliation of my father's fury.

"Your father had men out searching for you," she pointed out. "Whether you entered Waylria or ended up captured, the outcome would be the same. Death would be at your door no matter what you chose." She shook her head. "I still don't know what you did to deserve such a severe sentence, but that is motive enough if one death seems more merciful than another."

Then she seemed to understand the last part of what I'd said because her brows furrowed. "What do you mean about saving your family? What about telling us of your father's supposed 'plans' would save your family?"

I gritted my teeth, a war raging inside me as I fought back flashes of memories.

"I don't know how to save them. That is why I need to find an oracle." A beat of silence. "Just come, listen to the oracle. If she does not speak on my father's plans, take me back to Sandire as your prisoner, and all this can be over."

"How can I trust you will go back with me?" she asked. "How can I trust that you won't just run the other way when it comes time to return to Sandire?"

I stared at her. Trust? Trust was not something given to shifters, nor was it shared among others across the realms. Vikings trusted Vikings and were wary when it came to others. There would be no need to take me back to Sandire once she learned of the truth, but still, to swear an oath to a shapeshifter ...

"I can do nothing but swear to you—before my gods—that I will. We have no way to perform a proper oath swearing."

Zyra stared at me, picking me apart in search of a reason to hold onto her distrust. She must've found something, or her instincts forced her to hold tight to them because she jerked her gaze from mine. Despite that, she muttered, "Just don't make me regret this, or I *will* find it in me to rip open your throat."

Relief overpowered any desire I might have had to hurl back my own seething response.

She reached her hand out for me to set the dagger in her palm.

"You have your teeth. I get the dagger."

She gave a curt nod, letting her hand drop back to her side. "Fair enough."

Chapter Twenty-Five
Zyra

I SUPPOSED this was the only way. While Haiden might not be pleased by the deviation, I might be saving us from a greater threat. I didn't know what I would do if I found the Viking to be lying.

Perhaps kill him myself.

He was right about my teeth, but my claws could just as easily carve open his throat.

Either way, returning to Waylria unaccomplished was not an option. Not for me. Not without retaliation. Laughter. Being dubbed an outcast in a worse way than before. No one would claim or talk to me then.

I would be nothing more than a lone wolf.

Almost no better than the rogues we had just encountered.

The thought sent an ache through my chest. My pulse wild and mind howling, I cast a glance at the Viking out of the corner of my eye. Only to realize he was observing me with the same caution. The wolf inside me bristled, but I clenched my teeth to keep from baring them.

That was something I had always admired about my animal skin. My instincts. The wolf in me always seemed to know what it wanted and sensed how and when to act. It felt like having two selves. Two halves resided within my one body, which, I supposed, could be the idea the Great Spirit had in mind when it came to our human forms and our animal forms. My human form might not know when to have the conviction to react, but my animal skin did.

Neither of us had let our guard down.

Even now, despite my thoughts, my animal skin was wound tight, ready to spring into action despite the exhaustion over-taking my body. Riker kept a close eye on me. I kept a watchful eye on him. Our very nature screamed how the other was dangerous.

And yet, I could not shake the Viking's warnings of his father's intentions. More than that, I could not shake the underlying desperation he expressed at the mention of his family. He seemed shaken to his very soul—his very essence. If none of what he said was true, why would he be so uneasy? What could he be lying about? The concern for his family seemed raw and real.

My stomach rumbled with hunger, telling me I'd have to hunt soon.

The forest seemed to change within no more than a blink. The snow was behind us now, the forest thinning. Moss clung to the bark, and the farther we walked, the more it coated the trees. The dirt beneath our feet suddenly became uneven as roots littered the ground.

The Viking whirled on me. Eyes widening, I stiffened, sure to meet his gaze. He did not seem to like that, though, because he tilted his head away to speak. "We are weary travelers in search of a place to stay. This—this might be where I find answers. Don't try anything."

My mouth dropped open, ready to ask what he was talking about, when I spotted the rickety shacks. Even from where we stood, pieces of the outside seemed to be falling apart.

I racked my brain for a village between Nedfin and Waylria, only to come up with nothing. According to our maps, nothing was supposed to reside between our two realms.

"We look like shit," I said, gesturing to my dirty and tattered clothing. My whole body was dusted in dirt and dried blood. He looked no better. "There is no chance we *won't* call attention to ourselves."

He didn't listen, nor did he bother to respond.

Upon entering this village, I realized I was no longer on Waylrian soil. At some point, we had crossed the border. While I had never traveled far from the borough, the realization I was outside the boundaries of my home felt like a punch in the gut.

"Wait." I nearly made the mistake of grabbing his arm. He did not remove his hand from the dagger's hilt as he turned to face me. I could barely speak around the sudden dryness of my throat. "Do you really want to risk people asking questions? With your father trying to catch up to you?"

He seemed to consider this for a moment, looking back at the village over his shoulder. "I doubt anyone will stop me to ask questions. My father's men could be anywhere. That is what you are for."

He kept walking, and I was left trying not to dig into his answer.

The village was worn with weather and lack of care. Holes and puddles of water littered the compact dirt roads, making walking a treacherous feat in and of itself. One wrong move and I would twist my ankle. Yet the village bustled with people chatting, those focused on where they were headed, and … strange-looking characters who did not seem to have a grasp on where they were or what they were doing.

The likelihood of the Viking finding the information he needed, suddenly seemed slim.

Mostly, people just looked gruff and worse for wear. Their clothes were decent, but the people themselves were dirty, indifferent to their crumbling buildings and homes, and unbothered unless someone looked at them the wrong way. Not a single person seemed unarmed, either.

When I inhaled to taste the air, nothing stood out to me. No shifters. No Fey. No Vikings. Nothing but the musty scent of humans. The only abnormality was the Viking and me. Which meant everyone here was from Nedfin.

Still, while some looked at us with interest, others did not bat an eye.

Riker looked at me with narrowed eyes. "I have not had the chance to sleep in a bed in quite some time. I wouldn't say or do anything to put that at risk."

My eyes landed on the inn down from us. While I wanted nothing more than to sleep on a mattress for my aches and wounds, I doubted I would be getting a bed. Even worse, I doubted I would be let out of the Viking's sight.

"You can't possibly think you'll find out anything about an oracle here," I said as we passed another group of seedy-looking men.

"Even with oracles being banned from stepping foot into Sandire, there are still people who talk about them," Riker said as he pushed open the door of the inn.

Inside was even more stifling than outside. I cringed at what met my senses.

The space was cast in shadow, with only a few lit candles providing light. Nearly every long, dingy table was empty. A few stragglers sat alone with steins; some slumped over the table, asleep before they could finish. A man and woman stood behind the wooden bar, staring at Riker and me with dissecting gazes. They were no doubt taking in our wounds and filth.

The space was more of a tavern than an inn, but the stairs suggested rooms might be above us.

The man and woman behind the bar had tensed by the time we reached them. They pointedly kept their gazes off me. They knew what Riker was, and that was enough for me to be ignored. Though they still refused to meet his eyes. Likely because of how worse for wear he looked.

We might not be in Waylria, but others knew of the brutality of Vikings. Were Vikings feared and hated by other realms?

Riker strode right up and requested a room. I kept my gaze down in a feeble attempt to hide the bruises on my neck. Despite having no way to pay, he spoke with all the confidence of a warrior. As if the room was owed to him.

Waylrians traded goods, which left us with no way to pay for a room since the Viking's pockets were also empty. Once these people realized he had no way to pay, Riker would be dismissed. Maybe I could gain a chance to escape, or they would realize who he was and help me hold him until word could be sent to Slate.

"Half up front," the man barked, handing a glass to the woman in dismissal. He stared down his long, crooked nose at us.

I tilted my head enough to watch the exchange through my hair.

"I am here to look for work tomorrow. If you allow us the night now, I will reward you handsomely for it." The Viking was lying through his teeth.

The man took a moment to consider his words carefully when my gaze flickered to him. Despite how he spoke, he was still taking care of how he chose to act. "You could come back 'ere with nothing more than a potato as your so-called 'reward.'"

"Sir." Riker glanced around us, as if to ensure no one was close enough in the empty tavern to hear. "My woman here — she is not the most ... put together. She left half our things in the woods, for god's sake. I have no way to pay you half now, but I will have more than enough tomorrow."

I clenched my hands into fists, wanting nothing more than to punch him in the teeth. I had fought a rogue shifter, and an alpha, no less. Not to mention that I had taken *him* down more than once. I was pretty certain I could do it again. My hand was the only thing that didn't hurt, so it would hardly make a difference.

He better start proving what he's been telling me.

The innkeeper glanced at his wife behind him. "I can understand what you mean."

The man seemed to decide his life wasn't worth an argument over a simple key to a room and bent for something behind the counter. Then he set a key on the bar top.

"Just for the night," the man muttered.

Riker nodded. "Just for the night."

Those words struck a cord. Riker only intended to stay for one night and disappear by morning, likely before the sun rose. We were not to linger. We would get some rest, likely ask a few questions, and be on our way before the innkeepers came to collect.

I wondered if the keeper realized that, too, and was merely letting us have a room to keep his head attached to his neck.

My stomach hollowed out again at the thought of being in a room—a confined space—with the Viking.

He was pulling me upstairs before my mind could wander to the worst possibilities of what might happen tonight. I held in a gasp, forcing my wobbly legs to take me up each step. A hallway of bedrooms were at the top, above the tavern. There was no telling which led to a bathing chamber. I wanted nothing more than to wash the grime from my face.

Riker strode up to the first door to try the key, and the door opened to a cramped room. My prison for the night. He wrenched me inside, shutting the door in the same motion. My nails and canines sharpened, ready to defend.

The size of the room allowed for very little space around the bed. I stood in the center. Where did he expect me to go? I would not be backed into a corner without knowing what he would do.

I eyed the bed, then slid my gaze to the dagger at his waist. I had no intention of touching or going near the bed. It looked like one big lumpy trap.

Without warning, he pulled the tin can from my bag, which was still slung over his shoulder, and tossed it at me. I caught it. He was already turning away when I looked up again.

"I'll be back with something to eat."

I didn't bother reminding him we had no way to pay. Evidently, he was scary enough to get whatever he wanted in this village. Likely out of fear, he alone could pillage and destroy it in its entirety.

Without another word, he strode from the room, slamming the door behind him.

I heard the lock slide into place, as if that would stop me if I wanted to leave.

Only ... he knew I couldn't with a clear conscience. Not when my fear over him being right about his father outweighed my need to turn him in. For now.

Chapter Twenty-Six
Riker

My mind was still reeling from having saved her. I was not entirely sure why I had acted so irrationally. Something had just … snapped. When it came down to it, I couldn't let her die. I was unable to take her life, and I couldn't walk away when another had tried.

Killing the bear had been so easy. Second nature.

When I saw Zyra trapped beneath the rogue, an invisible force had shoved me into action. I'd heard another voice scream; another face flashed before my eyes. Blood hadn't even been spilled yet, but I'd seen so much blood. Crimson soaked through clothes, the rug, and stained the floorboards.

I couldn't bring myself to watch that much blood spill. I couldn't watch it pool from around my dagger.

My thoughts wrestled against one another, grappling for an answer for why and how this had been so different.

To keep my thoughts from gravitating to Sandire and the family I left behind, I stormed down the stairs of the inn and headed straight outside. The sun was only just setting, so people still mingled along the road between the buildings and homes. The whole place was a mess. Although, I refused to think the shifter might be right about getting answers here. We were close to the Nedfin Mountains—someone had to know something.

I walked up to the first woman I saw, who scowled and clutched her basket closer to keep it between us, then walked around me before I could so much as say a word.

I turned to the next person without watching her go. The man didn't so much as flinch away, but he couldn't bear to look me in the eye as he told me he did not know of any oracles. He seemed slimy and like he knew more than he was willing to share, but I let him move on. The next person I came face-to-face with was a burly man carrying an ax. With each person I approached, the more fatigued my body felt.

"I'm not looking for any trouble," he muttered in a gruff voice, going to push by me.

"I'm not either," I said. My words gave him pause, and he turned to me with a hand on his ax. I had fought enough battles over the last few days. He did not want to push me to go there. "I'm looking for information about … oracles." I settled on the name the shifter chose, hoping it was common enough to be understood. "Those who see the future. Do you know how I would come to find one?"

He eyed the dagger at my hip, which I had merely stuffed into my waistband. The wooden hilt was visible, though, which had etchings that had likely taken hours to carve. Sandire weapons were mostly forged from steel, which was where my love of my ax had come from—its intricate wooden handle.

"No," he finally offered. "I know they pass through some-what—for meals and fortune telling—but I wouldn't know how to find one. We don't leave here; we come here."

I nodded. "Understood. I appreciate your time."

He went to be on his way.

I turned back. "Would you want to trade?" I called after him.

The man paused again, looking back over his shoulder.

THE INN MIGHT VERY WELL BE RUNDOWN and in a shit town, but I thanked the gods for the bed upstairs and the ale they served downstairs. Though I had locked the girl in the room, I was certain a locked door couldn't stop the wolf. Only, in a village like this and with me downstairs ready to put myself between her and the door, she wouldn't make it far.

I hoped it wouldn't come to that.

I hoped she would heed my warnings.

After having slept in a cell for a few days, and the cold ground for longer, even a lumpy mattress called to me.

I missed my bed. My home. My family. It had all crumbled before my very eyes; before I could realize it or do anything. Even though I knew stopping it was beyond my control, I couldn't help thinking that I could. If maybe if I had done one thing differently …

The lack of answers from the villagers was amplifying the thoughts and causing a headache behind my eyes.

I walked right up to the bar of the tavern, the ax on my hip tapping against my thigh. Only the woman stood behind the bar, still scrubbing glasses, while her husband was nowhere in sight.

"What can I get you?" she asked when she looked up.

I nearly asked for a pitcher of ale.

"An ale and a few answers."

She eyed me warily, humming under her breath, then set down the glass and scooped up a stein in its place. As she filled it, she glanced over her shoulder. "We don't get your kind here. You have everyone scared shitless, walking in here with that girl. My husband included."

I took the ale and downed it the moment she handed it to

me. I slammed the stein on the bar top with a final gasp. It quenched my thirst but not my racing thoughts.

"Another?" she asked.

But now was not the time.

"I'm not here to be any trouble," I told her. "We're passing through. I'm looking for information about *völva* — seers of the future — and how I can find one."

"Hardly ever see them in this place." She nodded to herself, leaning against the bar top. "I would say you would have better luck at Nedfin, but no one would let you through the gates. We would know, seeing as we are all rejects of the realm. Everyone in this village — either not peaceful enough or not willing to follow Nedfin's every rule and organized arrangement. Only thing we have to worry about around here are rogues, but it ain't so bad."

Zyra had said something similar.

I had avoided her long enough.

The state and the people of the village suddenly made sense. Everyone here was just trying to get by. Live their lives the way they wanted. I was sure many in Sandire had considered doing the same, but there was nowhere to go — nowhere to hide — among the dunes.

"You have nothing else you could tell me?"

"Find the traveling wagon."

"Traveling—"

The door behind the woman burst open to reveal her husband. Somehow, she had already backed away and was cleaning more glasses and plates. Though he eyed me, he was meticulous in going about pouring himself a pitcher of ale, as if he did not want to move too suddenly for fear of startling me into attacking him. The moment he left to join a group of men at one of the tables, the wife set aside what she was doing with an eye roll.

"I don't know anything more," she told me. "That's as much as I know from the people around here. They find you."

I nodded in understanding. Perhaps the shifter had been right.

"Can I get some food, too?"

Waiting for food might give me the chance to prepare for what was to come next.

THE GIRL SAT up when I opened the door to our room. I crossed the space within a few steps and dropped the plate on the floor in front of her. Some of it fell from the plate. Surprisingly, she did not flinch.

"What, are you treating me like a dog now?" she sniped. "Why did you bother saving me if you were just going to—"

Where her wounds had been bleeding, there was a shimmer from the salve. Blood still crusted on the side of her face. Dried. Dark red. No longer bleeding but healing. My stare went to the holes in her shirt, wondering if her other wounds had stopped bleeding.

"Until you can prove—"

"Prove what? Shifters have not been able to deter your belief—"

"I don't know!" I suddenly found myself saying. I stood back then, crouching from a careful distance and making sure to keep my hands close to the ax. "I don't know why, but I couldn't kill you, and I couldn't let you die. But now ... now, it's time for me to question you."

Her eyes flicked to me, analyzing, questioning. She was still trying to figure out why I had said it. And decipher what it meant.

Change your mind about me? The question wove through the room like smoke, ready to choke us both.

I clenched my teeth. I should not have said anything. My

own thoughts were scrambled—all cluttered and fighting to be at the forefront.

"Don't worry, I won't resort to what you and your beastly friend did to me."

She let out a halfhearted "Woof."

Silence settled over the cramped room that only seemed to grow smaller. I found myself staring at the jagged scars on the back of my hands.

"Why doesn't Haiden hold the title of king?" I asked. "Why does he choose to be known as the Chief of Waylria instead?"

Her head tilted, as if she had not been expecting such a question. My questions should be easier to answer, too, unless there were more secrets than our realm had ever fathomed.

"Why do you want to know?" she asked. "Trying to decipher some sort of secret?"

"Aside from my father being a madman, I want to know the differences in their ruling." I had no idea of what was to come or how to prepare, but knowing how others ruled might be a good place to start.

Something final gnawed at my stomach.

To stop my father was to end him.

Somehow, the girl had narrowed her eyes even more. I could see her struggling with how much to say. She didn't trust me, that much was certain, but her hesitancy spoke of a lack of trust within herself more than anything.

"Haiden considers kings to be selfish rulers who make decisions that only benefit themselves. He doesn't want to be called a king because he wants the opposite. He takes the wants of his people into high consideration to do what's best for Waylria."

"Your insults aren't so subtle, shifter. It's no secret you hate everything about Sandire." From where I was standing, I wasn't sure I much liked Sandire either. At least not for how dangerous it stood now.

She exhaled a long breath through her nose. "You can't stomach anything that steps outside your idea of what I am—

who shifters are. And you lead them—or would have, if your life was not to be disposed of by the swift fall of an ax."

"I'm trying to stop that from continuing." I'd intended to spit the words, but my tone was even.

I met her vacant stare, wondering what she was thinking. Wondering if her anger was still eating at her—if she was still fuming over how she had failed to return me to Sandire. But her eyes gave away nothing, holding a distant look. I couldn't help but think it went back to the hesitancy—the self-distrust—from before.

She had every right to question her own reliance when I had taken her prisoner so effortlessly.

"Are you saying the sacrifices will stop if you manage to overthrow your father?" She let out a short laugh. "You have been hunting us for far too long for me to believe such a thing. That's what this is about, isn't it? You want to overthrow your father and take Sandire for yourself." She shook her head. "Yet you stand here and act as though you are any better than him."

"I don't want Sandire." It was never meant to be mine. I just wanted to protect what remained of my family. "You have your beliefs, as we have ours. Ending sacrifices is impossible in the eyes of our gods."

"And you truly believe that?" Her voice was quiet, but that didn't take away from a word she said. "You must have made plenty of sacrifices, and look at where you are—banished and wanted for treason. You've even been taken captive and tortured by your very enemies. Some help your gods are." She shook her head. "And now you're struggling to figure out how to stop your father. Is this where your sacrifices have gotten you? Or has killing innocents caught up with you?"

I clenched my jaw, my fury urging my hand to twitch toward my ax. After releasing a long breath through my nose, I said, "That was not the first time I had to endure something like that. Sometimes, an offering shows just enough appreciation to earn help in the next battle."

I had to believe that—grasp it to keep myself moving forward. Letting that go would leave me with nothing. As much as I'd wished the sacrifices had done something to protect my family, their unraveling derived from betrayal.

"At least our beliefs are not tied to the blood of others."

All I could see was Annora's blood.

I rubbed my hands together.

"What do you believe, then?" My voice sounded distant to my own ears—muffled and lost.

The shifter blinked, then stared down at her plate of food. "I ... I believe shapeshifters come from the Great Spirit. But the fruit ... eating it helps us find our skins from within. It does not give us that blessing; we are born with it. We are given the fruit as children to unleash our animal skin, but I believe we are warned against eating it as adults because that is all it does."

"You're given fruit from a tree as children?"

She nodded, unseeing. "It's a ritual we all go through. Some of us are more blessed than others."

I moved from my crouched position to sit on the floor, no longer able to ignore the ache of my own wounds. The salve was beside her, though, and I doubted she would appreciate such a sudden movement from me after being attacked. Even now, she watched me warily.

"What makes one animal more important than others?" I asked her.

Zyra's head snapped up at the question.

While Sandire had gained information about shifters since the sacrifices began, we were missing fundamental details. None of which I knew what to do with. There was no telling how far I would make it, if I would carry such information for long.

I grinned. "What? Didn't like the question?"

She looked away again, staring at the cold food on her

plate. I saw the debate about whether she should eat it. "Perhaps I've just had enough of your questions."

"I'm not done getting my answers. Don't think I didn't notice how you just reacted."

She clenched her jaw, and I couldn't help but wonder about her fangs. The way shifters could summon some of their animal characteristics without fully turning made my skin crawl. Though I couldn't deny how curiosity also pulled me in.

"No shifter is of more importance than the others," she admitted. "Not truly, anyway. Even Haiden is only so much more important because we would need him to keep the peace and guide us."

"How did you become one of Haiden's puppets?"

That was when she seemed to decide the food I'd brought was safe enough to eat, so she picked up a piece of stew meat, throwing it into her mouth before reaching for the bread. "I'm not. I pickle and make preservatives to trade with Nedfin."

A laugh burst passed my lips.

It was difficult to see from all her hair, but a flush colored her cheeks. For the first time since I walked into the room, she met my eyes in an unwavering stare.

"I don't believe that for a second," I told her with a shake of my head. A sour taste coated my mouth. She thought she could fool me. Even if pickling and shit was the part she played in helping Waylria, it only proved that all shifters were bred to kill. "Not after you took part in interrogating me."

The shifter shrugged before plopping another piece of meat in her mouth. "He sent me to die. That is how much of an asset I am."

Chapter Twenty-Seven
Zyra

"It's the only explanation."

The Viking sat in stunned silence. The Viking who was being hunted by his own father was stunned by how I was disregarded.

"Haiden has never found any use for me, not since my animal skin was revealed during the ritual I mentioned. He owed my mother a favor—she's the only reason I have any connection to him. Even when everyone turned from me, he called upon me when needed—kept me to assist him in trading with Nedfin."

"Why?" was all he asked.

Though I had been trying to meet his eyes whenever possible to keep him from wanting to kill me, now, I couldn't look at him. Something in the back of my mind whispered of how he would not harm me, not after saving me from being burned away in that fire. Perhaps I should have swallowed my fear and run for my life while he was downstairs. Fear kept me from doing more than I wanted to admit.

Regardless, something had shifted.

Him saving my life, asking me questions, giving me the salve … I was uncertain of what the change was, but I felt it.

The pull was heavy in the air. I felt it — could taste it — but I refused to reach for it to see it for whatever it was. No. I wanted him to fight me, snap back to the way he had been, but he failed to retort when I tried to get under his skin.

"Why what?" My voice came out hoarse, as if I had been screaming into the void. Maybe I had.

"Why did everyone turn their back on you?"

I'd hesitated when he left. I had hesitated to take back my freedom, and now I was trapped into answering things that ached to my very core.

"I'm a curse. My wolf is a curse." My voice — my self — no longer felt tied to my body. Flashes of memories raced through my mind, numbing my entire body against the withering looks from my parents, the shock that rang out after the reveal of my wolf, and against how others kept their distance. Lizeth and Corinna were the only ones to ever fully embrace me without fear or prejudice.

"Legend speaks of a wolf shifter who had fallen in love with a Viking." With my eyes locked on the wall across from me, my mouth moved of its own accord. "Everyone believed she was influenced by the Viking in some way to make it so. Because our kinds have hated each other for so many ages. By the time other shifters knew of the attachment, she had fallen pregnant. She was shunned by the other shifters, but such a thing had never happened before, and no one felt right about banishing her while she was with child. It is believed the shifter cursed the next wolf."

Feeling returned to my fingers in waves. Ignoring how they tingled, I formed fists as the Viking came back into focus. I blinked when I thought I saw concern in his gaze, but then it didn't exist.

I leaned into the wall, relieved to feel something, even if it was brick digging into my spine.

"Do your kind have mates?" he asked.

"We won't unite for life. Not all of us, at least." With how I was ignored, such a thing was never a concern for me.

He glanced at my plate. "Do you want more to eat?"

It took me a moment, but I shook my head in reply. My stomach was hollow, and no amount of food would fill it.

The silence of the room was palpable. I hated it. My teeth pinched into my gums.

"Did your wounds get enough salve?"

I looked up then. The salve had cooled my wounds, leaving them with a dull ache. My fingers twitched toward the tin. "Yes." After a long moment, I pushed the tin closer to him and pulled my hand back before he had the chance to reach for it.

I had hoped there would be a water basin in the room, but the bed looked creaky and the small table beside it would likely collapse if so much as a rag touched it. That likely explained the dust coating the top.

Riker grabbed the salve off the floor and stood to move to the bed, which did creak when he sat at its edge.

I wouldn't be getting much sleep tonight.

Though determination set his eyes, he looked ... utterly exhausted. The amber of his eyes was muted, only a spark for answers glimmering in them.

We both had taken the chance to ask questions, hoping to be indulged with answers. A tether of trust grew between us, but it went ignored—denied and tied with guilt.

When he went to lift his shirt above his head, I sharply looked away. My heart involuntarily strummed against my ribs. I swallowed back a hiss, reminding myself this was unknown territory. In such a tight space, I did not need to risk myself further. That tether felt taut now—or perhaps I confused the sensation with the ache in my chest.

I was already at his mercy.

"You wouldn't know which story to believe."

I hadn't been able to shake that statement either. My mind

was a cloud of confusion. I didn't know if I could withstand letting things go unanswered.

After some time, I heard the top of the tin screw back into place. I ignored the strange tingle that made its way down my back. He hadn't made a sound while tending to his wounds.

The bed creaked with the movement of the Viking lying down. "I sleep with a blade under my pillow," he said in warning.

I glanced at him out of the corner of my eye. His shirt was back on, and he was lying on top of the thin, basically useless blankets. "That doesn't sound too safe," I muttered.

"Says the beast with claws."

"What's wrong, don't want to share a bed?"

He scoffed, then let the silence blanket the room.

I lay awake most of the night on the cold, hard floor, my mind echoing memories and voices I had hoped to leave behind in Waylria. After the rogues, bringing up the curse, and thinking of Lizeth, I did not have the energy to feel much. Not even disdain for the brute I was sharing a room with. And I lay awake not because I was worried he would kill me, but because I couldn't quiet my thoughts long enough to doze off.

Chapter Twenty-Eight
Riker

I HAD BARELY MADE it to the edge of the bed before the shifter sat up, her green eyes trained on me. From the little window, the remaining moonlight crept into the room. I got up, sliding the ax out from under my pillow, and grabbed the satchel. She quickly followed.

More than just the lumpy mattress kept me awake.

The legend she spoke of haunted my dreams the same way Annora's death did.

Wolf shifters were curses. For one of presumably falling in love with a Viking. Such an offense was punished by the king himself. A betrayal of one's heart to the enemy was akin to betraying us all. And so, the king would carve out the heart of the betrayer.

We were not to touch a shifter for any reason other than to kill them.

Even now, I was breaking our laws.

I should not be letting my guard down in any way.

But here I was, walking alongside a shifter, and we had touched more than I would ever admit—to myself or otherwise.

When we reached the stairs, I did not slow. I kept my focus

straight ahead for the door at the bottom. I never took in the rest of the tavern. We had spent enough time here, and no one would be getting a thing from me.

I had more dire things to focus on.

"Find the traveling wagon," the barkeep's wife had said.

Time was slipping through my fingers. With the shifter being a trader with Nedfin, she had revealed a new use for me. Once we spoke to the oracle, she could vouch for my warnings.

As we walked the rough trails from the village to the forest, I focused on her every move.

I monitored the occasional way her steps hesitated, as if she were listening for something. And then there was the way she overanalyzed everything, even at the early morning hour, her head often tilted.

Everything about her screamed wolf to me now.

How had I never heard of the legend she spoke of? A Viking falling in love with a shapeshifter was unfathomable. It was not something that would go unnoticed or unuttered about among Sandire. Had my father—or his father before him—ordered it to go unspoken?

"When had the last wolf shifter lived?" I found myself asking.

Her steps slowed until she eventually paused. "Was that the first time you had heard such a story?"

I almost denied it; the dismissal was on the tip of my tongue, but it was pointless. "Yes."

She watched me for a moment, seemingly trying to decide something. "I don't know when exactly. It isn't talked about. They only speak of how repulsive I am."

Of all the legends and stories we had of shifters, the one she spoke of was not one handed down. *Do you think it's true?* I wanted to ask her. If I had never heard of the legend and no shifters spoke of it …

"I only know about it because it has been spat at me for so long," she added.

We turned back to walking. For some time, the story circled through my thoughts. I could not shake it—stop thinking over every word and wondering where it had been lost from Sandire.

As the sun rose higher with the day, I realized I hadn't seen any animals since we left Waylria Borough.

Few birds drifted through the branches, and if they did, they didn't make a single chirp. None of the trees rustled from another critter, and no faint steps reached my ears. The rays from the sunrise were empty, and shadows failed to reveal movement. It was only us.

I wondered if other animals could sense Zyra was something bigger and more dangerous. If I could clearly see the wolf within her, then surely they could sense it.

"ARE we going to talk about what we are doing now?"

The shifter's question bit at me as if she had taken a chunk out of my arm or leg. My head was aching the same way. It made it impossible to think. *"Find the traveling wagon."* That was all I had to go off of.

I was doing the very thing I did not want to do: aimlessly wandering the realms in search of an oracle.

I had guided us northeast, toward the mountains. Now I was doubting the journey, wondering if we should have gone west. Though the thought of heading in the direction of Sandire made my stomach hollow out.

"Did you grab more supplies before we left?"

I grit my teeth. She knew the answer to that. She watched me walk in last night and had just walked out with me this morning.

I had been too focused on getting answers. And the sloppy

meat and potatoes at the tavern had filled me up enough for the thought to not have crossed my mind.

"I got us a place to sleep—" I started. I didn't get far, which had my grip tightening around my ax.

"Oh, yes, the cold floor was much more comfortable than the dirt ground," she griped.

"Can't you hunt?" I challenged.

Her jaw locked when she surveyed the trees, still alert. Sometime in the night, she had worked to wipe away the blood and dirt from her face. "Can't you? My being a shapeshifter is convenient for you now? Or is this a trick where you'll kill me for hunting? A death sentence for bringing back a rabbit?"

The thought of her shifting at any given moment sent beads of sweat down my back.

"I haven't seen a single animal since we left. Why? What's out here?"

Her head whipped around, a grimace on her face. "You would have a better idea of what is out here than I do. I only know from stories. Rogues, bandits, maybe creatures from Annarr—does that really happen or are those just stories? Either way, I don't know what's out here."

Her words had somehow grown more brazen since our journey began.

I had never been within Waylria's borders, and now I was traveling farther north than I ever had. I could only hope we were heading in the right direction since it was impossible to tell from the trees. Every dirt patch, tree, and root looked identical. The thought of likeness sent an ache from my head to my chest.

I turned my focus to the shifter. Home and family were risky thoughts right now. I could not afford to get lost in them. I didn't want to exchange one forest for another far more dangerous one.

A forest shadowed in mystery, with monsters so horrific, they couldn't be described in legend.

Wandering into the shadowed realm of Annarr would be the worst of fates. Nothing the shifter could come up with would be worse than whatever awaited those who entered the sinister and otherworldly land.

Dunes and a dense-looking forest separated Sandire from Annarr. Children often called it the Dark Realm, as there were whispers about how calling the realm by its true name brought great sickness and even death. Such a name thwarted children from entering.

Even worse—those who dared to enter were never to be seen again. They never returned. What laid beyond the dark forest that encircled the realm was the greatest mystery to those who quaked at the thought of entering themselves. No one truly knew what became of those who never returned— whether they were dead or merely unable to turn back.

The realm was thought to have been in existence since the beginning of time itself, trapping and devouring victims from the first night.

"This is the farthest I've traveled," I admitted. And likely the farthest I would ever travel.

The very last thing I needed was to be forever trapped in a realm with a shapeshifter, with no way to save my family from what was to come. I would prefer the Dark Realm—Annarr— to remain a mystery to me. Even the shifter's friend had warned us to keep our distance.

Chills raced down my spine. There was no escaping the stress my body was under.

"Since neither of us know what is out here, we will find out together, I suppose."

She didn't seem to like that; her green eyes catching fire. "Did you even ask around about your oracle?" she asked.

"I asked the barkeeper's wife, and she told me to find a traveling wagon."

"Bandits? What would an oracle have to do with such a thing?" the shifter went on.

"I don't know." I sighed. "I don't know what any of it means."

I was doing everything I could think of. None of it felt like enough. Time was being wasted. My family's lives were at risk every day they were in Sandire. And getting them out was a risk. Even if I could get to Nedfin and have them provide a sanctuary for everyone but my father, their lives would be at risk during their escape from him.

The entire kingdom believed my father's version of what happened. And even if the truth of what happened stared them in the face, they would still believe whatever he said. Zyra would never believe the *true* story once she heard what everyone believed. Not with what she thought of me. Not unless I got her to talk to the oracle first.

Chapter Twenty-Nine
Zyra

As twilight settled, I announced, "I need to hunt if we want to eat."

The Viking paused to turn to me, flipping the ax in his hand. "Don't think I can stab anything with my ax?"

Not even a squirrel, I wanted to say, but I swallowed the words. "You're better off staying in one place. You don't want me chasing you after I've been hunting. I might not be able to stop myself from ripping your throat out, and I have a feeling I might be gone awhile with what you pointed out."

I bit back a grin that would flash my canines, my stomach doing a flip out of anxiety rather than hunger.

He grabbed my arm, but then hesitated, as if caught off guard by his own actions. "I don't trust you to come back."

I narrowed my eyes at him. If he ran off, it would not be the end of the world, but it would mean my head. If I ran off, it would mean his. "Trust your warnings then, and we won't have to starve."

Without another word, I shifted, racing off into the woods on four swift legs.

WHEN I BROKE through the trees from following Riker's musky scent, I had already shifted into my human form and was carrying a few freshly killed badgers. I wiped my mouth clean with the back of my hand. I wouldn't lie. I was both surprised and disappointed the Viking was still here.

I thought for sure he'd make a run for it.

"Are we really doing this again?" I asked at the sight of Riker dropping a few logs in a pile together. "Did you learn nothing of the rogues earlier?"

Perhaps Vikings were dumber than shifters ever thought.

He straightened, his eyes immediately finding mine. "How else did you expect us to eat what you caught? And I think the chances of another pack seeking us out are low, especially if they run into the bodies."

I glanced down at my fresh kill. I supposed he was right, but I was not about to tell him that.

I dropped the carcasses. "You impale and cook them, then. I did the hard part, so I'll keep watch." Then I dropped myself onto a flat boulder.

I did not know what to think or how to feel about where we were or that I was traveling with someone who could kill me in my sleep. I had to keep my instincts alert. Then, if this didn't go according to plan and he decided not to follow through on his oath, I would have to face Haiden's wrath. I would likely become one of the very rogues we encountered, banished for disloyalty rather than bloodlust.

Having to rely on nothing more than *trust* made my canines pinch my gums.

I watched him carefully as he got to work. While there was a precision in how he fought, typical tasks seemed clumsy. Hacking at a living thing was an effortless act, while piercing two dead badgers to cook them over the fire proved strenuous. I forced my lips to keep still. Though his movements were anything but graceful, I could not help but think about when he could barely walk. His burns. The burns Corinna and I had inflicted during his interrogation had slowed him down. If only I had not given it to him the first time ... he would have been too weak to overpower me.

"How far did you have to hunt?" Riker suddenly asked, dragging me from my thoughts.

My head snapped up, and I inhaled a breath to ensure we were alone before speaking. The ache of my neck had not gone away, it was just easier to ignore when there were other aches and pains. "I just wandered until I found something."

Just as I had lost track of time now, watching him.

I found myself staring at the jagged scars on the back of his hands. When he went to look up, I jerked my head to the side to stare off into the woods.

"What does it feel like to change—to be what you are?" he asked. I blinked, turning back to him, my thoughts still trying to unravel. I could not examine them enough to understand the underlining purpose behind them. When I failed to answer right away, he went on. "What is it like to shift?"

It was as if now that we had fought together, the fight between us had waned enough to make room for questions.

"You're asking an awful lot of questions for someone who hates shifters," I pointed out. "And why do you want to know? To turn around and relay information to your wretched father?"

I practically gulped once I realized I called his father "wretched," but if he was doing everything in his power to stop his father as he claimed, there was a chance he would think nothing of it.

A smirk stretched across his features, and the tightness in my chest released.

"What would my father have to gain from you telling me

how it feels to shift? He's going to kill me the moment we get there. I'll be lucky if I have enough time to breathe in the heat before he brings the battle-ax down clean through my neck."

I wasn't sure what his father knew of shapeshifters—whether he knew how our shifting worked or how it transformed us—but the thought of sharing something so personal ... sharing a feeling that could reach the Viking King's ears ...

Every shifter felt different when they shed one skin for another. Some felt exhilaration or absolute glory; some even felt utter, undeniable passion. We were the same, but different, reborn when we changed bodies. Those who were shy in their human skin could be daring and unafraid.

Shifting was powerful. The change brought out our strongest features, and sometimes, even the ones we kept locked inside ourselves.

When I shifted, I felt as if I were being set free. I could chase the wind, follow the moon, rush past trees until they resembled blurs of nothing, race until my heart was pounding furiously against my chest. Where my human skin held apprehension, my wolf skin held a fierce nature. One with no hesitation.

The wind in my fur. Being consumed by the scents around me. The dirt beneath my pounding paws. Allowing myself that breath of freedom.

Things I didn't allow myself to feel—to think about—in my human skin unraveled once I shifted. From the moment the warmth of my fur encircled me, the wolf inside me knew what it wanted, and she did not hesitate to reach for those things.

Before I could think, I found myself saying, "When I shift ... it feels like I'm bound to nothing—like I'm being set free. The light makes my skin tingle, and there's only a second of discomfort. It feels warm and strong. Exciting." I didn't dare look at him as I spoke. I didn't want to see anger, or any of the words he would use to describe me or my kind, swimming in his eyes. "But everyone feels something different when they shift."

Trust.

It was a word I never thought I would associate with a Viking. Everything in us had screamed that it was wrong, but sitting across from him now … I shied away from such caution. I leaned toward him.

"How do you shift?" His voice held no anger but mere curiosity. "And … where do your clothes go when you shift?"

I swallowed a laugh. I didn't exactly know the answer to the latter question myself. Our clothes just disappear when we shift into our animal skins and reappear when we shift back to our human skin.

But the first question …

"That—I'm definitely not telling you." His smirk flashed into a glare. I added, "Tell me about your father."

Something almost feral flared across his face, but before I could discern what it was, the look was gone. Like a sweep of a breeze.

"What? No. Why would I talk about him?"

"Because I asked. I want to know more." I would forever think of Slate as a cruel, heartless bastard, but I wanted to know if his own son had the same opinion as the rest of the realms. If I was going to share what it felt like to shift, the least Riker could do was offer me what he thought of his own father. "Is the legendary Viking King cruel toward his own flesh and blood?"

Riker stopped what he was doing, the meat halted over the fire. I opened my mouth to point out that he would burn our meal, but his eyes were ablaze—as if he couldn't hold back his emotion or contain his thoughts. It had been a while since I'd seen such anger in his face.

I leaned away from him.

"My father always has and will always live up to the

legends that are spread about him. He acts no differently toward his own flesh and blood."

"Why is your culture so merciless?" I asked. I didn't spit out the question. I tried not to—I didn't want it to feel like an attack. But he still took it that way.

"*My* culture is merciless? You're—"

Anger seeped away hesitation and any fear that hovered in the back of my mind. "Name something—name *one thing* we've done that you haven't! Yes, we interrogated you, but it was in the interest of protecting ourselves. Yes, I'm taking you back to Sandire knowing you're going to die, but your father will start a war if I don't, and I can't even fathom how much worse things would get for me. Your father is searching for you, and if I don't follow through with my orders, they might kill me!" I inhaled a steady breath. "Your legends are much crueler. You lie, you sacrifice, you pillage, you kill and maim for sport!"

"*You* shouldn't exist!"

I gritted my teeth, though I wanted to scream. I wanted to scream about how I knew that already. Since being attacked by a rogue at a young age, since being hated and feared since the time I could shift, and after another rogue attack, I knew I should not exist. I did not need his kind to tell me that when my own discarded my existence.

"You have no reason to think such things," I finally said. I was shocked my voice didn't sound more defeated. "You've been devouring every word your father's been saying since the day you were born."

His chest tightened, his lips forming a thin line. "You know nothing." He shot to his feet, charging past me into the woods. How he avoided brushing up against me did not go unnoticed.

I inhaled a long breath through my nose, then released it through my mouth before I turned. The food was nothing more than soot at this point. Speeding after him, I grabbed his arm and forced him to face me. I lightened my tone, hoping to take some of the edge off. It was easier than whatever this was.

"What did you mean before—when you said that I wouldn't know which story to believe? Every time I try to find out about whatever awful act of treason you carried out, it's the only answer you give."

"It doesn't matter."

"It does—"

"It doesn't matter," he repeated through clenched teeth. "Just because we fought a few shapeshifters together does not mean you get to invade my life."

I narrowed my eyes at him. "I'm getting tired of this."

"Tired of what?" he bit out.

"Of arguing with you. Of you getting angry every time I ask you a question."

Riker stared at me, unblinking, as if he were at a loss for words.

I tried to convince myself I owed him nothing, that I owed him less than nothing. I did not need to prove myself to the likes of him nor did my kind. Vikings could not be convinced their barbaric ways were wrong. Every day since encountering the Viking Prince of Sandire had more than proven that.

"I don't know why, but I couldn't kill you, and I couldn't let you die."

My hand was still on his arm. My fingers stiffened around his bicep. Yet, here I was, unable to disentangle myself from the gold irises locked on mine.

"I have nothing to hide," I said. "Is this concern for your family even real? Your mother, your sib—"

"Shut your mouth!" he shouted in my face. "I do not want to know you."

I didn't flinch—didn't move away.

For the first time since starting our journey, my voice sounded smaller than I intended. "If you think I do, then why did you fight with me?"

His jaw locked. Neither of us spoke, but words charged between us. Words tinged with temper under our forced, calm demeanors. I didn't understand—couldn't unravel his words and examine them enough to understand the underlining purpose behind them.

"I don't know why, but I couldn't kill you, and I couldn't let you die."

We had no choice. We were stuck here. Together. Until he was able to speak to an oracle and I could take him back to Sandire, or until we were caught.

I had already memorized the sound of his footsteps. His frame was ingrained in my mind. I knew what it sounded like when he rolled over in sleep in contrast to when he awoke.

I had no choice but to get to know him. At least in some sense, for the sake of my survival.

And he would have no choice but to know me.

Realizing we were likely the only Viking and shapeshifter to carry out a somewhat civil conversation made my skin crawl.

WITH BLOOD POUNDING through my veins and early morning light breaking through the trees, I kept an eye on the sky as we walked. Sleep had eluded me again last night, my body heavy from the endless walking and my mending wounds. The bite no longer stung or ached; not even when I moved to get up. Even the ache in my neck had since faded.

When I had lain down last night with only a few feet separating us, I was confident he wouldn't be able to move an inch without waking me. Even still, I had jolted myself awake every half hour to make sure he was still beside me, then checked our surroundings before falling back asleep.

Riker didn't move from my side. He tossed and turned in

the dirt, carefully avoiding the roots sticking out from the ground, but he didn't get up or try to go anywhere.

After I finally gave up on sleep, he must have known I was awake because he rolled over to tell me we had a lot of ground to cover today—we were not to stop until we reached the mountains.

From there, I had turned away, unable to stand looking at him. He seemed withdrawn deep inside himself since. Focused from the moment he turned over. I wondered if he was consumed with thoughts of his family.

The sun was the only way to know how much time had passed. With my eyes cast upward, it wasn't until I noticed the change in the air that I realized the terrain was changing as well. Snow was far behind us now, and Waylria's border was even farther. The only relief from such a thought was there was no mist—no eerie silence beckoning us closer. We hadn't wandered too far off track. Not enough for us to have walked into the unknown, devouring lands of Annarr.

We had begun our journey on snow, and the flurries had changed to roots sticking up through pine needles and dirt. Lush green grass nearly reached my hips now. My fingertips brushed against the swaying tops.

A shudder tumbled through my body, and I quickly hurled thoughts of home away, leaving them among the trees as I walked farther onto the plain.

We eventually approached a hill. Where, from the peak, purple leaves hanging from branches were visible for miles. White flowers towered over the blades of grass, reaching for sunlight. Then, beyond it all in the not-so-far distance, rested the Nedfin Mountains.

Riker glanced over at me. "You better be right about the oracles living near here."

I smiled, showing off my sharp canines. "Or what?"

"At this point, we both have a lot to lose."

I thought back to his distantly focused look earlier. How

haunted he almost seemed … As much as we both wanted to believe we owed each other nothing, the time for secrets had long passed.

"Why are you so worried about your family?" I asked. We were walking through the tall grass now, not exactly side by side but close enough. "If your father is the one to be feared, is he so deranged that you think he would hurt the rest of your family? I mean, he's already after you, why rid himself of even more?"

"Less people to stop him." A beat of silence passed. "He might feel like he has already lost so much, what is the difference if it means getting what he wants in the end?"

I nodded as if I understood. That could not be further from the truth. "End-it-all mentality."

Even with what I had lost—though it all still happened right before my eyes, the rejection and denial of existence—I could not fathom ruining everything around me.

"He thrives off it right now."

I had a gut feeling he knew why. Perhaps because of Riker's treason? Perhaps the Viking King had truly gone mad —stopped caring about such things like family. I supposed if he truly intended to force the realms under his rule—when compared to sending Vikings to die, slaughtering innocents, killing his own son for treasonous acts—his own family might seem insignificant. Especially when his son was a traitor. And telling their natural enemy about it.

Nonetheless, it made me sick to my stomach.

"Don't all Vikings?" I asked, my tone genuinely curious rather than accusatory. "If your father achieves what he intends, your realm will follow."

Riker glanced at me out of the corner of his eyes, his stare narrowed. He seemed to be debating how to interpret my tone. I tried not to tense at the stretched silence, keeping my attention on the soft tickle of the grass we walked through. It was such a good way to ignore the whirling in my stomach.

"Most will," he admitted. "My father has led Sandire his whole life. I grew up watching people follow his every lead. Even my every lead once he put me in charge."

"The way you fight … Have you ever led your own army?" My words were cut short; they were too close to a compliment.

According to Haiden, Sandire had armies with varying purposes. One was meant for safety, in case shifters or others ever planned to invade Sandire. Another was solely meant for hunting and sacrificing shapeshifters. Some served as guards for the royal family. I wondered if one of them had been secretly training for Slate's plans.

Trying to decipher what was true would only make my head hurt.

"I lead—led the *Illska Sanðr* quarter of my father's army." He paused to mull over his words. "I became one of my father's top three warriors by the age of fourteen, and that inspired him to give me my own army to lead."

This was the most information I had gathered from him since leaving the borough. I had no intention of not pushing further to see how far I could take this.

I couldn't help the tilt of my head. "What does illska— whatever you said, mean?"

"It means cruel sand."

My knees locked for a moment, and I had to force myself to keep walking. One step in front of the other. I glanced at the sky again. Sunlight streamed through the purple leaves. With the sun easing behind the mountains, we would have to stop soon. But Riker's steps did not falter.

I'd been trying so hard to prove myself, but what if it amounted to nothing? What if I was still just as weak as they all thought I was? What if William's death meant nothing? Would I be to blame? What if I was met with my own death and it came to nothing?

I glanced at Riker. What if there was something truly bigger going on? Vikings were known for their barbarity. Slate even more so, according to his own son. With each realm being separated, with the land going unnamed—pillaging and overtaking the mass as a whole by Sandire's king was not-so-far unimaginable.

Then there was Riker. Sandire's very own prince who ran into enemy territory from the realm of brutal sand. To escape, yes, but also to warn against his father. Perhaps the treason came from how he had stood against his father's intentions. Perhaps he had thought to use his army—*Illʂka San∂r*—to stop his father.

The very same Viking Prince who had saved me from a savage rogue.

A nagging feeling tugged at my gut.

Chapter Thirty
Riker

I EYED the shifter out of the corner of my eye. Standing among the purple leaves of some strange willows I could barely wrap my mind around after growing up among endless grains of sand, her dark fighting leathers stood out. She was hiding her exhaustion well, but I knew that deep-in-your-bones feeling. Eyes could not hide such a thing.

"How old are you when you're sorted into packs?" I asked her.

She slowed her pace until I was walking even with her, her head tilted to the side.

"We're not. All of us are connected, so there's no need for us to branch off into packs. Rogues are the only ones that form packs, and that's when they're banished." She paused. "We're usually only sorted into a pack when we're young. We're clumped together as children to learn the ways of our culture and how to handle discovering our animal skin."

I almost shuddered at the thought of young children morphing into completely different beings.

"One of the adults overseeing a group of us was the reason I shifted so early," she went on. "He went rogue. Another pack leader had said something that set him off, and he snapped. He went into a frenzy and started attacking everyone nearby. I was four years old, and it happened on instinct because my body knew it was what it needed to do in order to survive." She spoke quietly, letting out a bitter scoff. "He took a nice chunk out of my side. I still have the scar."

My gaze fell to her sides, landing just above her hips. I didn't know which side the scar was on, but I had a strong urge to look.

I didn't want to care—not about her. She had whipped and cursed me. Given me shit right back whenever I started something.

But … four. She had been four years old when she first shifted.

I couldn't imagine a tiny body against the savage canines of a grown wolf. I didn't *want* to imagine but … Flailing her small arms in an attempt to free herself from the jaws of her attacker, crying and screaming from such pain and shock. Only to shift into a wolf herself moments later. To survive. To endure the pain and blood loss and then be shunned …

The image was sickening enough to cause something in my chest to writhe.

My own childhood was called forth. My entire life arose.

"He acts no differently toward his own flesh and blood."

From the time I could lift a dagger, my father had started shaping me into a warrior worthy enough to be his son. He disciplined me through the different weapons we forged for hours—until my arms were trembling with taxing strain. We wouldn't stop even after my hands bled. Every horrendous thing he did, he followed all of it up by claiming it would make me stronger. He wanted me to learn endurance.

Endurance was a necessary quality if one was to survive.

And fear was an emotion that would lead to our destruction and eventual downfall. Sandire could not withstand such weakness.

It had always been my reality. I never thought twice about

it. Never agonized over the injuries. When pushed enough, it awakened my rage, but the things he had done ... He was the reason I'd matured into the warrior I was. Even if I still occasionally woke up in a cold sweat, swearing I'd heard one of my bones crack.

But all of that—none of it seemed as scarring as to how Zyra had earned the mark on her side.

A beast with uncontrollable bloodlust had wounded her harshly enough to leave a permanent reminder.

Sandire's legends spoke of the savagery of shifters, but what if our legends had always spoken of rogues, not knowing there was a difference in shifters? All this time, we'd been infiltrating the edge of Waylria to capture any we could trap for sacrifices, convinced we could hunt them to extinction or chase them back to the darkness they had come from.

From how our ancestors had feared those who changed to beasts—feared how their packs would raid their clans for the taste of blood, snatching and devouring their young and loved ones in the night—it was easy to understand where the terror had started. And how such hatred evolved from grief.

Our legends had to be about rogues.

Because Zyra—this shifter who felt regret for interrogating me but felt enough passion to protect those counting on her to bring the whip down over and over, who had brought me salve —was not a beast.

"Stop staring," Zyra said.

My focus was locked on the clothes covering her old wound. I wondered how much of it obscured her skin— wondered how it had healed over.

And still, everything I'd ever been told growing up didn't line up with what I'd seen of her. She regretted the torture. She was so determined to protect the people she cared about. And she was still following me to ensure that happened.

"How—"

"I'm not talking about the scar, so you can stop staring and ask a different question."

I bit back the flare of ire that rose.

Each new little bit of information sent my brain reeling. I wanted to know more. Questions were building on top of one another. Though, it wasn't because I thought to use the information to my advantage. No amount of information would be satisfactory enough to barter for my life. My father would never consider sparing me.

It was how little sense my mind made. I shouldn't give a damn about her—whether she lived or died. Not when I had helped my father capture and sacrifice shapeshifters for years. Not when I had helped, led, and instructed my men to find as many as possible to bring back to my father. A gift. A sacrifice. All that hate. All those years. All for Sandire. All for our gods. All for my father.

And yet, the rogue shifters seemed to be the creatures of our legends. They seemed to be the ones worthy of our hate. They were the creatures of nightmares. The creatures we aspired to destroy.

I could see that now. I could see the hint of truth there. But the theory couldn't erase generations of legends or the loathing of our realms.

Just as how my mind wasn't willing to dig deeper into the reasons behind my actions.

There was an answering pull in my chest at the uncertainty barreling down my thoughts. Something was whispering from the abyss. Murmuring the truth—the past entwining with my present motivations.

I just wanted to know. I wanted to hear her. I wanted her to want to tell me.

"How do you communicate?" She shook her head at that question, her lips tightening. So I asked a different question, finding myself wanting her to trust me. "What can you tell me about the … ritual? For when you shift."

Hel, I did not even know what I was asking.

She snickered, her eyes flicking to mine for a moment, revealing her amusement at my struggle for words, then paused before saying, "I've already told you a bit about the ritual and the fruit. It's a spring tradition. One that outsiders are not allowed to know."

She had turned her head away while answering, using her hair to cover her face, but not before I noticed the way her eyes clouded.

I tried another. "Why do you call it 'animal skin'?"

"Because when we shift, we are stripping ourselves from the skin of one form to take on another."

I could feel the tension beginning to drip from her. Still, I could not hold back my questions. "And your animal skins aren't inherited?"

"No. My mother is a grizzly, and my father is an owl." I opened my mouth to question that further, but she promptly sent a glare in my direction. "That's enough. I still know nothing about you."

I snapped my mouth shut, contemplating what I could tell her—what she would want to know.

She had stopped walking, but my thoughts were like a storm, where I stood in its center, unable to take in my surroundings.

"There is not much to tell. You must know a lot about Vikings already."

Her next words were spoken in a rush, though not as a challenge. "You thought you knew everything about shapeshifters, did you not?"

Her glare flashed into a smirk; she saw right through me. She fell silent, as if she were waiting for me to offer more. My heart jumped at the thought of telling her anything of the life I had been forced to leave behind. Sandire considered me a traitor when I wasn't, but I could easily slip up, tell her something I shouldn't, then truly become one.

Though, not to the extent my kingdom thought.

"How did you sneak up on me that night?" she finally asked.

"I know how to tread lightly while walking on sand." I spared a glance toward her to catch her reaction. "Turns out, walking on fresh snow requires the same strategy. As soon as I saw you, I ducked into the underbrush before you noticed."

She nodded, falling quiet for a moment. I followed her gaze across the grassy valley. The mountains felt much too far.

My chest tightened at the thought of being too late.

We had to keep going.

"I smelled the sand," she told me after nearly a full minute, speeding ahead as my steps slowed at the remark. I stared after her, my stomach dropping as the dread set in.

THE FARTHER WE WALKED, the more uneven the ground became. Walking down into the valleys and then uphill through tall grass had me tightening my grip on my dagger. Anything could be in the brush.

Eventually, though, far off past the trees, the mountains appeared in their full height. A storm thundered across the sky. Zyra's steps quickened in a graceful way, while I stumbled to keep up.

The purple forest dripped with raindrops.

The graying sky echoed with thunder and flashed with lightning. Zyra flinched the first time it shot and boomed across the sky, then rushed forward just before the sky opened up to rain down on us. Drops fell on our shoulders, onto our chests, and rolled down the curved branches of the trees, then made the air thick with humidity.

I ignored the way my heart sank with each step and how

everything twisted with the promise of being so close to finding an oracle. How was I supposed to find a traveling wagon? Just aimlessly walk in the hopes of running into one? We had not seen a glimpse of one since the start of our journey.

"Do you want to stop here for the night?" Zyra panted.

Rain was soaking through our clothes, but I did not want to stop. A restlessness had settled in the pit of my stomach. I wanted to tell her we had to keep going. We were too close to stop now. Even for the night.

I could only manage a nod, but a thought sent my heart shooting forward.

Through the downpour, I looked back at the mountains.

When I turned back, Zyra's eyes were narrowed as understanding sank in. She knew we were getting close now. "It's raining, anyway. We'll start again at first light."

Nedfin had to have more answers.

She went to sit against one of the many trees. We were immersed in silence as the sky darkened further and the rain progressed, drenching the ground beneath us. The shower brought a different kind of cold that could be felt through our damp clothes.

Leaning my head back into the tree, I schemed through tactic after tactic of how I would talk to the *völva* once light stretched across the sky.

Just to fend off thoughts of the family I'd left behind.

Zyra was curled into herself against the tree, knees to her chest, fighting off shivers. I thought to move closer but stayed stiff where I was. While she moved to lay down for the night, my eyes went to her side when the thought of her scar crossed my mind again. I still wanted to know which side it was on, how big it was.

When I'd lain down, I kept my distance but faced her back.

I reached toward her, but instead of touching her side, I placed my hand on her shoulder over the tear she had covered with salve. Once finished healing, it would likely scar over, too.

If she did not believe me or the oracle, I would return to Sandire with her. Without a fight. But there was a high chance my father would kill her. And my entire focus would be on my family.

There would be no room for mistakes. Not again.

I couldn't comprehend why I said it, but I spoke without thinking. "My father gave me many of the scars I bear." Each a story of how he had not broken me. Even now. I was stronger, above his words and punishments, and I would be above him long after he brought down the ax he was specially sharpening for me.

I wondered if my words were a warning. Even though I knew it was one she was aware of. I just needed her to know I could not save her. I would not have enough in me to save her. Not when so much more was on the line. Zyra had to save her own life if it came down to it. And I had full confidence she could. There was not a doubt in my mind she couldn't hold her own when facing my father.

Zyra went still. Unusually still. So still for so long, I decided she must have already fallen asleep.

But then she turned over to face me.

It seemed to take her a moment to think of something to say, but she whispered, "You deserved better."

Chapter Thirty-One
Zyra

Utterly out of my mind. I had to be utterly out of my mind to say such a thing.

He was wanted for treason. His crimes and Waylria's safety were the sole reasons I had traveled so far from home. They were the sole reasons I was lying beside him in the damp dirt. Why did I think he deserved better? It wasn't but a week ago that I thought he deserved to be burned and tortured, and now I thought he didn't earn the scars his father had given him.

Then again, a significant part of me understood what it was like to be treated so harshly by those who were supposed to love you the most.

And though I could never imagine admitting it aloud, it was why I was here.

You deserved better, you deserved better, you deserved better. The words echoed in my head all night, louder than booming thunder. They even overpowered the crack of lightning. Resounded over the downpour.

I didn't even know what he'd done. He'd evaded the question since his royal blood was discovered.

For reasons beyond simple curiosity, I felt I *had* to know what had taken place.

"You deserved better." He had closed his eyes afterward, as if he were savoring the words. As if they were the last words he wanted to hear before falling asleep. I stayed awake long after, unable to take my eyes off him. I was frozen, shocked, confused. I could barely blink, let alone sleep.

Though, the heat coming off him was comforting, even with the damp ground beneath me.

I scanned the peaceful lines of his face, wondering what images were playing behind his eyelids. His mouth was open ever so slightly, his long hair was down, tangled around him. I held back the urge to reach out and touch it, knowing the slight movement would wake him. He looked peaceful, but he was a light sleeper. Since leaving Waylria, I had learned that the faintest noises caused him to stir.

"You deserved better."

I stayed like that until I couldn't stand him touching me a moment longer. I shifted for the warmth of my wolf fur and lay under a nearby tree. Not too far, but at a careful distance.

Was I wrong to assume he was malicious? Like his father? I nearly shook my head. Was he really different from other Vikings? While I had never encountered one prior to him … Waylrian legends reflected the awful deeds inflicted on shifters by the hands of Vikings. Captures. Sacrifices. Torture. So much spilled blood, no matter the age.

But … the only true threat I'd seen from Riker was during interrogation. Only under pain did hatred shine from his eyes. Since then, that ire had dulled. The amber glow of his irises stared back at me as I drifted to sleep.

RAINDROPS FALLING from purple leaves was not what woke me. My ears perked at the sound of wheels crunching across dirt and twigs. The noise sent me flying to my feet so I could survey the trees. The clatter of wheels was off a little ways, and there were light, wandering footsteps on the soaked ground. When I sniffed the air, I sensed multiple people heading in our direction with a wagon of some sort.

My eyes fell to Riker, who was still lying on the ground. One of his eyes had cracked open a fraction and was watching me.

At the sight of him, something deep in me halted before giving a tentative pulse.

I bared my teeth the smallest bit to warn him to be quiet. He probably didn't like it or understand it.

He shot to his feet, reaching for his weapon at his hip. I could already tell he was convinced those approaching were the men searching for him.

Part of me would be relieved. I wouldn't have to be the one to drag him before his father. Regardless, I had no idea what or who was heading this way, but I had come too far to let myself be caught off guard.

The wheels were drawing closer. My eyes met Riker's, and I could see how he wanted to run. He didn't want to go up against whoever was nearing us. They could be men he knew —men he'd trained and fought with. His men from *Illska Sandr*. His friends.

But I could also see that he would fight if he had to. If it came to that.

Whether I was the one who took him or someone else, his fate would be the same … My chest tightened.

The wandering steps had found a purpose.

They were drawing closer. Heading straight toward us.

I whirled, moving to flank Riker's side. His hands were balled into fists, eyes watching the trees. I wanted to ask him what he wanted to do, but even if I was in my human skin, I would've been afraid of attracting attention by speaking.

"Goodness, I hope this was not your attempt at hiding," a

voice said before brushing passed the drooping branches before us, drops cascading around her. Holding back branches in front of her, she stood just yards from us, her eyes bright with amusement and curiosity as she studied us.

I blinked in recognition, my mind scrambling to place her.

Her flowing skirt skimmed the forest floor, and the jewels dangling from the hem and her wrists jingled. The top she wore was blue rather than the burgundy I had seen her in before. Had that really only been a few nights ago? It felt like she had left Waylria a fortnight ago at this point.

Beside me, Riker was tense, an unmovable force. I merely stood by his side, watching the woman as she watched us. She didn't have the chance to speak again before the horse carriage revealed itself and stopped some feet behind her. Another man jumped down from the back of the carriage. The boy handling the reins to the Paint horse stayed planted in his seat. Although, his eyes did jump between the woman, Riker, and me.

There was not a single doubt in my mind this was the woman from when the rogues attacked. The alpha had been holding her by the neck, and her clothes had been in tatters.

The broad man came to stand beside her, placing a hand on the woman's bare shoulder, his large hand swallowing her small frame. He didn't even look toward Riker and me as he asked the woman, "Who have you found, Skuld?"

Her gaze did not waver from us. The tension in Riker's body was growing stronger by the moment. My own urges were flaring in my veins.

"*Völva*," Riker muttered under his breath.

"A Viking," the woman, Skuld, said, her eyes falling on Riker. Then she looked to me, her head tilting to the side. "And a shapeshifter."

The carriage boy's eyes widened at me. My blood was racing, my heart pounding. My skin itched as my claws curled into the dirt beneath my paws. The wolf inside me was ready for a fight. I could feel that Riker was just as ready.

"A shapeshifter?" the man beside Skuld breathed, looking me over. To him, I looked like Riker's pet.

I was almost too afraid to breathe. While this man was with the oracle, something underlined the look in his eyes. In turn, I dissected him with mine. Broad frame with straight, very-dirty blond hair, as if he had been rolling around in mud.

He addressed the oracle. "What are they doing here?"

He sought a premonition from her, to debate how he should react, no doubt.

"Why don't you ask us directly instead of acting like we aren't standing right in front of you?" Riker seethed, but the man ignored him as he waited for her answer.

"I would be careful what you say, Viking Prince," Skuld warned, though there was still a flicker of amusement in her eyes. "You do not want to add to your predicament."

This caught the attention of the man and boy.

"Viking Prince?" The man's focus turned on Riker now. "I heard Slate wants him returned alive so he can kill his son himself."

The oracle pushed away from the tree, moving out from under the man's hand. "You are not to touch them, you selfish pig! It is not up to you to get them there."

Then, out of nowhere, I felt the slightest brush of fingers against the fur on my right shoulder. I tried not to jerk from the touch and fought not to spare a glance toward Riker.

Despite the oracle's warnings, the man kept on. "We could skin her—use her fur or sell it." He let out a backward cackle resembling that of a child's. Bold words for a man who was still refusing to meet my stare. "Shapeshifter fur must go for a high price in Sandire."

Riker inhaled a long, hot breath as his fingers brushed my fur again. Unable to fight the urge this time, I looked up at him. I knew he could feel the question rolling off me. His eyes were on the man who had spoken, narrowed, calculating, deadly. My heart thumped harder. Protective.

"We've been looking for an oracle," Riker said after clearing his throat. As if he struggled to get the words out. "I need help—guidance."

I snapped my eyes from him, trying not to think of how forcefully my heart was beating against my ribs.

I did not know what was to come, but the Viking had found what he'd wanted. Now we needed her for answers. Now I was faced with what I was to do from here.

When I looked back, Skuld had moved away from the man, drifting closer to us as she glared back at him. "There is no concept of 'price' within our culture. Being with the oracles means trading and living in equal peace; never taking more from others and land than necessary. We are not to touch them. We are not to mess with fate." Her voice did not raise but stayed sensible. "You have failed to let go of your scheming ways. I am afraid this is where I leave you, Fenris."

"Ah," the cackled one said. "I see. You've seen something. You've seen what's to become of them."

"Yes," she hissed, "and we are not to meddle with fate."

Fenris tilted his head. "How is it that you are able to see their fate so clearly? When I look at them, everything is blurry."

Every knot in my back locked up. Riker had to have felt it, too. This Fenris was not going to let us go so easily.

"It is blurry because you are looking for the wrong reasons. You should leave. Take the carriage and boy back to the others. Do not challenge me."

The oracle's spitfire attitude reminded me of Corinna. The comparison made my chest ache. Glimpsing the colorful tattoos on her hand had also sparked my worry, even though they looked nothing like my friend's sharp, angry lines.

We had to keep moving. My fingers curled at the thought of how Riker had touched my shoulder moments ago.

Chapter Thirty-Two
Riker

My teeth clamped down on my tongue, nearly drawing blood when I remembered his suggestion to skin Zyra. Shapeshifter fur sold for a hefty price in Sandire. It did not matter what kind of animal fur it was—mouse, jaguar, beaver, etc. Although, the size of the animal it belonged to was what truly mattered. The bigger the animal, the more expensive the fur. Larger furs were used to make coats for important, well-off Vikings. The smaller fur pellets were often strapped to our warrior's weapon belts. One for each shifter they brought back for sacrifice.

A shudder split through me at the thought of Zyra becoming a fur rug. Her wolf skin being trampled on by my father's guards and servants alike as she forever laid within his household.

"I'm not sure how trustworthy that information is, Skuld."

Tightening my grip on the hilt of my ax, I severely needed to plunge the sharp steel into flesh. As many times as I could until my arm trembled at the effort and force—until my fingers couldn't grasp the hilt anymore. My hand quivered with the force of my need—to cut and slash before observing the blood that leaked from every thrust of my ax.

I could hardly keep still beside Zyra.

Fenris gave us a hollow smile, his stare raking over Zyra in her wolf skin before darting to me and landing on the weapon gripped in my hand. "Not ready to go home, *Prince*?"

A growl rumbled through Zyra, growing louder until it echoed off the trees. Her stare never breaking, her nails buried in the dirt.

Beside us, Skuld gripped her skirts. She seemed weaponless.

Fenris continued closer. "I'm willing to bet against Skuld."

"It is not the way," the oracle jumped in. "It is not our way. You came to us for guidance —"

"Some things are more important. We are meant to be nomads, after all."

Within a blink, he was charging for her, a glinting blade in his hand. Before he could even take his third step, Zyra launched toward him with her claws extended. But it wasn't meant to kill. Only to stall. He roared in pain when her paw raked the place between his shoulder and collarbone.

Skuld's eyes widened, her mouth agape. Zyra and I were moving before his knees slammed against the ground.

I gritted my teeth as I ran toward him, my ax raised, ready to be brought down to cleave through him. For his disgusting suggestions. For his threats. For being here, thinking he could take us.

He pulled twin blades from a strap at his hip before reaching me, mastering them, moving them as one. Swift and sure, the blades stopped my own from coming down on him. He sent a gloating grin over our entwined weapons.

But I was done playing games.

The rogue shifters had been Zyra's to target; this piece of shit was mine.

Snatching my weapon from his, I steadily stepped back, taking a moment to assess where his weakness might be before making another deadly lunge. I rammed with my ax, prompting Fenris into movement. From what I could gauge in those few moments, if he had a weakness, it wasn't an obvious, outward one. His movements were fluid but not that of a skilled warrior. They were movements of a cocky pickpocket who had threatened others with looming death for nothing more than a few coins and wealthy possessions.

Fenris swiped out with his long blades, moving them as one, right for my neck.

I spun aside, raising my ax high, bringing all my strength down as I angled it to the side, down across his body. He leaped toward my ax and knocked it from its deadly course.

Then he feinted right, spinning his measly daggers to slash them down my side and darting left in the same moment. I whirled when I sensed him behind me, blocking the lashes coming for my side, and continued to turn until I was facing Fenris. *Coward.*

I pointed my weapon up to hack it through him, but he was knocked aside before I had the chance. The man landed on his back in the dirt, eyes widening at the wolf standing over him, crouched and growling, revealing sharp, vicious teeth that were more than eager to rip skin and draw blood.

When I looked back at the oracle, with my heart in my throat, I nearly breathed a sigh of relief to see her still there standing before the boy guiding the wagon, instructing him to leave, no doubt.

I heard Fenris's quick approach from behind again. He was aiming for Skuld and the boy. But then Zyra was there, a snarl ripping from her throat.

Something snapped loose in me. I didn't think. Adrenaline shot through my body, launching me into action.

"Zyra!"

Without thinking, I rushed forward to put myself in front of her the same way she'd done for me. In front of the oracle — my last remaining hope of protecting those I cared about.

My ax found its mark, forcing him to drop the daggers he'd

been close to plunging into her chest. Blood slipped down his fingers. Yet I didn't see the next weapon he'd pulled from his belt.

I had put myself in front of Zyra. Then I was blinking at nothing, gasping for breath as pain exploded through my chest.

Warm blood trickled down my torso, coating my suddenly chilled skin. And then I was falling to the ground, hard, the wind knocked from me.

A snarl ripped through the shadows, echoing off the trunks and leaves of the willows. A gurgling scream followed.

I fought to drag air into my lungs.

I had less than a moment to process the sight of Zyra.

Zyra, ripping Fenris to pieces in her wolf skin. Zyra, crouched over me in her human skin, gasping, fingers shaking. "So much blood. There's so much blood," Zyra was saying, gasping.

Forcing my eyes open, I found hers wide and panicked as she took in the sight of me. Her hands were on my chest.

It was a strange sensation—to see panic swarming in her green eyes and to have her touching me without fear or hesitance.

"Looks like you won't be returning me alive," I rasped.

"You're going to be fine," she said, and kept repeating those words as she wrapped her hand around the hilt of the knife planted in my chest. For so much pain and so much panic, the knife must have hit something vital. She yanked it out without so much as a warning, and I shouted, but my eyes fell shut a moment later as I was swallowed by the pain.

Chapter Thirty-Three
Zyra

I BREATHED HIS NAME, watching helplessly as the blood continued to spread across his shirt, soaking it crimson. He was unconscious—blacked out from the pain or blood loss. "Riker."

Heart racing with deranged panic, I shook his shoulder, touched his face, grabbed fistfuls of any part of him I could seize before rushing to place my hand over the wound in an attempt to stop the bleeding. Seeing it seep between my fingers made my breath come in ragged gasps.

With my lungs constricted, I ripped the bottom part of my shirt and placed it over the wound, but it was drenched in red within seconds.

I didn't understand the whine that tore from my tight chest.

Then, as if he could still hear me, I repeated the words I'd said to him before he fell unconscious, pressing on the wound harder. "You're going to be fine."

His blood was slick, staining my hands.

My mind jumbled, I tried to slow my breathing and racing heart enough to think through what I needed to do. I gasped. What *could* I do? I had no way to bandage his wounds, and salve would never help him while his wound was so open—

"Go!" Skuld shouted behind me.

I didn't bother to look up at who she was speaking to. If the words were directed at me, there was no moving me.

Skuld was beside me in an instant, stumbling toward us in her rush. "This fate was not carved into the tree."

My vicious snarl stopped her short. I moved closer to Riker, pulling his head into my lap and leaning forward to cover him from her sight.

I bared my teeth, keeping my sharp stare on her as I retained a rumbling growl. It stayed low in my throat, a warning. Every thump of my heart echoed in my ears now.

"I saw the vision too late—"

I scuffed. "Some teller of the future you are."

She narrowed her eyes. "I saw it as soon as it was a possibility, but the vision did not affirm itself until moments ago. And I have … other talents that consume a lot of my energy. I do not need a shapeshifter questioning my power."

"C-can you heal him?"

"I can tend to the wound." She took a step closer. "But not here. You will need to let me get close enough to help him."

I looked down at him, sheer panic still trembling in my hands. Even unconscious, his face was contorted in pain.

"We need to get to my home, now. I can vault us all there." Her gaze landed on my arm, where I was leaning over his chest trying to stop the bleeding. "Before he bleeds out."

My body had not eased from its constriction. "All right. All right, just—please help him. You have to help him."

I couldn't explain it, but I also couldn't deny it. My instincts screamed at me to protect the man in my lap.

She crossed the remaining distance between us, reaching out to me. "Take my hand."

I moved my blood-soaked hand from Riker's chest to plant my fingers around his arm, and blood spurted from his wound. My chest seized as I realized what was happening again. When I placed my other hand into Skuld's, she closed her eyes.

Faded-blue light swarmed around us in response. I grasped Riker's arm harder, turning away from the light to stare down into his face.

I told myself I only cared about what happened to him because I needed to present him to his father. Alive. That was what I needed to believe — to do what I had to in order to protect those I loved. And to get back to them.

He was going to be fine.

I needed him to be all right. Only because I needed him alive.

I cupped his cheek, the skin warm under my palm. A little fevered. Silently, I willed him to open his eyes and face me, then I asked him to assure me the knife hadn't hit anything of importance. The knife had been lodged deep in his chest, rather close to the center ... Not his heart. *Let his heart be wholly unharmed.*

Moving my hand from his cheek to his neck, I searched for the beat of his heart, hoping to find it pounding as intensely as mine. His pulse was there — strong with a slight hesitancy between beats. With my mind an irrational tangle of feelings and thoughts I didn't dare examine too closely, I let my hand trail down farther, stopping at his chest to feel it rise and fall with each intake of life —

The blue light snapped away.

My hands fell away from Riker, but his head still rested in my lap, with his body laid out before me. I looked up but didn't have the chance to take in where we were before Skuld instructed, "Help me get him into the bedroom."

She went to his legs while I stood to lift him from under his arms. Riker was a warrior honed by years of training, battles, and who knew what else with numerous other Vikings. Lizeth and I had struggled with his weight when we'd brought him back to the borough, so it didn't come as a surprise when Skuld and I strained to carry him into her bedroom.

We paused, sharing a look over his body, then nodded before heaving him onto the bed.

Skuld placed a delicate hand on his forehead. His face was drained of color, but I could see the heat festering beneath his pale skin. His entire shirt was soaked in blood now—every inch of it bright red.

"He has lost a lot of blood." She pulled away from him, starting for the door. "I need to get bandages." She paused, looking back at me. "You are safe here. You can trust me."

"Why?" I struggled to ask before she slipped out the door. I swallowed against the dry roof of my mouth to strengthen my voice before trying again. "Why should I trust you?"

"Be-because I have seen what is to come. It is not much, but the pieces I have glimpsed …" Skuld lifted her chin toward Riker, but I didn't follow her gaze. "And because you helped me before, when those rogues held me captive."

I recalled the colorful skirt and her bright hair from before—how the alpha had imprisoned her by her neck.

"He will live." Skuld nodded. "He must be present if what I have seen is to be prevented."

She walked out, and I glanced around the room, taking in the wooden chair and table on the other side of the bed. There wasn't a single window or anything else inside the small room. My eyes fell on Riker again. His body nearly took up the whole bed.

I sat on the floor with my back pressed against the wall, my eyes on the door. Fighting to keep my hands from digging into my curls, I settled on staring at the blood dried on them instead. The growing pit in my stomach was becoming impossible to ignore.

The only reason Riker was hurt was because he had let the knife go through his own chest.

I didn't have to close my eyes for the images to clearly play out in my mind.

When I saw Riker start to sway, my immediate concern

was getting to him. I had whirled on Fenris, taking his wrist between my canines before ferociously biting down with all my strength. He'd screamed, but not loud enough to satisfy my rage. As I bit clean through his wrist, it was Riker's shout that had echoed in my mind. More screams from the pathetic man. I'd snarled, throwing his torn fist far into the dark willows. That was all it took to send him scrambling back before running, his good hand gripping the forearm without a hand as blood poured.

My lungs became tight again, my breath coming in short, heavy gasps. My body chanted *my fault, my fault, my fault*, with the beat of my heart. I looked up from my bloody hands to peer at Riker over the edge of the bed.

Silence bled through the room.

The door opened again, and Skuld came racing inside with a handful of cloths, bandages, vials of colorful liquids, and water. I jumped up from the floor as she reached the bed.

"I need you to take off his shirt," she told me as she worked to set everything down on the side table. "I cannot have it in my way."

Knowing there was no way I could lift him to remove his shirt, I tore through the fabric, straight down the middle, with my sharpened claws. I cringed when I saw what laid beneath. Scars of all shapes and sizes; healed-over burns.

His words rang true. *"My father gave me many of the scars I bear."*

Some of the scars must have come from battle, but I knew many of them had come from the Viking King himself. I did not know how he'd gained such scars from his cruel father. How they were justified. Just thinking about it made dark anger simmer through my body.

Skuld came up beside me, abruptly snapping me from my stirring anger, desperation, and panic-stricken thoughts. My eyes landed back on Riker's bare chest. Pale jagged lines cut across his toned body. And blood—blood was everywhere, smeared among the muscles and scars. My eyes traveled along his torso and chest until they landed on the gap.

The knife had gone through one of the several burns Corinna had inflicted.

I snatched my hands from him as Skuld placed her palms on his bloody chest. Beginning with a soft cloth, damp with the liquid from one of the vials, she carefully dabbed at the wound, trying to wipe away the flow of blood to get to the stab beneath.

Skuld shook her head. "Fenris was meant to be my protector."

I took a step back, unable to remove my eyes from Riker's face and chest. My cheeks burned, and my heart pounded with wild hunger.

"I had grown fearful after the rogue shapeshifters had imprisoned me. Fenris was new to our community, and I … You had saved me from the rogues the other night, but … I had been asking him about his willingness to follow me whenever on outside business when we came upon you."

Silence stretched through the room. I couldn't bring myself to respond.

"The Viking is lucky," Skuld continued when she opened her eyes. She moved over to the supplies she brought and got to work picking through the things she needed. "It missed everything vital, but only barely. His heart is all right."

My heart quickened in response to this assurance.

I needed him to be all right. Only because I needed him alive.

Chapter Thirty-Four
Riker

THERE WAS nothing but the pain in my chest. Fever was eating away at my heart. Devouring it. Melting it. Heat pumped through the veins, spreading across my chest. I couldn't take in a deep enough breath to exhale the warm throb in my lungs. I had taken the knife for her. Allowed the knife to plunge right through me—past skin, muscle, and bone. I had done it for Zyra—a shapeshifter. My father would have beheaded me for that very act if he wasn't already out for my head.

Eventually, I felt hands on my chest. Then something being poured over the wound. A burning seized through my chest. The hole near my heart pulsed in anger. I lost track of time altogether as the heat seized my body, bringing me in and out of consciousness.

The burning only stopped when something soft wiped across my chest and shoulder.

Though the throbbing had subsided, my entire body was wrung tight with tension, my pulse slowing with loud thuds that echoed in my ears.

Suddenly, I could hear a female speaking, but it wasn't Zyra's voice.

"Clean him. I took care of the spot around the wound, but

he is still covered in blood," the female voice said gently. "Come out when you are ready. I will have food prepared. You must be hungry."

No response came from Zyra then, either. My chest deflated. I needed to hear her, to know she was here. But I couldn't reach her—couldn't open my eyes to search for her. The aching pang had me trapped in the fog of my mind, keeping me from reaching her through the haze.

I didn't care where I was so long as she was here, too. But I needed to know. I needed to hear her speak or feel her ever-observant eyes on me.

And I did.

I felt her beside me. She released a long sigh that sounded like my name. The sound of it on her lips tugged at me, like a merciful caress down my back. I could feel her eyes roaming over me. Then—then she touched me.

Her palm skimmed my torso. She was cleaning the blood from my body, the cloth leaving my skin damp, and my body relaxed under her touch.

When I fell back into the darkness, it wasn't so painful.

Chapter Thirty-Five
Zyra

A WHILE PASSED before Riker's wound was clean enough to bandage. The colorful liquid within the vials was used to cleanse the damage. I didn't have a clue what was in the tiny bottles—what made them bright pink or green—but I didn't protest when Skuld poured it over the gash. The sterilized solution was meant to prevent infection. With my eyes glued on her, she moved cautiously, taking care to be as gentle as she could.

I couldn't help but wonder if whatever she used was something I could use alongside herbs or preserves to strengthen our well-being.

I kept beside her, watching and handing her whatever she asked for without a moment's hesitation. The scab of Riker's burn had to be peeled away to get to the new wound beneath.

Something timid crept through my chest. A large part of me screamed that the way I was looking at him was wrong, but a smaller, stranger part of me denied this. Not when being near him felt so right—so reassuring.

Just being able to watch him breathe kept my mind, body, and heart resilient.

After having his blood on my hands from his protection, I couldn't deny it any longer.

When she was done taking care of the gash, she stood up, wiping the sweat from her forehead and unknowingly replacing it with Riker's blood.

With a tired sigh, she turned to me, placing a damp cloth in my hand.

"Clean him. I took care of the spot around the wound, but he is still covered in blood," she said. "Come out when you are ready. I will have food prepared. You must be hungry."

I merely nodded as she walked passed. As soon as the door clicked shut behind her, I raised my head. His body was stiff, his eyes closed, his chest and stomach still smeared with blood from the gaping wound.

Moving closer to the bed, I clutched the cloth in my hand, sighing his name. My throat thick, I slowly placed my trembling hand on his torso. His stomach was taut beneath my fingers. Pain woven into his flesh.

I eased the cloth over his stomach, and after a few strokes, his body relaxed beneath my touch. After sucking in a breath, I whispered his name again. The only response was his sporadic breathing. I stared at him for a few moments longer before wiping away the remaining blood. Each and every one of his scars were on display. The severity of them splayed for the world to see.

I shuddered at the sight—at the pain he must have felt. One scar started from below his shoulder and cut down along his torso before disappearing around his side. I ran my fingers along the large, raised scar. The longer I stared, the more I thought it looked to have been inflicted by a sword. I hoped it came from the sword of an enemy rather than that of his father. The Viking King was known to be cruel, but to do this to his own son—

Tearing my stare from his bare chest, I slowly pulled my fingers away.

Stepping back, I glanced under the bed and found a spare blanket. Since his shirt was in tatters on the floor, I didn't want to leave him exposed like this. Though he was still sweating, I knew shivers would soon follow. I spread the blanket over top of him, sparing an extra moment to carefully cover his chest.

I swallowed the feeling that tugged at the thought of leaving his side, and drew back, reminding myself I only cared —only needed him to save Waylria and nothing more.

So I backed away from the bed until my shoulders hit the door.

Behind me, I fiddled with the doorknob. Once I managed to get it open, I whirled to leave the room. Without glancing back, I made sure to take in everything I had bypassed when we carried Riker's body inside.

Noticing the warmth, my eyes first went to the crackling fire going in the fireplace. There was a single window on the other side of the blackening wood, and half of it appeared to be consumed by vines snaking across the view. The room itself was rather small, and the only furniture within it was a table and set of chairs Skuld was already seated at.

Her back was to me, and though my steps were silent, she somehow knew I was there.

"Let him take the time to heal while you come sit," Skuld said, and I moved farther into the room. Her smile was as equally warm when she looked up at me.

I came around the table to face her, then slowly took the only other seat at the table—the seat across from her. She was weaving something between her hands, the tattoos on the back of her right hand expanding and relaxing as she guided the rope.

Everyone gushed over oracles' ability to read empathy, tell fortunes, carry out psychometry and retrocognition.

It was said that if an oracle possessed true magic, they could vault between the world to appear in other realms. From a simple touch, images of a person's possible future played out in their minds. Though such things were not set in stone, as it was theorized that with each person, came a different foreseeable future due to the strength of the images. They could be vaguely cryptic or rather specific, but it solely depended on the person. An oracle's job was to analyze the images and give predictions.

Skuld's widening smile snagged my attention again as she neatly placed the thread on the table in front of her. Her voice was tranquil when she spoke again. "You look worried."

My brows furrowed, images racing to recount everything that had happened leading up to the knife sinking into his chest. "It happened so fast."

"He lost quite a bit of blood, but, thankfully, the blade missed his heart."

Something inside my chest sank into my stomach at her lack of reassurance.

"Why are you helping us?"

Riker—*we* had been looking for an oracle. We had spent days traveling on foot to hear the truth—and one had magically shown up.

"How did you find us?" I added.

"Do not fret. We are still in the Willow Forest. The only way to find us is if we find you, my dear, and I did—at the correct time." She leaned back in her chair, her eyes on the thread. "And I already told you why. He must live." She paused. "An-and because when I laid eyes on you and the Viking, I knew I was meant to tell you some of what I know. I am meant to help."

The Willow Forest? We had been traveling closer to the Nedfin Mountains when we ran into her and Fenris. Where were we now?

My eyes jumped around the room to ensure we were indeed the only ones in the cabin. "What do you mean?"

Her gaze moved from the thread to catch my wandering

stare, and she reached across the table with her palm facing up. "Give me your hand."

I didn't move at first but inevitably placed my hand in hers. She turned it over so my palm was facing up. She placed the thread over my palm, then sucked in a breath and settled into her seat, leaning forward—closer to my open palm as she examined it closer. Though I could not see whatever she did, my heart picked up speed. What was this thread? Where did it end? I could not see where it ended; it continued long after her, winding around the room. What was it for?

Her eyes snapped shut as her grip on my hand tightened. "I see him entering darkness."

"Him?" Dread settled in the pit of my stomach, and my eyes shot behind Skuld—to the door separating me from the person I was supposed to force to his death. "Riker?"

Her eyes snapped open, but there was nothing upsetting in them, only gentleness. "Riker, yes. But not. He is the darkness. He is the savior. His family ... Something doesn't feel right with his family."

My heart plummeted. *Riker is the darkness?*

"He mentioned feeling fearful for his family," I told her. "He's worried for their safety. That's why we're here. He wants to know how to stop his father. Slate is planning something—"

"I know ..."

The darkness could be death. The darkness could be pain. Darkness could mean torture.

"Stop thinking in such a loud panic," Skuld told me, her eyes still closed. "You are making it difficult for me to see past you."

She ran her hand over the thread again, caressing the woven cord with the pad of her thumb.

I closed my eyes and pushed back against the image of Riker with pain in his eyes. The image that surfaced in its place was of him lying next to me mere nights ago, closing the distance between us.

"Good," said Skuld. "Keep your mind calm."

Silence beat through the room. My back stiffened with each moment I sat unnaturally still. The wolf in me huffed with restlessness.

"You are narrowed to the paths before you, so you are not focusing on any of the possibilities before you." I nearly flinched at the suddenness of her voice. She gave a light squeeze of my hand and opened her eyes to face me. "There is no true right choice right now. The thread could end soon or at a later time. This is up to fate. When the time comes, it is up to the Norns just as much as it is up to you."

"Do you see what awaits us in Sandire?" I asked her, almost in a whisper.

"Unspeakable things await you there. Things you are already prepared for, but also one you are not adapted to handle. It will cloud your mind. Everything will catch you off guard from then on. You will not know what to believe—which story is the truth."

My blood ran cold.

Riker's words echoed over hers. *"You wouldn't know which story to believe."*

"What did you say?" My voice sounded breathless even to my own ears.

"You will not know which story is the truth."

I couldn't stop the shudder that racked through my body, and snatched my hand from Skuld's. She watched me, her mystical eyes lit with wonderment and despair. For me. For whatever else she saw in my future. I banished it all to the dark corner of my mind.

"What did—" She hesitated, breaking off with the tilt of her head. "What did you feel when you saw him lying there; hurt?"

I didn't allow myself to think of that either. Panic. Shear panic. I didn't analyze it. I didn't answer her, sinking back into my chair instead.

She pulled back, nodding as if she realized I was done listening to her reveal the cryptic future ahead of me.

Only … I couldn't be.

"Can you tell me of Slate's plans?" This is what we had come here for. I had come for answers. I just did not know what I would do with them once I had them.

Skuld clasped her fingers together. When she pulled them apart, a glowing thread appeared. After a few moments, it dulled to look like the thread she had been caressing before.

"But," Skuld continued, "I can only see how *your* life and fate intertwine with Slate's. I cannot see beyond that. If your fates do not meet or influence one another in some way, there will be nothing for me to see."

"You cannot tell me if what Riker says is true?" I asked, my voice small.

"What does he claim?"

"That Slate plans to send the realms into ruin for his own gain."

Skuld met my gaze without wavering.

"Maybe if you're here, and if what Riker says is true, you can help me convince Haiden of what is coming for shifters."

Skuld pulled back. "You must be hungry, let me fix you something."

My stomach sank with how my heart nearly stopped dead.

I couldn't think of eating, but I said nothing as she left me alone at the table. She went to the wood stove in the far corner of the room, the farthest from the fireplace. A large pot rested on top of it, its contents quickly rising to a boil as Skuld tended to it.

I turned away to stare at the closed door in front of me.

The cruel Viking King did not know what he would be unleashing. He did not know the lengths the shifters would go to to remain free or how vengeful Haiden could be—what wrath would be unleashed upon him and everyone else who stood in the way of that freedom.

And when my thoughts turned to Riker … It was foolish to even go down that road. To think of him differently. Especially now, in the face of warfare. He was my prisoner. He was to be executed.

There should be no other choice or thought but to take him to Sandire. Not when the safety of Waylria was in my hands. There was too much at risk to be foolish. There was too much at risk to think of him as anything more than my prisoner.

Then why, despite knowing this, did my heart squeeze in answer?

AFTER LOOKING over everything in the cottage and deciding Skuld wasn't a threat, I slipped back into the bedroom. I sat on the floor and leaned against the wall beside his bed—keeping a careful distance—so I was facing the door. No one would be able to set foot in this room without waking me.

I looked over the side of the bed at Riker, easily seeing in the dark. He was still unconscious, his body relaxed under the blanket I had covered him with. I was tempted to check for a fever, but he looked neither cold nor feverish.

I looked down at my clean hands, thinking of the trembling panic that had consumed them earlier. I didn't know what to make of it. Not entirely.

I did not want to explore what was behind it.

But … I still knew the truth. Deep down. Even though I kept forcing it back, I knew. I especially could not deny it now. Not after watching him collapse.

I let those thoughts drift back.

Watching the blanket rise and fall with his breath, I leaned my head back against the wall, eventually closing my eyes with the hope that Riker's would be open when I awoke.

THE FAINT SOUND of a click sent me shooting forward. Crouching low in my wolf skin as my eyes adjusted to the darkness of the room, I released a low growl that rumbled from my throat. Skuld stumbled to a stop at my warning, and I froze at the sight of her, then shifted back to my human skin. "I'm sorry," I said. "I didn't realize it was you."

She nodded. "It is all right. I should not have snuck up on you." She held out the bandages she was carrying, the candle in her hand illuminating them. "I only came to redress his wound."

I nodded, holding my hand out for them. "I'll do it. You've done so much to help us already."

She smiled, placing them in my hand before giving me the candle. "If you are sure, I will see you in the morning." She turned to leave. "And my apologies again."

"You shouldn't be the one apologizing," I whispered back. "I'm the one who almost attacked you."

She flashed another smile before slipping back out the door.

I stood in the dark for a moment, holding the binding fabric, staring at nothing as I worked to collect myself. My heart was pounding in my ears—with the need to protect. I had shifted on instinct when I heard the door open. I had reacted quickly and without thought.

But everything was fine. We were safe.

Releasing a breath, I came out of my trance and walked to Riker's side. When I pulled back the blanket, I was relieved to see blood hadn't escaped the dressings. After placing the candle on the table, I reached for the bandages, slowly peeling the spotted strip back. Blood didn't seep through my fingers.

Instead, cool fingers caressed the back of my hand and trailed across my wrist.

Jumping at the contact, I nearly dropped the fresh bandages. My gaze fell to his face, my heart thumping through me. Riker's eyes were cracked open, his lips parted as he weakly stared up at me.

As I met his golden stare, relief overpowered all thought. "Riker."

I swallowed against the lump in my throat. Relief. That was all it was. "I was just about to change your bandages. How do you feel?"

"Like you owe me." Every word—every breath held strain.

My heart sank, hoping he wouldn't ask the impossible. I couldn't let him go. I had to take him to Sandire—for Waylria.

"You seem to need quite a bit of help," he added.

It seemed he wasn't beyond taunting me even in the state he was in. Even with a weak voice. I probably shouldn't have been surprised. After all, he had insulted and spat terrible things during the hours of his interrogations.

"I've taken you on multiple times now and won," I reminded him. "If you think I need help, then you are sadly mistaken."

"I've saved you from being killed *twice*. You should show a little gratitude." He glanced at the wound in his chest but made no move to touch it. "And you won a few of those fights with unfair threats."

"If I have to make threats to get you to shut up and behave, so be it. Now, let me change your bandage so we both can go back to sleep."

He lay back into the pillows, defeated by exhaustion. I removed the last part of the bloodstained dressing, keeping focused on my hands. He didn't flinch or make a sound as I worked to replace the strip of white cotton. I could feel him watching me, yet he didn't speak.

It wasn't until I was finished that his hand brushed against mine again. I didn't jump this time—but went still. An accident, I decided but didn't pull away.

Reaching across him again, I plucked the candle back up. "You're all patched up. Try not to move, I won't get up to change it again."

With slow, deliberate movements, I eased my hand out from under his. He matched my stare, neither of us saying anything with our eyes, or our mouths. After a drawn-out moment, I blew out the candle and backed away from the bed to my place against the wall, facing the door.

There was silence. And I was about to close my eyes when he said, "Thank you—for helping me."

A pause. "Thank you for saving me."

Silence settled between us. I leaned my head against the wall again, a smile tugging at my lips as I relaxed back into sleep.

Chapter Thirty-Six
Riker

MY ENTIRE BODY was stiff from lying flat on my back for so long. Keeping my eyes closed, I moved my fingers first before carefully shifting my shoulder. Pain radiated from the gash in my chest, and I struggled to catch my breath.

Blood loss had weakened me, but the fiery agony had dragged me under. There was no telling how much time had passed before I'd woken to Zyra standing over me with fresh bandages.

I'd heard and felt her when I was struggling with the pain and temperature of my body. She cleaned the blood from me. Her every move careful not to disturb my injured chest. Then there was the way she sighed my name under her breath. Sending a different shudder through my limbs.

I opened my eyes, looking for her, but I was alone in the room.

She was not propped against the wall as she had been when I saw her last, with her head tilted back and eyes closed in sleep.

Forcing the rest of my body into action, I propped myself up by my elbows and scanned the room more thoroughly. Zyra would not have left me alone somewhere she didn't think was safe, but I still wanted to know where we were. I only knew I was alone in a nearly empty room, lying on a bed in some sort of cabin. The smell of the wood structure was dominating from the recent rain.

As I rose, the blanket covering my bare chest slid to my waist. I stared down at it for a moment, trying to prop myself the rest of the way up. There was a tug of pain with each movement, followed by fatigue from the loss of blood and stress on my thumping heart.

The knife had come so close. But Zyra was fine. Zyra had been up and walking, tending to my injury. I'd reached her in time, and she took care of the bastard. Her ferocious snarl suggested how she'd torn him to pieces before racing to get to me.

Filled with the sudden need to find her, I moved to get out of bed—where I stepped on my shirt. When I picked it up, it practically fell apart in my hands. The fabric was shredded. I cast it aside, not acknowledging the twinge as I pushed to my feet and made my way to the door.

I walked as quietly as I could on the wooden floorboards, creeping toward the door to listen to what was going on in the other room. Pressing my ear against the door, I heard nothing on the other side. Zyra and I couldn't be the only ones here. I'd heard another woman's voice in the agonized haze.

Now, I didn't hear Zyra's voice or any other. I didn't hear movement either.

I yanked the door open, my stare quickly sweeping the room. Little to no furniture, one window letting in sunshine, and from how bright it was, I guessed it was late morning or heading into midday. There was also a single door leading outside. My eyes stayed on the door for a long moment before landing on the woman sitting at the only table in the room.

Her back was to me, but I knew she heard the door when I swung it open. Her hair was pulled back over her shoulders, long and dark; she wore a shawl over it, covered in jewels and beads of bright colors. My jaw almost slacked at the sight of the woman who had been traveling with the very men who'd attacked us. The same woman who had run from the shapeshifters we'd encountered not long before that.

"Hon er úti," Skuld said in the Nordic tongue without looking up. She was moving something in her hands. *"Hon sagði at hon vildi lauga, svá ek senda hana til rennanda pollsins þarna."*

I slowly stepped around the table to face Skuld. She was moving threads around in her hands, not looking up at me.

"How long was I unconscious for?" I asked in the same tongue. My voice came out hoarse, though I hoped she would keep speaking in my language since it had been so long since I last heard it. That was when I realized I had barely spoken my own language since leaving Sandire. Even at the village, they had understood the shapeshifter language and used it to speak to us. Just as Skuld was doing now.

"It has been two days since you last woke."

Two days spent wrapped in silence. Two days of my body struggling to recover.

"Where did you say Zyra was?"

"She is across the way, at the pool."

I started for the door, but then the threads in her hand paused their shuffling as she finally looked at me.

"What do you see? When you look at her—do you still see the beast your ancestors scorned and hunted? Do you see the past you are fighting to forget? Do you still wish to destroy her, or are you finally glimpsing the heart beneath the skin you have been cautioned against—taught to fear and hate? Perhaps —" A blink of certainty. "Perhaps it is a blend of everything and you are uncertain of which voice to listen to."

I froze, holding the knob in a tight, impatient grip. Something in my chest squeezed, causing the stab wound to spasm. I stared at her, mouth dry, a heavy feeling in my stomach. I tried to swallow against the sudden discomfort in my throat, ignoring the race of my pulse and the weakness in my knees.

She flashed a knowing smile. "The one you are running from will find you, Riker."

My blood ran cold. I gripped the doorknob tighter, practically crushing it. "Is there something I can use to stop him?"

"This him you speak of is not the him to be concerned with," she said, her eyes flashing to mine. "You cannot hide from your spitting image."

Without another word, I stormed out the door, hot anger roaring through my veins. While each step was a limp, I kept telling myself it was nothing.

I had no future.

Not unless I could find a way to stop my father and prove to Zyra his intentions. Before he used her to lead the extinction of Waylria.

I turned to slam the door back open.

"I have waited too long to talk to someone like you to let you get under my skin," I snapped. "I know Keyon was involved in what happened the night Annora died, but what does he have to do with what my father is doing?"

Skuld smiled up at my looming form in the doorframe. "I cannot convince your shifter of your father's plans when they are not *his* plans."

I LIMPED through trees and stomped over ground cover. The oracle said Zyra was across the way at some pool of water, so I walked in a straight line, trying to shake off the brooding thoughts bearing down on me. I continued to take deep, hot breaths, feeling none of the pain from my wound. My anger was too thick for the pain to get through.

I didn't snap out of the stifling of my anger until I heard the sound of rushing water. I nearly sighed with relief at the need for distraction. To let my anger drift to the back of my mind. To be able to focus on Zyra.

When I glimpsed the pool through the trees, I stopped dead, my anger vanishing.

Zyra was in hip deep, the surface rippling around her.

Without a stitch of clothing above her waist.

In nothing but undershorts.

At the edge of the water laid a clump of Zyra's discarded clothes and a long cloth. Rimmed with stones, moss, and ferns, a trickling rush was splashing into the pool, disturbing the otherwise calm pond.

Zyra reached back, running her hands through her curls, smoothing her hair so it rested in the center of her back, her curls wetting but not straightening. Lean and delicately muscled, her back curved with lines of faint and prominent scars of different sizes.

Then there was the scar on her right side. A large dark spot that was healed over with claw marks swiping across the top. The scar from the shifter who had gone rogue when she was a child, triggering her to shift for the first time. Looking as if it was painted on her almond skin, it told the story of a young shifter being brutalized.

And there was the tattoo. The black birds started from the right side of her waist, just out of reach of that scar. They flew up her back before coming to a stop at her left shoulder. Some of the birds were not following the others — some were flying a little ways from the trail gliding across her back in a curved line. The inconsistent pattern made them look all the more real.

My breath caught in my chest. Stolen from my lungs.

I couldn't think or see anything but her.

With my eyes glued on every curve of her back, I went to pull my shirt over my head, forgetting it was in shreds on the floor somewhere back at the cabin. I walked out from the trees in nothing but my undershorts. No longer storming; no longer angry; no longer limping. Everything else had faded away. I only wanted to get to Zyra now.

Then she turned, sinking until the water came up to her chest before I even reached the large stones that opened up and led into the pool.

Wicked amusement gleamed in her eyes at the sight of me.

We both knew she'd been aware of my presence all along.

"What are you staring at?" she demanded, her eyes light as she watched me wade through the water toward her.

I stopped a safe distance away. My mouth had gone dry. My blood roared in my ears. My eyes were trained on her in the same way hers were trained on me. Hel, she was looking at me through her lashes. Not glaring; not threatening with bared canines.

My eyes fell to the water, taking in her scars. Her gaze followed mine, and I spoke before she had the chance. "Did they hurt?"

I imagined my own scars—thought of the pain that had come with some of them. I only had one scar to compare to hers, and the thought of that pain made me want to hunt down the rogue who'd caused her such agony at such a young age.

"Some," she admitted. She moved her hair until it covered her chest before standing in the water. Glancing at me, she turned so her right side was facing me. I fought not to suck in a breath. "I'm … trying to be proud of them." Her voice was barely above a whisper. "Each one shows how I've survived. Even if I am an embarrassment to my family and shunned by others, I'm still here."

Claw marks above the dark scar were prominent.

My hands curled at my side with the urge to touch it.

She tilted her head, her gaze falling to my chest. "You have one of your own."

I didn't so much as glance at the jagged pale scar down my side. Another gift from my father. He had decided to show me how dirty Vikings could really fight. I hadn't been as young as

Zyra when she'd received hers from the rogue, but it was a barbaric lesson to give a youth.

She looked as if she wanted to touch my scar in turn, and the possibility caused my breath to knock from my lungs again.

There were unspoken words throbbing between us.

And those eyes—those brilliantly observant green eyes.

I waited for the internal struggle. To be repulsed by our closeness. To be repulsed by the urges wrangling inside me. But there was nothing but this sudden and bizarre fascination. I no longer felt conflicted.

It had taken me a while to realize she was beautiful. But once I got up close to her, once I spent so much time around her, finding those sharp, green eyes watching me with a threat or the spark of something else—there was no going back. I had broken through her barriers and my own prejudices, and there was no undoing it.

Those green eyes were watching me now, looking up at me through dark inviting lashes as the air between us singed with something that had been building long before today.

Chapter Thirty-Seven
Zyra

I GAZED BACK into those gold eyes as they studied me slowly, carefully—devouring as they took me in. The air around us was charged with an approaching storm. Remembering how to breathe and to think of anything beyond the storm—his closeness, his bare skin, and my own exposure—took effort.

We were somehow gravitating to each other through the water, our movement subtle but not unnoticed.

I thought nothing of being so openly bare in front of him. He was ravishing me in other ways. His eyes locking with mine, roaming over the scarred skin of my side, lingering on parts of me I wouldn't expect. Scars. Marks of survival. I knew it was impossible, but it felt as if his eyes were raking over all of them. I could feel the heat—the weight—of his stare. The intensity caused my breath to quicken, leaving me surprised my lungs still knew how to work.

"You have a tattoo," he said, his voice coming out hoarse. His fingers were moving over the water. I watched the slow movement, wondering if he were imagining skimming them across the birds on my back.

"And you do not." My eyes drifted downward, skimming his features. All scars and muscle. Scars upon scars. Healed-over jagged lines, holes, and burn marks. Marks caused by years of training, hunting. Some caused by me.

He closed the remaining distance between us.

I blew out a rush of air, then inhaled slowly, drinking in his scent. Sand and the musky scent of wood. There was also a hint of blood, which caused my gaze to fall to his bandaged chest. He inhaled, his broad chest expanding, not flinching at the movement. His eyes flared to a burning gold.

There was no denying what resided in them.

And I found myself wondering … if I tasted him, would my tastebuds sting with the saltiness of sand? Breath rushed out of me at the thought.

He lifted a hand—hesitated, then brushed back a strand of damp hair that had fallen across my face, his scarred, calloused fingers caressing my cheek.

The charge between us sparked, lighting up every cell in my body and sending my blood scorching through my veins.

All the air rushed from my lungs.

Then my body locked up, and I pulled back.

"I-I need to change your bandage."

He nodded in answer, distancing his body from mine. My body felt like it was burning from the inside. I forced myself to leave the pool, grabbing the cloth Skuld had given me before I'd left.

As we dried off at the edge, we caught each other's side glances. My heart skipped a beat each time I felt his eyes on me.

Then, when I looked up to catch him, his eyes locked with mine.

I swallowed, refusing to let my gaze drop as my next words spilled from my lips. "I … thought you were repulsed by me."

Riker's brows furrowed. "I—No."

Normally, I would have raised my brow in challenge, but a flutter in my chest halted any other thought.

I turned to continue down the path, but Riker's light touch caught my wrist, so I faced him again.

"I don't know what is to come. What I do know is that something has changed. I ..." He paused in thought of his words. "I don't think we have to be enemies. I *do not want* us to be enemies."

I stopped short.

Something was growing between us. We fit where we hadn't before. The charged energy—it felt like the storm was close and was going to rip everything apart. A tornado would sweep by and separate me from everything I ever cared about.

All of it was dangerous.

The charged storm, Riker, everything that stood between us, our differences and our similarities, Waylria, Sandire, the Viking King, Haiden, torture, and the waiting arms of death— all of it was waiting for us to walk out and face it.

And yet, I was plagued by the thought he was only saying these things so I wouldn't take him to Sandire. "This oracle has given me no reason to trust what you've spoken of your father's plans."

"Then let's go back." He tugged on my wrist, and I let him.

We were quiet as we walked back—my heart pounding louder and harder than I could have fathomed—and then, once we made it to the cabin, Skuld looked up from where she was tending to a plant in the corner.

I forced Riker to sit to let me change his bandage. He took up the chair I'd sat in while Skuld had given me glimpses into what awaited me. My chest clenched at the thought of Waylria lying in ruin—of shifters gone from the realm and the world.

I pushed back against the image as I slowly peeled the damp bandage from Riker's chest.

"I do not want us to be enemies."

But what if, deep down, he still wanted that—to be enemies? What if something had changed and he knew the oracle would not attest to his claims? What if he was only saying this to save himself from execution?

His gaze bounced between us as he sat sideways in the chair to face me. His eyes narrowed whenever they fell to Skuld. Though, when he looked up at me, his eyes weren't brooding. They watched my hands work to change his dressings while being careful not to brush the wound or cause much irritation. Although, I knew he wouldn't show an ounce of discomfort. He was stubborn and far too good a warrior to flinch from the cleaning of a wound. I would have cooled my features and kept my back equally as straight.

Once the bandage was switched out, Skuld sat at the table across from Riker, her eyes glistening with possibilities and knowing. "You should tell her of what is to come."

Riker looked up at her, his expression blank. He did not get the chance to say anything, though.

"That is why you came in search of me, is it not?" she pressed. "To get answers and convince her of what is to come?"

I stared at Skuld from across the table. She stared back as if she knew my every thought, as if she could see the tear forming. The tear I felt between Riker and my duty. Between my heart and my need to prove myself.

Neither path felt right. No matter what, something was lost. There wasn't a right choice or even a choice I felt I could live with. Not at this point.

I stood, ignoring the numbness that flooded my body. "What do you have to tell me?" My voice sounded distant—distrustful—to my own ears.

His silence only made my panic fester.

I found myself speaking before I could think better of it. "You were never going to go back to Sandire with me. All this has been a lie? Does your father even plan to attack us outside of the normal hunting and sacrifices? You better start talking, Riker, before I come up with the worst answer I can think of."

I didn't want to think about our realms, the rivalry, the

sacrifices, or about how I was a shapeshifter and he was a Viking Prince. I didn't want to think about how I was the one commanded to take him — to the death that waited in Sandire. I didn't want to think about my duty or everything at risk.

I wanted none of it.

I didn't want to feel or think or fear.

Without another word, I stormed from the room that suddenly felt too small and slammed the door to the bedroom once I was safely behind it.

How much of it was a lie? How much of this journey had been a trick? How much of what he had shared was fake? How much of what I had revealed would be used against me?

I crossed the room for the wall I had propped myself against while I'd watched over Riker's healing. Once settled, I let my head fall into my hands.

But I could only fight off my spiraling thoughts for so long.

I woke to the click of the door opening. I straightened, my spine rigid as Riker stepped into the room. He looked surprised to have found me asleep, but I hadn't been out for more than a handful of minutes.

As he stood propped against the door, he felt so far away.

I didn't want to feel the miles between us.

I didn't want to feel the realms between us.

"We could leave," he quietly offered, each followed by a pause as if he were picturing it. "Disappear together. Leave and never look back — pretend none of the realms are in danger and never get involved."

"How does that solve anything?" I asked, unable to look at him. I wasn't sure I wanted to see his face. "Your father will still target Waylria."

"He's waited years to declare war on Waylria. Ever since I was a boy. He's only now been ready to attack."

I tilted my head. "And how is that supposed to make me feel better? There hasn't been a day that's gone by where you haven't warned me of an impending war. How is running supposed to make this situation better? What aren't you telling me?"

He sighed, closing his eyes for a long moment. "There is a bigger problem than my father. That is what Skuld was talking about. This is only a glimpse of what I'd meant when I told you that you wouldn't know which story to believe."

My heart plummeted. "Tell me."

He shook his head. "I can't. And I can't go back to Sandire. Skuld told me how to stop the carnage coming, and I can't risk being caught before I get the chance to find what she told me."

Before I could press to know what he meant, he went on.

"But maybe you could come with me. Perhaps we can think of a way for us to walk away from Sandire with our heads." He crossed the distance between us to crouch before me. "I'm asking you to seize what you want." A pause. "I know you don't want to hand me over to my father. And I know you don't want Waylria and the other realms to suffer. So seize what you want. Don't just do what you're told. Do what is right for you. Do what your very blood screams at you to do. If that's handing me over to my father, so be it. I'll find a way to escape again. I can defy the odds."

I shook my head, closing my eyes against my spiraling thoughts. "I don't know. I don't want to see anyone hurt, but I don't know what else to do. I—" I took a deep breath to steady myself. "You're asking me to trust you blindly."

Without knowing everything, making a decision was too big a risk.

His expression was careful—without hope, but I saw something else beneath the surface. He reached out, capturing my cheek in his palm while his fingers wove into my hair.

I didn't want to feel or think or fear.

Because we fit. His roughness against my fierceness. The looming danger over both of us. Despite everything standing against us, we fit. Something was thundering between us.

"Sleep on it," he told me, hauling me to my feet against the exhaustion I felt. Both mentally and physically.

These last few nights, sleep had been scarce. I woke several times to look at the bed beside me. Just to be sure he wasn't in danger of an infection, and to be sure no one else had entered the cabin.

Every time I closed my eyes, I saw nothing but blood. Everything from my hands to Riker's chest and the bed had been stained bright crimson with no end in sight. The walls had been smeared with it.

Now I climbed in beside Riker, careful not to touch him as I moved across the mattress on my hands and knees.

He was beside me soon enough, keeping close without touching me, like he had given into something but not fully. I folded my arms across my stomach. He propped his head up with his arm, looking down at me while I looked up at him.

Since he didn't have another shirt, his tan chest was still bare. Each and every one of his scars were on display—including the burns I had a hand in scorching into his skin.

I inhaled through my nose, then shut my eyes with his scent wrapped around me.

Chapter Thirty-Eight
Riker

I DIDN'T EXPECT AN ANSWER. I'd meant every word. I wouldn't ask that of her. Demand she choose. I wasn't my father. I was the enemy. I'd never ask Zyra to choose me when we had been brought up to hate each other.

I was the enemy. Yet, despite everything that had occurred between us, here we were.

Lying beside her, our legs touching but not tangled, I knew the last thing I wanted was to put her in danger. The mere thought sent anger racing for my heart.

But I had seen her mind at work, turning over my every word, weighing her options. The weight of her thoughts thickened the tension in the room. Each and every word bore no exception. I wouldn't have said the things I did if I hadn't meant them. I wanted to take the stress pinching between her eyes.

I couldn't defy the odds a second time and make it out of Sandire with my head still attached to my shoulders. Hel, for escaping, losing my head would probably be the least of my worries. My death wouldn't be so easy if they had to chase me again. Public execution would be forgotten, and I would be subjected to imagination.

I would be powerless against torture methods long before death was bestowed upon me. All of which would probably end with me being blood eagled. That was likely to be a public event, as it was often used as a warning.

My chest was tight. My breath stirred her hair. I felt her body move with her every breath. They eventually evened out while I lay awake beside her.

I could tell Zyra, and she might believe me, but all that could end if she saw how everyone stood against me. My father would spew lies until she believed what he did. He would convince her I was using her. He would convince her I was a good-for-nothing son who deserved to be punished.

He would cloud her judgment, confuse her mind until she saw exactly what he wanted.

Closing my eyes, I bit back against the rage spreading through me. I could picture it all-too clearly.

I didn't want her to think I'd lied to gain her sympathy—that everything had been a lie and I had been manipulating her the entire time. I wanted—*needed* her to see the truth. The real truth.

I wanted more than for her to know that none of it was a lie. Something had snapped between us. Something had changed, bringing our hatred for each other to an abrupt halt. But it could be reversed if she didn't believe me.

It couldn't be reversed for me, though. She could hate me again, but I couldn't go back to hating her. I had tried before and hadn't been able to keep myself from caring if she were hurt. It was too late for me.

I released a heavy sigh.

Only one way to find out.

I had to tell her. I had to show her, strip myself of everything and show her how deep my scars truly ran.

Then she could decide.

If it went well, I would share Skuld's riddle with her. *"A flame in the center of darkness will spark, lighting the way for what is to come, but it has no wick or oil to fill.*" If Zyra rejected me, I would have to decipher it on my own.

My chest caved with the decision to tell her in the morning. The moment she woke.

Unable to resist, I moved my head closer to hers, trying not to disturb her. With my nose resting against her neck, I relaxed into her warmth and reveled in the smell of her.

If moonlight had a scent, there wasn't a doubt in my mind it would resemble Zyra.

HER WARMTH WASN'T against me. When I realized this, I opened my eyes. My hand was sprawled across the mattress, searching for her, but the bed was empty. I sat up with her name on my lips.

The room was empty, the door shut. She must have just slipped out and the click of the door caused me to wake. I pushed back all thoughts of falling back asleep and forced myself to get up.

Yanking open the door, sunlight came pouring in. I shut my eyes against the sudden light, blindly walking forward.

I opened them again when I heard a growl from my right.

The first thing I saw was Zyra in her wolf skin, crouched in the corner by the fireplace, baring her canines as she growled for my attention.

My heart jolted at the sight, practically launching out of my chest as dread overtook me. I reached for a weapon that wasn't at my hip. I was without a way to save Zyra.

The two men didn't have weapons drawn, but they each carried a chain as they approached the shifter, looming over her. Zyra snarled and snapped, trying to hold the men back enough to keep them from reaching her. That familiar fire was burning in her eyes.

A laugh snapped my attention from them. I took in the rest of the room, my hands clenched at my sides. I didn't know where to turn. I hadn't the faintest idea where to search for a weapon.

Skuld was on the other side of the room, wrenched against Fenris, despite the knife at her throat. I braced, gnashing my teeth together.

"I did not see them. *I did not see them,*" she kept repeating, panicked. "They did not decide. I did not see them."

But my eyes were on the man who stood in the open doorway casually leaning against the doorframe with a Viking war hammer slacked between his fingers. One of my own weapons. His gaze met mine from across the room, dark pleasure bathing in the gold of his eyes.

Eyes that matched mine.

With no more than two words, everything came crashing down around me.

"Hello, brother."

PART III

DANGEROUS CRAVINGS

Chapter Thirty-Nine
Zyra

I HADN'T BELIEVED it at first. I'd walked out of the bedroom, leaving Riker in the bed behind me, only to walk in to find Riker standing in the center of the cabin while Fenris held a knife at Skuld's throat to keep her silent. Apologies had stumbled from the oracle's mouth, but I heard none of them. My eyes remained locked on the other Riker, my heart stumbling over itself.

Now, my heart was pounding, and I was burning for a fight.

I dared the Vikings with a fierce growl. They did not fear me. They had caught shapeshifters before—perhaps dozens—and then helped slaughter them. They could do the same to me.

They had corralled me into the corner after Riker laughed at my reaction. I shifted on instinct and was now fighting to keep them at bay. It wasn't but a few moments later that Riker stumbled from the bedroom, shutting his eyes against the sudden light.

Desperate to catch his attention—needing him aware of the danger surrounding us before one of them decided to attack, I growled to wake him. His eyes had widened upon taking me in, absolute dread washing over his features. He only looked away from me to survey the rest of the room before his eyes landed on the Riker standing in the doorway.

Both Rikers in the same room. Face-to-face.

They stared at each other for the longest moment before a smile slowly broke out across the face of the Riker in the doorway. *"Góðan ðag, bróðir."*

Bróðir. Brother.

My blood turned ice cold, but there was an unrecognizable wildness in me begging to attack.

They looked exactly alike. Their hair was the same dirty blonde with dark roots. It was the same length and had the same slight wave. The Riker in the doorway even had the same dark scruff and the same strong build with broad shoulders and strong arms.

A perfect build for a Viking warrior. A perfect reflection of Riker.

What tugged at me the most, though, was that he had Riker's gold eyes.

I had known that the Viking King of Sandire had more than one child. In fact, he had three. But I had been completely and utterly oblivious to the fact that two of them were twins.

"What are you doing here, Keyon?" Riker practically growled, speaking in my own tongue.

"Careful," his brother said, switching to my language as his golden gaze flicked to me. "You're starting to sound like the dog you've been traveling with."

Riker's jaw tensed, his eyes blazing, never wavering from his brother.

Instead, I snarled at the two Vikings standing in my way. They only smirked when I snapped for their hands again.

Oh, how tempted I was to tell them how the man holding Skuld in the corner had lost his hand.

He'd found us. I had made the mistake of letting Fenris get away while he knew where Skuld lived. Somewhere along the way, he ran into those searching for Riker and informed them of where the Viking Prince was.

If I could get past the Vikings, I would rip him apart. Piece by piece so he felt as much pain as possible. Losing his hand would be nothing in comparison.

"I'll come with you if you leave Zyra alone," Riker said.

I snarled at the suggestion, and Riker's head whirled toward me. I saw the fear boiling beneath the surface of his eyes. There was desperate panic there, too, flaring for no more than a second when his eyes met mine.

He wanted me to understand every word of their exchange. He did not want there to be any surprises.

Keyon's taunting smile widened. "Why would I leave a perfectly good sacrifice here? And you're not in a position to negotiate. You're coming with me no matter what I do to the shifter." He snapped his fingers, and the two Vikings advanced with purpose. "You'll come with me without a fight, or I'll kill her before we ever leave this cabin."

The one nearest me jumped forward with his chains. I lunged to meet him, snapping my canines, ready to taste flesh and blood. I whirled on the Viking stalking behind me, launching at him with my claws, mouth wide open.

I knew I had him as soon as I lashed out, my claws cutting across skin to reveal the blood beneath. Then, without giving myself the chance to think twice, I reached for his face with my teeth. It all happened within a blink, as if I were acting on instinct alone.

I turned to face the other in the same moment he fell to the floor with a thud.

Then the other Viking was on top of me.

His hand was around my throat, and somehow, he had me shoved up against the wall. I clawed at the hand around my neck and flashed my teeth. I shifted to my human skin in a feeble attempt to pry at his fingers with my own.

Over the Viking's shoulder, I saw Riker start to launch toward me, but Keyon was there, stepping between us.

I gasped, trying to bring air into my burning lungs. I kicked against the wall, but there was no leverage for me to push off. The Viking only squeezed tighter, his expression indifferent.

"Stop this!" Riker shouted at his brother. "You've done enough already."

Keyon's head tilted to the side. "Care about what happens to shifters now?"

They stared each other down.

My eyes went to Riker. He was struggling with wanting to rescue me and needing to protect me by acting like he didn't care what happened to me. He didn't want his brother to see an inkling of what we had established and use that to his advantage to control and hurt us.

Even if neither of us had fully admitted it aloud … He was battling against himself as much as he was in a power struggle against his brother.

Keyon's head tilted farther. "She doesn't know? You didn't tell her what you did? Tsk, tsk, brother."

The hand around my neck loosened enough for me to draw in a hiss of breath.

Riker exhaled hot air, his chest expanding as he got in his brother's face. "I didn't tell her because I didn't do it. We both know that. We *both* know I don't thirst for the title of king."

"Yet it's your head the kingdom wants. Everyone wants a piece of the eldest Viking Prince." Keyon spared a glance in my direction. The pressure around my neck released. "Is that the reason you didn't tell her why our father wants your head on a stake?" His smile grew wider, already knowing the answer. "You didn't want to go up against her, so you kept your treacherous actions to yourself? You didn't want to be ripped apart by the teeth of a mongrel?"

Still gasping for air, I used what little I had to snarl.

Riker's mask slipped as Keyon turned to me.

"He killed our sister," Keyon said at the same time Riker said, "Don't believe a damn thing he says."

Everything went muffled—distant. Even my own breath. I had no words. Shock. Disbelief. Anger. Confusion. Every feeling rammed into me with the force of a stone wall. I had asked him again and again and again. He had refused to tell me. Never giving a straight answer. *You wouldn't know which story to believe.*

He was wanted for treason.

He escaped Sandire and ran across the lands until I captured him in Waylria.

He had committed a treason so terrible he was wanted alive so his own father could carry out his death sentence.

He killed his sister.

My chest tightened as my thoughts scrambled to understand.

"Our sister was heir to everything that came with our father's title," Keyon went on before I could fully collect myself. "Riker betrayed our entire family—turned the guards against us all and used them to plot our deaths. Our sister was killed by our own guards as she tried to protect our parents, and Riker did nothing but watch. He wanted us all dead so he could take our father's title."

I stared at Keyon, unable to look in Riker's direction as each word sank to the pit of my stomach. I didn't want to see his expression, look into his eyes. The way he had looked at me while bathing in the pool yesterday ... The eyes of a traitor. The hands of a cold-blooded murderer.

And yet I ... I had wanted ... I had been tempted and felt something between us. I had felt the temptation of the very curse I have hated and been hated for.

I couldn't look at him, so instead, I shut my eyes to block it all out.

It couldn't be true. His brother's claims couldn't be true.

But some dark corner of my mind whispered … *then why else would his own father aspire to behead him?* Why was he wanted for treason? Why had his own people turned against him? My chest tightened further, my lungs striving to crush my heart.

My mind wrestled back and forth, incapable of fully believing he was innocent or guilty. *"You wouldn't know which story to believe."*

I needed to hear what Riker had to say; hear his side of this horrible story. I couldn't trust his brother, but my mind shied from the thought of trusting Riker, too. A pang came with the thought of what he might tell me. A pang came with the thought of everything that had led to now. Everything leading to now had been a lie. And I was afraid of being hurt. I was afraid of whatever was evolving between us.

I was afraid of the truth.

And I was afraid I had done all this—betrayed my realm—for nothing.

"Why don't you take the wolf outside?" Keyon suggested to the man holding me. "I'll bring my brother out in a moment."

I growled at the threat of being separated from Riker, even if I wasn't certain where we stood.

"No." Riker stepped forward. "Just leave her, Keyon—"

He shook his head. "No. I think I'll use her to keep you cooperative since you seem so fond of each other. And once I don't need you to behave anymore, she'll be an excellent sacrifice. So will her friend. I'm sure many will gather to see their hearts ripped out."

My heart plummeted further.

"My friend?" I gasped out.

The only other person who had been sent to Sandire—Corinna. Was she here? Had she been kept alive but held captive? Had Riker's brother been waiting for such an opportunity, somehow knowing that would get me to bow to him?

Keyon gave a curt nod to the man, who pulled me from the wall. My mind raced as my eyes flicked between everyone in the room. I took that moment to let my gaze flash to Riker's. His eyes had lost their glint. And that was all I had the chance to decipher before I was thrown to the ground. I slid when I hit the floor, letting a snarl rip from the deepest part of my chest. I could have sworn the sound shook the house as I flared my sharp canines.

The Viking, however, was not fazed as he yanked his chains free from his belt, which many pellets hung from. He was following orders. We were enemies, and therefore, he was more than happy to follow them. He was smug as he grabbed me, roughly locking the iron chains around my wrists and then a larger one around my neck. Seething, trying not to show my discomfort and humiliation, I kept my head low, letting my hair cover my face.

If there was any pain from being strangled, I didn't feel it. My anger and confusion were blocking anything I would be aware of later. My whirling thoughts were probably contributing to the numbness, too.

Everything I felt—they weren't only related to being locked in chains.

My mind was still reeling, my emotions out of control, tugging my heart in every direction imaginable. I tried to put a leash on every feeling flooding through me, but it was damn near impossible. Every one that lashed out at me was overwhelming.

I paid no heed to where I was being led and heard nothing outside the whispers and screams of my mind. I physically felt nothing while every emotion hurled through me like a thunderstorm.

When the Viking shoved me into the back of a prison wagon, I was grateful to be able to curl into one of its corners. There was one door with a single barred window, so I was almost completely swallowed by darkness when the door slammed shut behind me.

He was wanted for treason.

He killed his sister.
There had to be more to the story.
Riker couldn't be a stranger to me all over again.
And Corinna … she had to be alive.

Chapter Forty
Riker

EACH INTAKE of breath was coming fast and hot. My glare was locked on my brother, who watched as Zyra was escorted out by chains and cuffs around her wrists and neck. I could only imagine what she felt as she was forced from the cabin in such shackles. I couldn't bring myself to look at her.

I wanted to kill my brother for his lies.

I wanted to kill him for putting Zyra in chains.

I wanted to kill him for making her think I had betrayed my family, the entirety of Sandire, by having my sister murdered.

If only we didn't share blood—if only he wasn't my brother. If only I didn't still love him despite everything he'd done … I wouldn't hesitate to punish him the way I would any other man. I would not have thought twice about snapping his neck.

He deserved a stab wound for every lie he'd told. For painting me as a greedy, selfish murderer who cared about nothing beyond the title that was never meant to be mine. Annora was the rightful heir to the title of Viking Queen of Sandire. Neither of us were meant to be king. The title had been hers from birth. I hadn't wanted it, and I still did not want it. I never would.

After seeing Annora's blood spilled on our mother's carpets, and after hearing her body slump to the floor with a lifeless thud, I wouldn't ever want it.

I could still hear my mother's scream echoing in their bedroom …

At the sharp pang gripping my heart, I pushed back against those memories.

If I could stop looking at him as my twin brother—the one person who always stood in my corner, fought and ran beside me among the dunes, kicking up sand—I could storm up to my father and tell him the truth without giving my actions a second thought. Lay out every detail of Keyon's treachery without feeling a lick of regret.

If I could forget how he was the one who endlessly teased but also comforted and tended to me when our father was cruel, I could kill him where he stood. I had spent our lives defending him far more than he had defended me, and that need to shield him was not something I could ignore now.

"I'm going to kill you," I ground out, making a promise to myself as much as to him. I would make him pay for what he'd done to Annora. Once I found the willpower. Even if it required my last breath, I would find a way to make him pay for what he'd done to our family. He had changed. He wasn't the brother I'd grown up with. He had become someone I didn't recognize. "It might not be today or tomorrow, but somewhere down the line, Keyon, our lives will collide, and only one of us will walk away from that sandstorm. And it will not be you."

His eyes darkened, the cruel smile remaining. "You sound rather confident for a Viking stripped of his army."

"I won't need an army to take you down—only my ax and my strength and Annora's spirit beside me."

"Too bad you won't make it past sunrise tomorrow. I would

have liked to have seen how that would have turned out for you, brother." He gestured to the door. "Shall we start our journey home? Father is awaiting your return, after all."

I clenched my hands at my sides, wanting to get them around his neck to see how he liked it. But, uncertain of who my brother had become, he would probably take some sort of sick pleasure in it.

He pulled leather handcuffs from his belt, and I almost chuckled as he stepped toward me. Before he could strap them around my wrists, I snatched him by the hand, stepping closer until I was right in his face, my eyes boring into his. "You've taken enough from me. If you so much as think about hurting her, I will make sure you have the most miserable ending I can think of."

He took a step closer. I couldn't believe this was the same person I had grown up beside. I couldn't understand how my twin brother had become a Viking crueler than our father. We had shared everything. We looked exactly alike—unless one examined our scars closely and aside from the tattoo on Keyon's left shoulder. Now, my brother was unrecognizable. He had become someone entirely different from me. A murderer and a traitor.

"I intend to do more than hurt her, brother." He strapped the cuffs around my wrists before I had a chance to do much else. Leather rather than iron was used for Vikings since there was no need to prevent shapeshifting.

Fury bursting my control, I swiped my hands to the side, breaking his hold on me. Stepping into him, I brought my fists up until they connected with his face. The force sent him to the ground. I stood over him, burning to do more. Yearning to leave him bleeding out on the ground as Annora had.

But Zyra was outside. If I took things further, she could suffer for my actions.

I fought back the urge as Keyon propped himself up, blood dribbling from the corner of his mouth. He looked up at me over his shoulder to see I had not tried to run off, nor was I advancing to cause further harm. He smiled as if he knew the answer to some deep, dark secret, as if he knew he had won something.

Keyon slowly picked himself up off the floor, wiping the blood from the split corner of his lip, keeping eye contact with me the entire time. I shifted my weight, bracing myself for an attack. But he only snatched me by the straps connecting my cuffs, like Zyra had done so many times before, and yanked me toward the door.

On our way out, he glanced at the man still holding Skuld —the very man I had put myself in front of when he tried to stab Zyra. "You can do what you please with the oracle. She is of no use to me, and neither are you anymore."

Fenris's eyes widened behind the emotionless Skuld. "What of the reward?" he asked.

"The reward is walking away with your life," Keyon said, slamming the door shut behind us.

Outside, carefully placed out of view of the window and door, sat a prison wagon. The black stallion leading the front was restlessly digging its hooves into the dirt, ready to feel sand underfoot again. The wagon had a door with a single window in the center, and there was a giant bolt on the side— to ensure no way of escape.

My heart sped up with each step closer to the wagon. Once the door opened, I would have to face her. I would have to face her questions, her harsh words—I was prepared for everything she would say and unprepared to hear them all the same, knowing each one would cut me open like one of her claws.

But it all would be well deserved. I wouldn't blame her for being furious with me. I was her enemy, and I had kept this from her. I didn't expect her to trust me ever again—

Keyon opened the wagon door and told me to get in. Zyra was sitting in the far corner with her knees drawn up to her chest. Her stare moved between Keyon and me, her face unreadable in the shadows. I should have known better than to think she would look scared.

My chest caved wide open.

I could not stand the thought of Zyra regretting not mauling me that first time we laid eyes on each other.

It was a thought I could never have imagined.

I climbed into the back of the wagon, and Keyon immediately shut the door behind me. The only source of light was from the small window. In the moments before my eyes adjusted, I could barely see Zyra. I stayed near the door, almost positive she wouldn't want me any closer. There were so many things running through my mind—so many things I wanted to say, but none of them seemed enough. I didn't know where to start.

I had wanted to tell Zyra this morning. I was going to tell her every word of what had happened and how it all reared its ugly head; tell her how I'd escaped it all. But when I'd walked out of the bedroom to find Keyon … Of course, Keyon got to her before I could.

Everything I had to say would be taken as a lie now. I didn't know how I could convince her that everything about our journey here had been true up until this very second and that every word my brother spoke was an absolute lie. Nothing —including anything about myself—had been fabricated. I had given her nothing but the truth from the moment she caught me in the snow.

The same thoughts from last night echoed in my mind.

I wanted—*needed* her to see the truth. The real truth.

I needed her to listen to what I had to say before Keyon poisoned her mind further.

The thought of her hating me—being so close to her now and not knowing every thought that plagued her—was unbearable. There was a tightening in my chest.

"Zyra—" I started in the same moment the wagon jolted into movement.

Zyra spoke up before I could defend myself or argue my side. "Did you trick me?" Her voice was raspy and uncertain. *"Did you use me?"*

"No," I breathed. Then spoke again, louder. "No!" I made to move across the wagon toward her, but a vicious snarl echoed between us. Something inside tugged at me, leading me to her. There was nowhere for her to go. She couldn't pull away, but I didn't reach for her—not yet.

When she spoke again, her voice was stronger. "You never once mentioned you had a twin brother. Not a word. Not once. I knew you had siblings but ..." She ran her hands through her hair. I wanted to pry them from her curls. "You wouldn't tell me what you'd done, and now your *twin brother* is here, and he's saying all these things—"

"Zyra. Zyra, look at me." I couldn't help it—couldn't stop myself. I reached for her, taking her face between my hands and forcing her to meet my eyes. "Nothing my brother has said, or will say, is true. You can't trust him. He's the one who's done all those things, and he's pinned it all on me. He's the reason everyone in Sandire wants me dead, because he's tied all those terrible things back to me. And that isn't even half of what he's done."

I could only imagine what my eyes revealed right now.

Close enough to see her eyes in the bit of light coming through the window, I paused to search the depths of them, needing to know what she was thinking. I needed to be sure she was hearing me. "If you don't believe me, then I will spend every second I have trying to prove it to you."

Zyra shook her head. "How can I be sure you aren't lying? How can I be sure anything you've told me is true? You could have been deceiving me from the start."

She didn't know what to think, but her trust in me hadn't shattered. Not yet.

My heart pounded furiously. My hands were practically shaking, and all I could think was that I had to find a way to get her to trust me again—to believe me. And despite her panicked words, she was scrambling to regain her confidence in me. She wanted to trust me. She only needed something to hold onto and wanted assurance that she could.

My focus was on her.

"I haven't been tricking you or lying to you. Yes, I kept why my father wanted me for treason from you, but I did so because I needed you to listen to me about his plans; not about why he wanted me dead. I could never—" I had to stop, finding it difficult to talk around the sudden lump in my throat. "I would never hurt my sister."

When she said nothing, my heart felt heavy and slowly sank to the pit of my stomach. I couldn't swallow around the lump lodged in my throat.

"You have far more reason to trust me than you do my brother. I need you to see the truth. I need you to believe me." I took her hand in mine, avoiding the chains and focusing on her smooth, warm skin. "Please. I would never do anything to hurt my family, least of all my sister. I'm not a traitor. You can trust me."

"I don't *not* trust you. I trust you far more than your brother. But I'm worried. I'm worried about Corinna now, about what's going to happen, about … Tell me. Tell me now," she said, gripping my hand in her tight grasp. "How did you get away? What really happened? What did you do?"

I swallowed, struggling to get words out.

She waited for my answer, her stare moving between my eyes and our clasped hands.

I released a defeated sigh, images from that night already haunting me. My gut twisted, my chest tight. I could have sworn my heart faltered a few beats. Zyra went to pull away, but I tightened my grasp. I needed her to sincerely listen to what I was about to tell her. To know what we were stepping into once we left this wagon.

I inhaled a deep breath before continuing. "The night my

sister was killed, the guards were after our father. Annora is —
was a light sleeper and likely woke as soon as they stepped into
our home. She was a blessed fighter. We were all personally
trained by our father, but Annora had taken to fighting like it
was second nature. It was in her blood. Any weapon she
picked up was an extension of herself, and you had better hope
you weren't at the end of her blade. She always won and did
not go easy on anyone for any reason. She could take down a
dozen men with only a dagger—while wearing a dress, I
might add.

"She was well aware of how extraordinary she was. So
when the guards slipped by her room, she took up her weapon
and followed them. She knew our parents were asleep and
unaware of the traitors that crept through our house.

"I woke to her yelling at them. I was out of bed and down
the hall faster than you could believe, Keyon at my heels.
Neither of us had grabbed weapons, but we were enraged
enough to fight with our bare hands." I paused, swallowing
against the lump restricting my throat. "When we burst into
our parents' room, they both were sitting up in bed with
weapons trained on them. My mother was screaming as she
watched Annora and the guards. My father could not move
without risk. Not for his weapons and not toward Annora.

"Annora had planted herself between our parents like the
fighter she was—like the queen she was meant to be. A force to
be reckoned with. She met them without fear, protecting our
parents, only to have a spear ... go straight through her. It
happened so fast—there was no way any of us could have
reached her in time.

"Her blood was—everywhere. Keyon and I had already
turned our rage on the guards. We moved through them
quickly until the floor was slick with their blood."

I stopped, suddenly unable to keep going. My mind grappled for memories of my sister while also flinching from them.
All I could see was Annora's blood. How our mother's skinned

animal rug had been coated in the thick red liquid steadily flowing from around the spear. Annora's favorite nightgown ruined.

My voice was hoarse as I said, "My father had talked of expanding our land for Annora but truly seemed to spiral into that belief after her passing."

"I-I don't know what to say, Riker," Zyra finally whispered, her breath warm against my cheeks. Her voice freed me from the haunting images of that night. Of my sister sprawled with glassy eyes.

"She is with the gods now" was all I could muster.

The wagon remained silent for a few moments, Zyra allowing me to get a grasp on my thoughts while I clenched my hands as if I could crush my emotions—bury them in the deep, forgotten corner of my mind. Crush them as I had crushed those guards.

After several moments, Zyra spoke up. "How can your family think you were responsible for what happened?"

I shrugged. "I don't know. The next morning, I was dragged before my father. They would only tell me about there being evidence proving I was the one responsible for orchestrating the attack. That I had turned the guards against my father to take Sandire for myself. That I was the reason I had my own sister killed and why the guards were there—to kill my father." My teeth ground together when I recalled how Keyon had smirked at me from behind our father. "My father didn't even hesitate when he declared my punishment."

My mind was spinning, my heart pounding with the violent hatred and confusion that came with thoughts of my brother. Keyon left me disoriented—uncertain of how we had come to this. How we had gotten here. If he had been *anyone* else, I would have charged for him that morning I'd been forced to my knees before our father, and stabbed the life right out of his eyes.

I had done my best to ignore thoughts of that night until

now, focusing on my father's plans. But now … now that I was saying all this out loud, perhaps it wasn't my father after all. I had not wanted—still did not want—to believe my brother could be capable of such atrocities.

Not when we had always feared our father. Not when I had always shielded him as best I could. Not when I had taken the brunt of everything up until the moment I fled.

"Keyon is the one responsible for the attack," I went on to admit. "He practically said as much when my father had him question me. I think he planned on having me killed that night, too, but never got the chance. Instead, he ended up planting evidence to have me accused of our sister's death and the attempted assassination of our parents. He never thought Annora should be the one to rule since she was a woman. He had imagined us ruling Sandire together when we were young boys, but it seems his plans have turned more selfish." My teeth gritted together harder.

Zyra rested her palm against my cheek, forcing me to look down at her. And, for a moment, everything outside the wagon fell away. "Sometimes, the best revenge is to walk away and let fate take care of the rest. You did just that. You got answers from Skuld—"

"Yes, but nothing direct. She merely gave me a riddle and warned me to watch out for my brother more so than my father. This isn't over yet. Not by a long shot. Not once we step onto sand."

Chapter Forty-One
Zyra

I SMELLED the sand long before I saw it. At first, I thought it was Riker's scent wrapping around me like his warmth since we were crammed together in the wagon.

Minimal words had passed between us since he shared the full story. Tension was still rolling off him—anger, grief, and his appetite for revenge. Although, I could also tell my words had an effect on him, running over and over in his mind, causing him to revisit his thoughts and hunger for violence. There was something else pulling him from his desire for vengeance.

I let his thoughts run wild, knowing he needed to relive it all before we reached the place that was once his home. The place he had escaped to save his life—where his sister had been killed and where he was hated by the very people he grew up beside.

All of it was difficult to swallow—so heinous and gut-wrenching—but I believed him. I trusted my instincts more than anything, and as I listened to his words and tone and saw how the grief had washed over his body, something deep inside me knew every word was true.

His brother had merely planted a seed of doubt, and Riker had trampled it before it could develop any further.

I trusted him more now than I ever could have fathomed. Because, somewhere along the way, we had stopped hating each other. I'd seen almost every side of him now, and I trusted everything I'd seen so far. I would trust him with my life, which he had saved twice before I had saved him in return.

I had no reason not to trust what he said. He hadn't given me a reason to.

I didn't care what the consequences were.

When I felt the crash of sand under the wheels, I pried myself from the wall to peer out the small window. I felt Riker's eyes raking over me as I took in the barren, desert land. I wished he was looking at me like that under different circumstances. Humid wind blew, and the wheels kicked up the sand from under the wagon, whirling the grains across the ground.

"It won't be long before we reach the village."

I glanced back at him. "What are we going to do?"

I couldn't read his eyes, but I heard the distress in his voice. "I don't know, but if you have a chance to get out, I need you to promise me you'll take that opportunity and not look back."

I stiffened. "I won't leave without you. If I have the chance, I'm making sure we both get out."

"They'll kill us. Forget about me. You don't deserve the horrific death they'll—"

"Would you leave me if you had a moment to escape?" He didn't answer. He couldn't lie when we both knew the truth. "You don't deserve to die either, Riker. I won't leave without you. Either we both escape, or neither of us do."

He shook his head. "You are something else, shifter."

There was no disgust when he said the word now.

"We'll make it out of this," I said. "If Corinna is here, maybe we can help her get out—send her flying back to Haiden to get help."

"My father is already going to start a war. Haiden should know as soon as possible now that we're prisoners under Sandire."

The wagon began to slow, and my heart sped up in reply.

"If I can help it," Riker said, "I don't want them to use us against each other."

Eventually, the wagon came to a stop. My heart lurched, but I stayed focused on Riker in an attempt to keep my breathing even. I would make it out of this. I would not die here.

Riker seemed to be thinking something similar. He was close, leaning into me, but careful not to touch me. His body heat radiated across my arm. Bumps rose, my hairs standing on end. The charge between us was back—the same charge from the pool—and it was tempting me. I wanted to pull him in.

I wanted to eliminate what remained of curses and judgment and the hatred we had been spat our whole lives. Because this—this was something I could not ignore. This was something bigger than I could explain. And I was more than confident I was not the only one who felt such an urge for the forbidden.

No matter the consequences.

I dared to lean into him—

Then the wagon door opened, and I glimpsed the fear that flashed in Riker's eyes.

Then we were being ushered out.

My chains dragged across the floor of the wagon as I followed Riker out, then they thumped to the sand once I was under the burning sun. Riker stayed a careful distance away.

My senses stayed trained on Keyon and his Viking companions as they rounded up their supplies. Keyon threw a black cloak at his brother, telling him he needed to look somewhat presentable. Riker said nothing as he clenched the cloak tight enough to turn his knuckles white. Though he was still cuffed, he managed to wrap the cloak around his shoulders to cover his bare chest.

I tore my gaze from him, keeping my face blank while my eyes wandered over everything around us.

The realm's capital rested in the bottom of a nook of surrounding sand dunes. We had already entered the village and were standing before the largest of the houses. Glancing back where we had come from, there was an entrance of two wooden posts dug deep into the sand with two shorter pieces connecting at the top to form a triangle. There were carvings etched into the wood. A shield hung from the planks connected at the top. Antlers and bones also hung from the lumber by strings, blowing with the sand that whirled by.

The village was not barren. Children were poking out of the doors of their homes while women and men alike stared at the prisoners Keyon had returned with. Some of the men and women watching were dressed in fighting leathers, but most wore dresses and tunics that reminded me of the farmers of Nedfin. Most glared, their hands gripping the hilts of their weapons. I did not balk, or even blink, under the gritted scowls I was met with.

I took in as much as I could, but the structures of the thriving village were endless. Though nothing was around for miles, everything was constructed from wood. Some were longer and bigger than others, but all of them were triangular and made from thick tree trunks. A few were decorated with antlers while most had weapons and large wooden shields resting outside the door.

I suddenly felt the distance between where I stood and my home. Beyond, sand covered the land as far as the eye could see. The valleys were far behind us, and Waylria was even farther. The grains whirling in the wind would never touch its soil.

Keyon and the other Vikings led us toward the largest

structure they'd stopped the wagon in front of. The ritual house resembled an overturned ship—its structure long and wide, with a line of shields resting against its outer walls.

I glanced at Keyon, who was leading me forward by my arm, then at Riker.

Their father was inside. Waiting for the son he believed to be a traitor.

Onlookers watched and murmurs spread through the crowd gathering. Though I couldn't understand what they were saying, I could guess. Despite receiving glares and sneers, their talk was of Riker—of how the traitorous Viking Prince had returned. The prince doomed for execution.

Riker kept his focus straight ahead on the door separating us from his father.

If my stomach felt hollow, I could only imagine how he felt to be standing in the realm of his home.

Despite the dread creeping through my body, making me feel numb and shaky all at once, I kept my body steady, determined not to let anyone see and think I was weak. The weight of the chains kept me grounded and from slipping into the panic slowly coursing through me.

Torture. Chained up and prodded with different weapons. Sacrifice. Riker being beheaded. Ripped apart and blood eagled. The possibilities loomed over us—taunting, whispering, causing our imaginations to run wild. Images of how our lives could end flashed across my mind. Pain. Suffering. Watchful eyes. The yearning of the executioner.

It all made my body jerk with the need to tremble. Yet Riker and I managed to keep our backs straight and our heads high as we were shoved inside. We strode inside like warriors despite being wrung with tension. The way Riker stalked across the room—exuding confidence and snark—reminded me once again of his graciously strong feline movements.

The sand had been replaced with wood floor. My eyes

flicked to the large fur pellets pinned on either side of the lengthy walls. I averted my gaze, trying to ignore the sudden nausea churning in my stomach.

In the center of the room sat a dug-out fire pit with a few charred logs stacked inside. Long tables stood on either side of it, pushed up against the wall with benches lining them. At the far end of the room was a rectangular table with chairs facing the rest of the ritual house.

There was a single chair placed in front of the table at the end — one larger and adorned with intricate carvings.

The Viking King of Sandire stood in front of it.

Slate paused when he saw us nearing, his hands clasped behind his back. He studied us from head to toe. He was especially careful as he examined Riker, as though he were able to see every detail of what his son had experienced since fleeing Sandire.

I studied him in turn, taking in his long, dark hair that resembled Riker's and Keyon's roots. His beard was equally dark and did well to hide his age. He was dressed as the other male Vikings of his village: dark pants with a deep-blue tunic.

He looked to be a peaceful man, but those who knew him were aware of his rotten core and burning desire for cruelty. His looks, though, were meant to fool those who first met him into thinking that there was no evil lurking beneath. His form was broad, and he looked as brutal as Riker had when I'd first tackled him in the snowy forest.

Keyon, with a painfully tight grip, jerked me to a stop only a few yards away before shoving me to the ground. The iron dug into my skin. I bit back a snarl when my knees hit the floor. Feeling several pairs of eyes on me, I looked up with contorted features to show my fury.

My blood was burning rage and disgust for being forced to my knees in a room full of sacrificed shifters.

I was going to get out of this and would enjoy ripping apart those who stood in my way.

They would not be able to get near my heart.

They would not be able to keep us here.

They would not kill us.

I looked up in time to see Keyon brush past Riker with a challenge in his eyes. I swallowed a growl. Riker kept his expression blank, but his bound hands were white with restraint.

I should question how far I would go to get Riker out with me. It's what a shifter would do. Corinna and Lizeth wouldn't hesitate to save themselves over a Viking, and perhaps my willingness to risk my life for his made me spineless in their eyes, but I would do what it took to get to him.

And that certainty was so strong—and so unlike anything I had ever experienced before.

Keyon crossed the room until he was standing beside his father's chair. The other Vikings had drifted from Riker to stand among the small crowd that had been allowed to glimpse the traitorous prince and the shifters in enemy territory.

The tension in the room was thick, but when Slate spoke, it became almost suffocating. *"Svikall sonr minn ok varúlfr fúll hans."*

His narrowed eyes slid to me for no more than a moment.

And then I was forgotten.

The Viking King's attention was solely on Riker.

"Dauði er með þér," he said with a nod to his kneeled son. *"Øx þín mun rísta háls þinn í dagan."*

Riker said nothing. I didn't need to see more than half of his face to know he was consumed with rage. The veins in his neck throbbed with it.

"Nǫkkut at segja?" his father continued, his eyes hardening.

Still, Riker remained stiff with outright defiant silence.

I was tempted to look between them, oblivious to the one-sided conversation and the true cause behind the thickening tension.

"It seems he will refuse to speak unless his pet can understand," Keyon drawled in Waylrian.

Riker finally spoke. "That is exactly correct."

Jaw working at this, Slate turned his gaze on me. He looked at me with an expression I recognized from his own son. From when I had interrogated him. Each word was deliberately slow, cold, and hard as ice. "We only went through the trouble to learn your foul language through the generations in order to spit on you before taking you to slaughter. It has been very helpful in torturing information from you."

I didn't give him the satisfaction of answering. Though it took effort not to send my own spit in his direction.

With his hands still clasped behind his back, every step he took was slow and deliberate as he made his way to Riker. "Then I suppose your filthy creature will have to listen to the dirty details of why your mother has failed to show herself for your glorious return. She decided that her heart couldn't take being here. She can't bear to look at your face."

The tension in Riker's shoulders was evident. However, his face remained blank. The pain I knew was whirling in his very being was nowhere in his features. Slate was only saying this because Riker had demanded he speak in the only language I understood. And now he was trying to get under his skin — hurt him with the use of his own demand — rather than show his full outrage.

"You're already dead to your mother. I, however, am glad you've made it home in somewhat one piece." His eyes darkened, moving over him as if he could see all the burns and bite marks I had given him. But I had seen Riker's scars and knew he didn't care that his son had a few more scratches on him.

"I'm glad you've made it back in one piece," Slate continued, "so I can peel you apart myself."

I clenched my teeth together, my skin beginning to itch as the wolf inside me cried to be released. It wrenched inside me, whining in encouragement and assurance that I'd enjoy seeing their blood spilled. Chillbumps rose on my skin. Still kneeling on the ground, I fought against the urges racking inside me.

I couldn't fathom what impulses Riker must be fighting against.

"Tell me how you expected to get away with this," Slate continued when Riker stayed silent. "Did you really think I was going to let you get away? Especially after the raven let us know you were supposedly on your way? There isn't a distance I wouldn't cross to find you. If Keyon had not offered to go in search of you along the way you would have come from Waylria, I would have started searching for you myself. It seems he was just as eager to avenge his sister. You *know* you must be punished."

"*I didn't do it!*" Riker's voice echoed around us.

Against my better judgment, I tore my glare from Slate to look at him. He was struggling to hold his composure now, desperate for his family to believe in his innocence. He hated how quickly they had believed in his guilt and wanted them to see he hadn't betrayed them—that he hadn't had his sister killed so he could take over Sandire.

But I knew he wouldn't throw the guilt of his brother over to them. At least, not yet. He wasn't desperate enough. His brother, the true traitor, deserved to be punished—deserved to be kneeling where Riker was. Perhaps he hadn't fully accepted Keyon's awful treachery and could not give him up. Perhaps he could not watch Keyon die after already having lost his sister.

"There were documents in your room! Letters of your correspondence with others you had turned to your side!" Slate bellowed. "Guards confessed to working for you in the hopes I would show them mercy. Explain that, Riker! Stop lying. For the goodness of your sister, stop lying!"

Riker's jaw clenched. He didn't want Keyon to receive any sort of punishment. He couldn't bear to be responsible for his death after the loss of Annora. He couldn't bring the ax down.

"I'm not lying," Riker shot back. "I am *not* responsible for Annora's death! I would never—"

Slate merely shook his head and turned away from his kneeling son to look back at Keyon. "Take him. Make him break."

Keyon's gaze jumped to me, a feral glint flashing through his eyes as a smirk tugged at his lips. "What of the shifter?"

"We can celebrate tomorrow with a sacrificial feast."

My blood ran cold.

They wanted to celebrate Riker's death with my heart as a sacrifice.

And then finish the day by eating over our bodies.

Slate stormed out, most of the others following his lead. I was still on my knees, barely worth acknowledging. Keyon grabbed Riker roughly while I was merely manhandled by another who had stepped forward.

The Viking who grabbed me stared me down, his long hair shadowing his face but not enough to hide the impulsive craving that plagued his eyes. I kept my head low until he forced me to look at him, grabbing my chin and tilting my face up to him. "It's a shame you're such a revolting creature. I could have had fun with a pleasing face such as yours." He grinned, the look full of foul suggestion. "You look more than able to handle my roughness."

I opened my mouth as if to smile at the brute's suggestion, only to realize I could not bare my canines at him. I released a low growl instead.

He gripped my arm in a bruising grasp.

I could hear the steady pulse of his heart thumping loudly in his neck, encouraging me to tear into the skin there. He was aware of what I was capable of, but I would make it so much worse for him if he made any further remarks. *I would hunt. Him. Down.*

We turned our attention to the others to follow them wherever they intended to hold us until they were ready for our slaughter. Keyon wore a wicked smile while Riker's blank expression hadn't wavered.

They led us through the rows of tables toward the back of the ritual house. Behind the head table rested a large trapdoor. One of the remaining Vikings in the room stepped forward with a torch when Keyon yanked the door open. He took it without looking at the man and shoved Riker forward.

He was the first to go down.

They had dug through the sand and stacked stones along the sides to keep the grains from caving in. It was too dark inside the pit to see what was at the bottom of the ladder propped against the stone wall.

As Riker climbed down, he slowly slipped into the dark, eventually disappearing.

Keyon followed before I was shoved forward. The only source of light was from Keyon's torch, but once my feet hit the ground, I found him walking down the single sand-and-stone tunnel, using the torch to light the others resting on the wall. The air was damp and cold, reminding me of the passages to Haiden's quarters.

The Viking leading me thumped down from the ladder and pushed me to walk deeper into the tunnel. My iron was heavy, especially the one clasped around my neck. That did not stop me from wanting to reach out to Riker as I passed.

Once the torches were lit, Keyon came back to grab Riker and pulled him deeper into the tunnel with us, toward one of the half dozen doors lining the tunnel. As I approached the fourth door, Keyon and Riker stopped at one short of mine.

All the doors were open except one. My heart leaped into my throat, my hands suddenly gripped and clammy. As they brought me into the room beside the one with the shut door, I swallowed, feeling as if I couldn't get enough air in my lungs. My mind screamed, my thoughts raking down the sides.

I whipped my head around to look back at Riker, heart fluttering. Neither of us said anything. Our eyes merely locked, wide and uncertain of what would happen next. Then Riker was pushed into one room while I was shoved into another.

Riker's door echoed shut, followed by mine. But I could not stop thinking about the room beside mine and whether that was where Corinna was.

And I couldn't get enough air to stop the fluttering from raging inside my stomach.

Chapter Forty-Two
Riker

WHEN KEYON SHOVED Zyra to the ground, a blaze of fury had ripped through me. I struggled to clamp down on it and cool my features until I appeared indifferent. For her safety.

Now he had us separated into different rooms. After the horrendous things Ake had said to her before leading her down here, I was furious by the single wall that divided us. Keyon knew it, too.

"We have much to talk about, brother," he said, lighting the torch to brighten the room. Alone, he had swiftly switched over to our language. He turned to me, still holding his torch high.

All I could bring myself to ask was "*Why?*"

The amusement on his face vanished at the question. Resilient, brave, serious but empathetic and playful—that was the brother I knew. I didn't know when this other person had taken hold. Someone selfish and heinously amused. He had kept this side of himself locked away until his greed overtook the brother I had grown up beside. The brother who watched my back and honored Odin when I went out to hunt our enemy; not the brother who planted evidence of treason to make me look guilty.

He had Annora killed and then left evidence for others to find, leading everyone to accept I had betrayed my family. My own brother had aimed the guilt in my direction so I would be the one punished. After my execution, he would be the only surviving heir for our father's title. Sandire would be his.

"You selfish bastard, tell me why!"

In that moment, I didn't care that my hands were bound or that he had several different weapons strapped to his body. I wanted to give him the same death he had given Annora. I wanted him to pay for it. Then I could die knowing the right man had been punished.

"You know why," he seethed, stepping toward me as he hung his torch on the nearest hook. "She didn't deserve to rule. How could she have led us and taken care of everyone? She didn't deserve to be heir. No woman should carry a ruling title in Sandire. How can you not see how weak they are?"

"I've fought alongside women since I was given *Ill*s*ka Sandr*, and most are braver than half my men!"

"You and I deserved to rule together. You never saw that— how powerful we could be together. With my ambition and your sensible tactics, we could have ruled over the realms." He paused, his eyes matching mine. "But you were never on the same page, so I decided to take it all for myself."

"And have Annora and I killed." The words were bitter on my tongue. "With both of us dead, you didn't think our parents would be suspicious of their only surviving child?"

"That was why I was glad you managed to stay alive that night. I was able to turn you into the traitor our father needed to punish. I was still able to get you out of my way. A traitor can't be king. And when Slate announced your punishment would be the same fate you had given Annora ..." His lips twitched up at the corners. "It was too good to be true. I still become heir, and I will still be king. Everything will work out for me in the end."

"I'm not dead yet, brother."

"You should have tried harder to disappear." He looked down, the snarky exterior gone, suddenly unable to look at me. "But maybe you don't have to die. I could still kill Slate, and we could take Sandire for ourselves. We deserve it. He deserves it. He deserves to have everything taken from him—"

I shook my head, astounded by this sudden change. "What are you talking about, Keyon?"

He assumed I had run to disappear. I was not about to tell him any different.

"If you don't want to rule with me, then I can let you leave after I take Slate's title."

"We both know Father won't let me live past tomorrow night. Why the sudden change of heart? Why spare me after having our sister murdered?" I spat. "Why not give *her* the option to flee?"

His jaw worked at the question. Then something flashed across his face, quickly smoothing to nothing before I could read what it was. Keyon had always been difficult to read. He was the quieter of the two of us, the less brutal twin. Twenty-seven years together, sharing the same features and everything else we had, and I hadn't seen this ... fiendish part of him that had been festering. Not a glimpse of it during all this time.

"What are you keeping from me? Why did you do it? Why did you have her killed if you're just going to let me go?" My voice rose higher and higher the more I went on—until I was shouting. "Why did you do it, Keyon?"

"Because she wasn't our sister!" he shouted. "She would have tried to stop me. The way she ran to her parents' aid that night is proof of that!"

Ice poisoned my blood. My voice was barely audible over the static of my abruptly halted thoughts. "Wh-what are you saying?"

He started backing toward the door. "She wasn't our sister.

We share no blood with our mother and barely did with our sister, Riker. It's just us and Father. It's always been the two of us."

The shock that slammed into me caused my arms, hands, and even my fingers to tremble. "I don't … I don't understand. They're our family —"

Keyon shook his head. "You have much to realize, brother."

My heart was like rolling thunder against my ribs, but I did not know how trustworthy his words were. There was no way to know. The look in his eyes gleamed to know something more. There was a certainty there I had not seen in a long time.

I found myself saying, "Tell me what it is you know."

His back was against the door, his hand gripping the handle tight enough to turn his knuckles white. He stared at me for a moment longer. Words rattled in my mouth, questions ready to burst, but my blood was cold with fear of what he knew.

"Tell me," I pressed again. "Why are you saying these things?"

I went to step closer — to stop him from walking out the door. With that step, he pushed the door open and was gone before I could take another. Crossing the small, boxed room, I slammed my fists against the door separating us, shouting for him.

"Keyon! Come back, Keyon! Tell me what you know!"

"Because she wasn't our sister!" My brother's words wouldn't stop echoing through my mind. My heart thundered, lightning cracking through my chest every time the sentence resounded.

I was lying in the sand against the far wall, my gaze locked on the door while I kept my arms crossed tightly over my chest. Nothing but a wall separated me from Zyra. I didn't hear anything coming from her side. I wasn't sure if she could hear me, but I wanted to know. I wanted to be close to her somehow.

There was almost no way out without being caught or killed. I knew because I had kept watch over the shifters imprisoned down here or instructed my men to guard the sand above these very rooms. If any of them managed to get out, they did not get far. For right now, there was nothing I could do except check to make sure she was all right.

I sat up, moving to the wall dividing us to thump my knuckles against it, and waited.

"Can you hear me?" Zyra's muffled voice asked a second later. Her voice barely reached my ears.

My chest deflated with relief. "Yes. Are you all right?"

"I'm fine. He left with Keyon. Are you?"

I briefly shut my eyes. "I'm not hurt."

"We aren't going to die here, Riker."

I didn't answer her. She sounded so certain, yet my mind was too overwhelmed. I wanted to get her out of here. I didn't care what I had to do. But first, I needed to get Keyon to tell me what he was keeping from me.

"We just need to wait for the right opportunity," Zyra added when I didn't reply.

"We'll have to make our opportunity," I told her. "We can't wait on them to slip up."

I could not feel her, and that was a torture in of itself I did not quite understand. The only thing I wanted in this entire world was her, and I couldn't touch her or feel the stroke of her hand, the coolness of her fingers. Instead, I felt the coolness of the wall as I leaned against it. Still, I couldn't block out the words that kept echoing and the images of the night when everything had gone to Hel.

And I could not stop thinking about the wall separating me from Zyra.

I ran my hands through the sand until my fingers scraped a flat piece of wood. The remnant was flat enough for carving, if I got lucky enough to find a sharp enough rock.

Chapter Forty-Three
Zyra

IF RIKER COULD HEAR ME, then that had to mean Corinna could. I edged myself to the opposite wall, despising how heavy the collar felt around my neck. I followed what Riker had done and rapped my knuckles against the wall I assumed —hoped—Corinna was on the other side of.

"Corinna?" I muttered.

Silence met my ears. With the wall between us, hearing anything from the other side was next to impossible.

"Zyra? No. No, no, what are you doing here?"

My heart soared at the sound of her voice.

"How are you even here?"

"How am I here?" I questioned. I propped myself against the wall, resting my head to relieve some of the pressure from the collar. "How are *you* here?"

"They shot me out of the air when I was delivering the letter." She let out a bitter laugh. "I was shot right out of the sky, so I can't believe you made it this far with that Viking."

I wasn't going to pretend that didn't hurt. I might not have made it here exactly how Haiden had instructed, but we were here, and there was no undoing that right now.

"William is dead," I admitted. "Riker killed him not long into our trip."

The second those words landed in the sand between us, I regretted them.

I had used the Viking's name—made my words too personal. But ... was it that obvious? Was it obvious I had feelings for him? Even while I was processing that I could feel something other than hatred? While I grappled with bringing the curse to fruition?

"Then how are you alive?"

I shut my eyes, grappling for an answer I could give her.

"I—" *I can explain* rose to my mind, but there would be none of that. Not for Corinna. Explaining would take far too long.

"How fucking dare you," Corinna seethed after reading into my silence. I could hear a squawk festering in her chest from the other side of the wall. "Tell me what I'm thinking is wrong. My assumption better be wrong."

My heart had left my body. "It's not what you think—"

"It's *exactly* what I think. You've betrayed your people for another traitor—for our *enemy*."

I could not think—conjure what to say.

"Is this why it has taken you so long to get here? What were you planning to do, run away with the brute?" Each word sank into the sand between us like poison.

My stomach was in knots. I had nothing to say. I did not need to.

Her voice grew louder, less controlled. "You had one job, Zyra. What were you thinking? Do you have any idea what this means? What Haiden will do?"

"We went to find an oracle first," I said. "I wanted to see if the Viking was telling the truth."

"You think *they* tell the truth?"

I don't know. I don't know. I don't know!

I wanted to believe Riker. He spoke with such conviction,

with such a need to prove his father's supposed plans, that I had followed him. Everything about it had felt wrong at the time. Now ... now I wasn't so certain. My gut wasn't against Riker anymore. Not when my heart beat something different.

I did not know if I could ever trust them, but I knew—with every part of my being—that I could trust him.

"He saved my life," I answered weakly.

"Is that all you have to say for yourself?"

My chest gripped, urging me to bow to Corinna. Only, I did not want to. I was a wolf while she was a mere bird. Haiden might value her, but she had been shot down by the enemy.

"You are the curse."

Her voice was faint. A declaration to herself. A realization she was struggling to grasp. And with it, my whole world blanketed in darkness, narrowing my vision until I saw nothing but the tiny grains of sand beneath my legs. I had become the very thing everyone feared. I hadn't even realized it. It had all happened so fast—how I went from looking at him as the enemy to something more.

"It's not love," I croaked out in defense. Though I knew where this was headed if legend had anything to say about it. I could deny it. Perhaps I would. If I ended—

"I have nothing more to say to you, Zyra," Corinna snapped. I barely heard her; everything felt and sounded distant. "Let's just focus on getting out of here."

I did not respond. I couldn't. Shock coursed through me at how she was considering escaping with me by her side. It made me think my true punishment was to come, and I couldn't help but wonder if my fate might be better off in Sandire than Waylria.

I wasn't woken by a tapping on the wall or by Riker whispering in my ear, telling me we were getting out of here before they could lay a finger on us.

No. I was woken by the door swinging open.

Wired alertness had my eyes wide. I was still in chains, but I was on my feet and ready to fight. I couldn't shift, but I wouldn't be dragged from here without a fight.

Within two strides, Keyon was across the small room. The only reason I was able to distinguish it was Keyon was thanks to the force he walked with. He walked with motive—and that motive was to hurt me. He was in my face as soon as he crossed the distance.

"I hope you're well-rested."

"What do you want?" I spat.

He moved so fast there was no chance to prepare myself. His hand cracked my face, snapping my head to the side. I grabbed his hand before he could move to strike me again and blocked the other hand he'd raised, and yanked backward.

I had no idea where any of it came from. I could only assume my wolf was crying out to me, forcing me to move on instinct.

Bringing him with me as I stepped back, I thrust my knee out and knocked him to the ground. He went down hard, but I had no choice but to let him go so he would fall, and once I did, he had his hand wrapped around my chain. He wrenched me down with him. I rolled, trying to catch myself. Sand stirred up around us. I kicked out and clawed at whatever skin I could reach.

"Zyra!" Corinna shouted from the other side of one wall.

Riker bellowed from behind the other wall and slammed his fists against what separated us.

Keyon managed to get me onto my stomach and had my wrists pinned into the sand, splayed above my head.

He spat in my language. "I presume you're talking about

that beast calling for you. Don't worry, you will be reunited soon enough."

My teeth rattled when I clenched them. A snarl rumbled behind them, and the rapid pounding of my heart had my blood screaming with the need to buck him off me. With the need to claw at his face until it did not match Riker's at all.

His fingers wound in my hair, wrenching my head back by the grip he had on my wild curls. My chest ached against the ground as I wrestled to breathe. His face close to my ear.

"Of course my brother would find a soft spot for a shapeshifter," he murmured. He must have been aware of how thin the walls were. "I was always the strongest of the two. The youngest, but the only one willing to do what needed to be done. Riker's always been hesitant to take what he wants. But" —his breath caressed my ear—"he seems to have taken quite the claim on you."

I said nothing, only clenched my teeth harder.

"My brother's army was given to me that day he left. The next day, I was named heir because my traitorous older brother could not lay claim to it. You've laid with a traitor, shifter. A traitor has made your heart beat faster, has made your palms sweat, and has caused you to cry out into the night." He pulled my hair back from my face to look at me. "I suppose it shouldn't be a surprise since such things are in your nature, but still, what if I told you I could spare your life? What if I offered you the chance to lie with a king?"

He spoke with such pride at the title, as if the realm were already his.

"Zyra!" Riker called to me from the other room. "Zyra, what is he doing?" He was furious, striking the wall with all his strength.

Corinna was harshly silent.

I inhaled a sharp breath so I could speak without wheezing. "I would rather die than lie with a liar."

Above me, Keyon clicked his tongue, pressing me harder

into the sand. He was so close, our legs brushing as he pressed even closer, either trying to intimidate or be ready if I attacked again. "Are you certain you don't want to reconsider? I could have both you and your friend. You'd never have to worry for your safety again—unless, of course, you ever betrayed me."

"Never." I spoke with force, hoping it angered him. I wanted him angry. I wanted to see the urge to fight me rise in him so I could rip my fury into him.

I was tired of this malicious stranger wearing the same face as Riker. I didn't want Riker's lips telling me awful things he'd stopped saying. This twin's golden-eyed stare held a darker tint to them—one that sent my skin crawling.

I wanted to strip this person of Riker's face. Claw my hands across his skin until he looked nothing like the man I had come to know.

The wild need to fight coiled through my body. A savage recklessness that'd been building in my blood, my bones, my skin since we arrived.

Keyon said nothing before shoving me into the nearest wall. My shoulder popped with the force, but I swung around to face him, a growl rising in my chest. My wolf was screaming for me to shift.

He was on me within a second, holding me against the wall by my neck.

I refused to react to the throbbing in my shoulder or to the minimal air my lungs were taking in.

"You branded my brother. I saw the healed-over marks. Slate preferred to cut, not burn."

I tried to shake my head. "No. No" was all I could get out.

"Deon!" Keyon called without looking away from me.

The door opened to a Viking I hadn't seen before—large like the rest but with long, raven-black hair and a tattoo under one of his assessing gray eyes. He carried a freshly hot iron. A small brazier rested outside the door behind him.

Riker exploded in the other room. "Deon, don't. Deon! I'm asking you as a friend, do *not* help my brother. Don't do this!"

Deon ignored his friend and handed the iron to Keyon. Fear flashed through me at the sight of its orange tip. The tip was branded with indecipherable runes.

Riker continued to shout from the next room, aware of what was taking place; able to hear it all but unable to stop it from happening.

Keyon held the iron up, a smile playing on the edges of his mouth. Riker's mouth. Riker's cruel eyes. "We usually mark our prisoners before sacrificing them. Burn the evil from them and whatnot and to mutilate you in case you get away."

His touch was sudden, and for a second, I barely felt anything when he pressed the brand against my thigh. Then he pressed the iron against me harder. Everything went distant for a moment. Everything sounded far away. I only felt the burning of my skin. And I was reminded of how Corinna and I had done this very thing to Riker.

There was only the hissing of my skin as the runes melted my flesh.

I tried to clamp down on my screams—to hold them inside, but eventually, they ripped from me.

Chapter Forty-Four
Riker

Her screams rattled my bones. My blood curdled against the sound. An all-consuming wrath burst through my body, spreading to every inch until my fingers were curling into fists. I felt like I could take down the wall between us, but I couldn't go to her yet. I had to wait.

Gods help him when I got my hands on my brother.

I was going to absolutely obliterate Keyon.

The rage taking over was meant for him and any others who dared hurt her.

Or tried to keep me from getting to her.

When she finally stopped screaming, the silence that followed was thick. I could taste the triumph Keyon felt. I didn't have to see him to know he'd let her fall to the ground. I knew he wore one of the very sneers I had seen him wear since he found us in that cabin.

My arms trembled with restraint. I needed to get to Zyra, to get her out of here before they could harm her further. The pain of having a hot iron forced against my skin was unforgettable. I remembered the smell of my skin burning. Smoldering heat and sweat had consumed my body.

She did not deserve to feel that scorch. I thought she did

once, but something had tilted our worlds closer. We were more similar than either of us had wanted to admit before this point. Now, I could not stand to hear her pain.

I had hoped they wouldn't brand her, but it was tradition. Before we ripped the hearts from their chests. Before we threw their bodies on the massive pyre that would consume their monstrous plague.

We branded shapeshifters before sacrificing them, marking them to ensure the gods would know Sandire had been responsible for eliminating them from the land. Most were adamant to sacrifice to Thor for strength and protection.

A tradition I was sure Keyon was more than willing to carry out in order to hurt me. He had seen what gleamed between us. Seen how protective we were of each other.

They exchanged a few murmurs from the next room, but neither voice belonged to Zyra. She had probably fallen unconscious to escape the searing brand. Rage flared through me again while it had merely been festering, waiting to be wielded like a weapon.

Deon and Keyon fell silent before I could make out what they were saying.

They shut the door to Zyra's prison as they made to leave.

But a pair of footsteps stopped outside my door.

"You've always gotten everything you wanted, Riker. Everything. And I … I've waited my turn," Keyon said from the other side of the door. "My turn is now. I deserve the title. I don't want to kill you; I want to spare you. Otherwise, there will be no one left to watch as I take it all."

While I wanted nothing more than to get to Zyra, annihilating Keyon was a close second. He was my brother—my blood—but killing him would put a stop to all this. Neither of us would be heir then. Annora would be avenged, and all our father's children would be dead, either murdered or executed for treason. Because I would never get away then.

But still … the thought made a part of me shrink back.

"What *started* this Keyon? What's happened to you? You aren't the—"

"I found out we've been lied to our entire lives, brother. It changes a person." A pause. "It will change you, too."

Under the door, I watched as the shadows of his feet moved away. A few moments later, the trapdoor slammed shut.

EACH MINUTE SEEMED to pass with a slowness that twisted my gut.

Zyra's screams were still rattling through me. My brother's vague confessions were still ringing in my ears.

"Because she wasn't our sister!"

"I found out we've been lied to our entire lives, brother. It changes a person. It will change you, too."

Eventually, I lost track of the passing minutes since Keyon left. I listened for any stir from Zyra, with my head cocked against the wall. No matter how hard I listened, though, I heard nothing. Not even the subtlest movement came from the other side of the wall. The room I was confined to swarmed with silence bound to plunge me into insanity. Waiting for each minute to pass was excruciating. Waiting to hear Zyra awaken was agonizing. Though it was nothing compared to the brand seared into her skin, keeping her trapped in dark unconsciousness. I was all-too aware of the severe pain she would feel once she did.

Sitting in the far corner of the small room, trapped, unable to do anything and knowing nothing, was its own form of torture. Barely able to stand it, my thoughts ran wild with gripping, petrifying worry for Zyra. Then, more often than I would have liked to admit, my thoughts would involuntarily turn over Keyon's strange confessions. They made no sense.

I needed to know more. Keyon had to tell me what he knew. He had to tell me the great secret driving him deeper into madness.

I needed to know Zyra was all right. With the wall separating us—not knowing what she looked like on the other side was bearing down on me more than any confession from my brother. I needed to be beside her when she woke.

I needed to get us out of here.

I was going to get her out of here.

Then I heard a muffled shout of "This is such bullshit!"

"Corinna?" I muttered before I could think twice. No other sounds responded. I turned back to finding a way free.

The guards would be waiting outside the trapdoor. Two at most, because it never required more than that to keep shifters detained. But more could be posted to ensure the treacherous prince was kept contained.

It was a risk. Especially if Zyra was unconscious. But we couldn't stay here. Corinna might also be a force to be reckoned with. She'd more than proven her capabilities when she interrogated me.

Which seemed a lifetime ago now.

But no matter what happened, it was worth the risk. If we stayed here, we would be killed. Our deaths would be excruciating. If we made a break to escape, at least there was a chance we could get out alive. If we could get past the guards, make a dash for the dunes, the death we would be handed would come from an arrow through our backs. A quick and nearly painless death.

It was a risk I was willing to take.

I was going to get us out of here alive.

I would do whatever was necessary.

On my feet and stalking toward the door, I let my festering anger rise until my chest rapidly rose and fell. I held on to the rage stirring in my gut, using it to anchor me— letting it fuel me as I rammed myself against the door. The hinges barely groaned. Deep claw marks were raked down the door; proof that previous sacrifices had fought to break free.

Fought for their lives without making it beyond the claw marks.

I backed away to ram my body against it again and barreled my weight into the door each time, but it remained standing. Nothing beyond the occasional groan.

My body slowed while my breath came faster, and I backed up one last time, taking a few extra steps back. I was looking at the door but seeing something else—the girl with forest-green eyes who could hold her own in a fight, the wolf, Zyra. I saw what they would do to her if we didn't get far, far away from here.

My heart pounded for her. My heart even twisted with the thoughts of what she looked like on the other side.

I thrust my shoulder against the door.

It still remained standing.

And I was sweating, my shoulder throbbing from the force of my efforts.

It did not matter how consumed by Zyra I became, the barrier did not budge.

I went back to leaning against the wall. Terrified of how things could unfold. Terrified we wouldn't make it out alive. Terrified I wouldn't get to her in time. The thought of failing her made me sick to my stomach. I tried to push back against the panic that rose, but it wasn't long before it took hold again.

I couldn't win against the thunder in my chest. I couldn't breathe around it.

Until it all came to a halt when the door opened.

Endless hours could have passed since I last saw him. But there was my brother, strutting through the doorway.

I stood to face him on my feet, analyzing the stranger before me now. The brother I no longer recognized.

"What do you want?" I should be relieved he was here with

me rather than in the next room with Zyra. I knew it was only a matter of time.

For the both of us.

It wouldn't be much longer before my father demanded we kneel before him again. Now that a few feet separated me from Keyon, I couldn't feel anything outside the bitter fury poisoning my blood. My hands shook with the rushed heat in my veins.

"Is that any way to greet your favorite brother?"

"My *only* brother," I gritted out. "If you weren't my blood, I would kill you where you stand right now." *And wouldn't mourn the kill for a single second.*

I would probably come to regret my weakness. Regret sparing him. But some part of him … some part of the brother I knew, had to remain. Even in my anger, the past—our blood—did not outweigh my thoughts and feelings.

A single brow raised, but his hand didn't move to touch a weapon.

He pulled the door shut behind him, barely having the chance to face me again before I advanced, lunging for him.

However, he seemed to be expecting my attack in some way because his hands caught my shoulders when I plowed into him. We skidded across the ground, grains of sand sliding beneath our feet.

Grinding my teeth, I grabbed his arms to throw him from me.

Shoving my chest, he tackled me to my back, driving me to the sand. Pain sparked where my chest was still healing—where the knife had nearly stopped my heart. My vision blurred at the hurl of pain, and once it cleared again, I felt and saw a dagger at my throat. "Relax, brother. Don't try to move. I can't promise I won't cut you."

"I thought you said you didn't want to kill me."

"I don't. I can have Slate killed before sunrise, and we will be free to take Sandire. Together. Stay, brother. Rule with me."

I shook my head. "No. I never wanted our father's title."

"Enough with this—this nonsense. How can you not see it?"

"Because she wasn't our sister!"

"I found out we've been lied to our entire lives, brother. It changes a person. It will change you, too."

"Tell me." I grabbed his shirt, wrenching him closer to me, challenging him with my eyes as I shouted, "Tell me!"

He smirked. "There is no unhearing it, brother. Are you sure? Are you sure you want to hear the sickening thing these people did to us?"

Dread swelled with the anger still pumping through my veins. There was nothing more I could do but nod. I wanted to know what had poisoned my brother—turned him into this person who couldn't see past the blood he wanted to spill. "I want to know what it is you know."

Suddenly, his eyes glazed over—looking at something far in his mind. "He killed her."

I waited, holding my breath as he struggled. "Killed who?" I pressed when I couldn't take the silence any longer. Something tightened in my chest.

"Our mother."

My heart slowly sank in my chest until I couldn't feel it anymore. Every inch of my body felt foreign and numb. I could not move to cover my ears.

"Slate killed our mother."

Disbelief held me to the ground. Each of those four words suffocating. Breathing became nearly impossible as he kept speaking.

"Father had fallen in love with a shapeshifter, but the moment she fell pregnant ..."

The silence was torture—a deafening, overwhelming mist that hung over us like impending death.

"After that, Slate killed his shapeshifter lover for the

babies, to keep Sandire's secrets, and to ensure no one else could have her if he couldn't."

"Why?" I gasped out against the blade warming my throat. The buckles secured around my wrists didn't so much as rattle.

Keyon's eyes snapped back to me. Rather than answering, he said, "Haiden is responsible for the separation of shifters and Vikings."

Faster and faster, my heart and lungs worked. Everything seemed to be getting farther and farther away. Until everything except my echoing heart sounded muffled. Until everything felt numb and unreal.

Lies or a deep truth that had broken him. And he was sharing this pain of knowledge. Not wanting to be alone. Not wanting me to continue to believe the lies I had swallowed these twenty-seven years. Wanting me to understand this sudden change in everything.

The truth appeared wide to swallow me whole, and I pushed away from it—fought against it. Because it couldn't be true. It was nothing more than an outrageous claim that held no proof. I had never felt evidence of a change—of another creature lurking beneath my skin.

I did not want to believe a word of it.

"Who ... who were the babies?" I asked when I snapped back into myself. I knew the answer, but I had to hear him say the words aloud.

"Slate snuck back to Waylria," Keyon continued, "to meet with her again. Had strung her along for months while she'd carried us. From what I've gathered, they hadn't been together for long before he slaughtered her like an *animal*." He spat the last word, recoiling as if he could remember it all, as if he had been there.

"Slate took us to raise us as his own. He took us to have the upper hand in case war ever came to Sandire. He's never given a damn about us because we were raised to be his pawns. He took us for his own gain. He beat anger into us and tried to make us fear him. I know. I read enough about it in his private documents."

Every word stripped me. They enveloped me. Suffocated me. Shock, dread, anger, and so much more overtook me. A sadness for people I had never known. Anger for so many years of lies.

Keyon let the silence pass between us, merely watching as everything came crashing down around me within a few moments. Unease crept into my veins, poisoned my thoughts, as my mind wrestled against everything Keyon said. I couldn't accept it—couldn't grasp it as truth or lie. I wanted to deny it all with every fiber of my being.

Because if this was the very thing that had destroyed my brother from the inside out these last months ... I could almost understand how such a secret had changed him. In Keyon's eyes, our entire lives had been a mirage. We had been thought of as mere pawns to our father.

Our entire lives ... stripped from us and fed nothing but falsehoods.

Discovering he was something we were taught to hate—it had destroyed Keyon. Sent his entire world upside down. Forced him to hate himself. Made him fear for his life every minute he was surrounded by people who would kill him if they knew the truth.

"That isn't true. It *can't* be true!" I finally said.

"All we've ever known is Sandire, Riker."

"And Annora?" I choked out.

"Slate and Ingrid's only blood child. She was already two when Slate brought us home to our new family," he seethed.

It felt like the world had fallen out from under me to reveal in inescapable black abyss. A labyrinth I would wander blindly inside forever.

Somewhere in his deluded mind ... Keyon had cast Annora

aside for being a woman and for not being fully related to us. For being weak and unfit to rule. Because she wasn't our *true*, full-blooded sister.

And, because she was human, she might have turned on and hated us for our blood.

Though I could see from the rigid way Keyon wrestled against it, and how his pain revealed his honesty, I was struggling to believe it as he did. Even though I could see how he truly believed these discoveries, I was convinced I would have known if I was the very thing I had loathed all these years.

"But I've never shifted."

"Neither had I until a few months ago."

Before Annora's death. Before my life went to shit. All of it because of him.

The desire to ask about his animal skin rose, about why he had kept this from me for so long, and why it had led him here —but it all died in my throat when a door creaked open.

Keyon pulled the knife away, suddenly embracing me, sending a startling tremor down my stiff spine before he released me and sheathed his dagger into his belt. He backed up to the wall, leaning against it before sliding to the ground and running a hand through his hair before gripping the strands close to his scalp.

I pushed up from the sand, fighting the urge to touch the cool part of my throat where the blade had been. A door had opened. My door was still shut. Sealed tight. Then another door opened. Dread slowly caused my heart to sink. "What—"

He looked up at me, his face empty. "Father instructed me to stay with you during the sacrifice."

Hearing those words—I could not identify a single feeling that tore through my body, but everything felt like a vicious sandstorm. One that swept away every life in its path.

All I knew was my father was not the one to defeat. Keyon was the one manipulating everything. He was behind the conquests—the overthrow of the realms. He was the one who was power hungry.

And I couldn't risk waiting any longer.

I propelled to my feet before Keyon could discern my intentions.

Chapter Forty-Five
Zyra

I COULDN'T TAKE in enough air around the heat pouring from the brand scorched into my leg. I had to force my eyes open. The sand blurred beneath my hands as I summoned what little strength I had left to push myself up.

Something thudded against the wall separating Riker from me. I gasped out his name, my heart clenching at the thought of him being harmed without a way for me to reach him.

I swallowed against my dry mouth, fighting to push back the fever snaking up my leg. Each step sent a flare of heat racing up and down my branded limb.

Clenching my teeth at the scorched rush, I forced out "Riker? Corinna?"

I fought against my lungs to avoid gasping. Sweat and hair clung to my forehead. Reaching the wall, I propped myself against it.

When I looked down, the brand seared into my thigh was that of a rune.

ᛞᚢᚢᛉ it read.

Had they done the same to Corinna? I could hear nothing of her despite the thinness of the walls.

The sight of the brand sent my heart plummeting to my

feet. I fell with it, crashing into the sand in a heap, my eyes shut against the fall. I could not move. I could not speak. And couldn't open my eyes, even when I thought I heard a door open.

All I could do was sweat and listen to the muffled shouts from the other side of the wall.

Chapter Forty-Six
Riker

I HAULED Keyon from the sand. His legs stumbled under him in a struggle to righten himself. His shirt clenched tight in my fists, I shoved him into the wall with every bit of strength I could muster. The buckles on my cuffs clanked together, and there was only enough time for Keyon's eyes to widen as he rushed to reach for one of his weapons.

Even so, I didn't let him get that far.

I couldn't grasp hold of a thought long enough to comprehend it. My mind was grappling. I was falling and had nothing to grab hold of to stop myself from plunging deeper. I was being flooded—overwhelmed by everything tearing its way inside me. Sand ran through my fingers, the grains scraping my dry, calloused palms.

They had Zyra.

I stared at the stranger before me and found myself speaking before I knew what I was doing. "What happened to you? Do you even care anymore? About anything?"

Keyon's eyes darkened, and he rushed to speak before I could act. "You're my blood. You're all I need in this world and the next. You and Ingrid are the only ones I love. Even though she isn't our mother by blood." He swallowed loudly. "I love *you*. I couldn't care less about anyone else. They will get what's coming to them. It won't be long." He shook his head. "So, I won't kill you. I need you here."

"What do you —"

"I don't want to be alone anymore, brother." I waited, watching him as he held my stare, as if willing me to read deeper into his words. "I don't know very much about what I want, I have ideas, but now I know I want you there to see them set in motion."

Keyon had always been an honest soul. He used it to his advantage whenever he thought it would benefit rather than come back to hurt him. As he was doing with me now.

"You may not care what people say about you when you die, but don't you care now?" he asked with dark curiosity. "Don't you want to be remembered? Hated by many but loved by even more?"

I shook him against the wall. "After what you've made me out to be, no one will ever stop loathing me. *Everyone* has turned on me because they think I tried to have my own family slaughtered in their beds!"

Because going against the lies, voicing disbelief in the presence of the king, would put not only your own life but the lives of your entire family at risk. These risks were the very reason most had turned their backs on me. Even those who I had called friends. But I did not blame them. I wouldn't wish the pain of loss on anyone.

Zyra was the only one who had not turned her back on me. Even though she should have. Even though she had nothing more to go on than my word. With her ever-observant eyes, she had listened to my side of the story, given me a chance. Then believed me without drifting away.

"I need you alive." Keyon turned his head slightly, as if he couldn't stand the sight of me. "I have something much more important intended for you."

I stopped letting him waste time and cracked the crown of my head against his forehead.

In a single motion, I had him on his feet against the wall, then finished with him slumped under my hands. I rammed him harder into the barrier, my fists tightening, my jaw stiff, then pulled in a long breath before slowly releasing it.

If I didn't get to Zyra in time ... I couldn't even finish the thought without bile rising in my throat.

I had seen enough death—witnessed enough sacrifices throughout my life. I would rather die than watch Slate strut into the pit with Zyra's severed head clenched in his hand. His fingers matted in her dark curls.

I flinched from the image.

I would rather die than feel that harsh helplessness again in this lifetime.

I backed away from Keyon's slumped body.

I would regret it. I knew I would, but I couldn't bear to kill him when I had lost everyone else.

Incapable of standing the sight of him, I put as much distance between us as I could in the confines of the small room. Stomach in knots, I was close to hyperventilating as a result of my racing heart and constricted chest.

I heard muffled movement above and from the other room, but nobody had lost themselves in the thrill of spilling blood. Yet. Which meant I wasn't too late.

I had no idea what would happen or what I would find once I made it out of this room.

I had no plan beyond getting to Zyra.

Uncertain of how long he would be out, I took Keyon's shirt for myself on my way to the door. I made for Zyra's door, which swung open while a man strained to pull her out.

My heart thundered against my chest, simultaneously sinking in the pit of my stomach.

I kicked the figure into the room, catching Zyra in my arms

before she could fall. She had braced herself with the edges of the door to stay in the room.

She looked around frantically, even trying to climb over my shoulder. "Corinna. Where is Corinna?"

I took her face in my hands.

My heart was pounding furiously, and my hands were practically shaking.

Before I had time to act, the warrior was back on his feet. I didn't waste a single second and had the man on the floor again —where he would stay—before he'd known what happened.

Once I was back in front of Zyra, remembering how to breathe took effort. Her green eyes were wide with wonder, drinking me in.

I closed the remaining distance between us.

Relief choking me, I wrapped my arm around her waist and slammed my lips against hers before either of us could remember to take our next breath.

Her body locked up beneath mine, and for a moment, I feared she would pull away—shove me away, reminding us both we were supposed to be enemies. Her hesitation vanished, seeming to decide to stop denying what we had already known, deep down.

Where her lips were soft, mine were crushing. Where my hands ravished her, touched everywhere open to me, her fingers gripped my arm like she needed something to hold onto. Lithe and strong; honed and ready for anything.

I gave into the intense heat thundering through my blood, pulling her ever closer.

The kiss was slow, thorough, and over all-too quickly.

I pulled away at a rush of sound. People storming the pit.

Zyra's eyes widened even farther.

"I'm incapable of being repulsed by you," I rushed to tell her. "No matter our histories, no matter what the future holds —you can hold true to that. And hold true that we will survive, and fate will lead us back to one another."

She didn't have time to respond before identical hands to my own snaked around me from behind. While I had the chance, I released the wood in my hand to let it fall to the sand between our feet.

My gaze never wavered.

Zyra was the last thing I laid eyes on.

Chapter Forty-Seven
Zyra

I HARDLY HAD time to meet Riker's eyes, which were flared into a burning gold. His lips had been crushing—rushed with urgency before we could be parted. He had known what was coming. So had my gut.

Yet I still reached for him.

And I hated Keyon's matching eyes and how they seemed to smirk as he dragged Riker from me.

But not before my gaze fell to what Riker had dropped at our feet.

I collapsed to my knees, shouting for Riker and Corinna. Both of whom had been ripped from me now.

In Keyon's absence, a swarm of other warriors barged into the room to haul me to my feet. I kept the wood piece clutched to my person and hidden from prying eyes as they held me down.

A SCORCHING PAIN in my thigh.

Words echoing through my mind before spreading throughout the room.

"*Hjarta.*"

"*Elðr.*"

"*Fórn.*"

"*Hjarta ðýrs.*"

"*Loganda reykr.*"

Everything but the pain felt distant.

I couldn't break the surface of unconsciousness or push past the barrier to wake and fend them off. I was burning but still fully aware of their presence. Their closeness.

They lifted me.

I was floating—light as a cloud—as they moved me.

Fire shot up and down my leg and simmered in the pit of my stomach. Warmth climbed across the left side of my body.

Then a deep familiar voice spoke. A few moments passed before I realized it was Slate. He hovered over me, a single, foreign word poised between us like a razor-edged blade. "*Fórn.*"

Chapter Forty-Eight
Riker

"A FLAME in the center of darkness will spark, lighting the way for what is to come, but it has no wick or oil to fill."

Darkness was where I was headed. This was a worse fate than death at the hands of my brother or father. I almost wished we had come face-to-face for that. I would be with Zyra then and have a chance at saving us. I would have a chance at stopping Keyon before his disease could spread.

Once the darkness of the wagon was replaced with the darkness of Annarr, my only hope was that there was a spark of flame to light the way.

Chapter Forty-Nine
Zyra

I COULD FEEL the weight of the room. The press of the bodies. The intensity. The heat. The crackling of nearby flames. The impatience. The restlessness of it all was suffocating.

Although I could feel the thickness consuming the room, it all felt distant. I was isolated in the shadows, trapped and submerged within my own mind. I fought to break the surface —to wake. I called upon my claws to rake them down the sides of my mind.

Because this couldn't be it.

I had to find Corinna. And Riker.

Someone leaned over me again, a cool steel pressing against my exposed skin. Murmurs of words I didn't understand were being chanted. Bits and pieces of a ritual blessing.

A gasp escaped my lips when the cool blade slid across my skin.

My eyes snapped open when the murmurs came to an abrupt end.

I didn't take the chance to see those hovering above me. My instincts howling, I shot my bound hands out to catch the wrist about to plunge the blade for my heart, descending far too fast for me to roll away. I growled when I recalled I couldn't tear my nails across the man's throat.

I couldn't move. I couldn't feel the rest of my body. Neither could I move it.

But someone else was there, too.

Corinna rolled on top me, shoving me away from the wrist straining in my hand as it tried to overpower me. I lost the battle, and Corinna didn't push me away in time. The knife struck my lower abdomen, blood instantly flowing over my skin and seeping into my clothes. I sucked in a sharp breath, unable to scream. My vision narrowed.

Somehow, Corinna was already on her feet, free of her chains. I couldn't comprehend how. I was struggling to focus as it was. But it wasn't a shock that Corinna managed to break free from her bonds.

My eyes drifted to the man beside him. Slate only gave me a slow smile when he saw how the blade was wedged in my side. Gritting my teeth, I didn't give myself another second to consider it. I yanked the blade out, and a growl ripped from my throat.

I rolled, but Corinna's voice stopped me.

"Can you stand?" she asked without looking at me over his shoulder. "Can you walk?"

The crowd no longer stunned, chaos had erupted through the ritual house.

"I-I think so," I managed around my dry mouth. My heart was like thunder against my ribs, its thud echoing throughout my entire body.

Before I could finish, a Viking was on top of Corinna, with another swiftly coming up behind her. I held back my fear. Too many—there were too many to fight off. We were surrounded.

But at least she was here and alive.

I needed to help, or we would never make it out of Sandire.

I willed my body to regain feeling, pushing against the pain in my abdomen. It was nothing compared to the searing rune on my thigh. I pulled myself up, forcing my way across the floor, and the hilt slid across the floorboards. Slate's laughter followed me, but I did my best to ignore it.

My body shuddered under my weakness, but I couldn't reach for my wolf. No matter how badly my skin itched.

Regardless, I would be something to fear. I would not be the weak thing everyone believed me to be. Even if Corinna felt differently because I had bowed to the cursed legend.

Instead, I allowed the itch under my skin to spread. Corinna spared a glance in my direction.

I crouched, prepared to lunge for the Viking sneaking up behind her.

Though I was bound, I would make the most of the dagger I had.

But before I could launch for his back, I was struck—kicked onto my side. I swallowed a yelp, but a pained moan still managed to slip from my mouth. My leg was on fire. My abdomen throbbed, blood trickling to collect on the floor beneath me.

Slate walked toward me, sword gripped in his hand. I scrambled to get my legs beneath me again, trembling with agony as I stood. I held the dagger between us, panting through clenched teeth. The blade did not tremble, but I knew I looked nothing like Riker.

"Disgusting mongrel," he seethed, prowling closer. "Just when I thought Riker couldn't fall any further, he has sympathy for a shapeshifter. Cares about a *varúlfur* enough to try and save her. Revolting, but I suppose expected. I should have expected everything, really. Though not long ago, he couldn't even stand to touch one of your kind to bring them back as a sacrifice."

I kept myself planted where I stood, refusing to back down. I was not fearful of more scars. Of disappointment. Nor was I fearful of him. He lived for cruelty. I would not give him what he wanted to see. He would not see fear in my eyes, or sneer in victory as I backed away from him. Neither would Keyon.

Not after I had learned of Riker's scars. Not while I stood and breathed.

I would rather die than cower to these men.

He tapped his blade against mine, testing my grip. "I'm going to enjoy his reaction after I run you through. Though, I suppose it will be a while before he finds out you've died. It's a shame he isn't here to witness this."

I snarled against the sinking feeling his words caused, challenging him to come closer.

I tried to ignore the hollow feeling in my stomach at not knowing where he was.

For now, I would tear through his father to get to him.

Next thing I knew, Corinna was between us, chest rising and falling rapidly with heavy breaths. I fought not to growl at her for getting in the way. She had risked herself enough to be here. And I did not need her to save me.

I moved to strike, but Slate's sword was there, blocking the edge of my blade from slicing across his esophagus. Someone must have come up behind me because Corinna moved to put her back to mine. Right now, her anger toward me did not matter. We had to come together to make it out of here, or we both would die. Could she get over our last conversation enough to do so?

I did not dare look around us, knowing we were surrounded.

Backing down wasn't in their blood. Fear wasn't present.

It was as if I were watching a Viking legend unfold. This moment would probably live on as its own tale.

Everyone was pressing closer, as if they knew not to interfere with this fight but still felt the need to protect their king.

My heart struck against my ribs before clutching.

I zeroed in on Keyon. Though I could not reach my wolf skin, my instincts were skeptical about what I was seeing.

Something was not right about Slate being the sole one orchestrating all this. Keyon was always there — waiting and watching from the shadows. Something about it was unsettling.

Among the pellets, keys dangled from his belt.

The only way we might make it out was if I could shift.

I didn't allow myself to think. I merely reacted.

It was the only way out.

I shoved up against Slate's sword. When it came back down, my dagger was gone, landing at my feet in time for me to raise my shackled hands. The chain connecting them fell away when his blade came down to meet them. Corinna whirled with my movements, taking my place in front of Slate.

My eyes were locked on one target — the man who reflected Riker in almost every way.

I sensed more than saw several weapons and bodies launch toward me but paid them no mind. My focus did not waver. I did not care if I ran into anyone else before reaching him. No one would stop me. Not now. Not when I was so close.

"Leave her to me! Block the doors!" Keyon shouted.

Once I could shift, that would not stop me.

Just before I reached him, Keyon pulled an ax from behind his back. Pure, hot rage coursed through my veins. I did not care whether he was intentionally trying to copy his brother or if they shared likes and dislikes enough to prefer axes as their weapon of choice.

Seeing it made my heart beat so fast it hurt. The pounding in my ears was deafening.

I slid on my knees, ignoring the pain in my side long enough to raise my dagger to meet the blade of his ax as he swung down. The force of his blade meeting mine strained my arms. I felt the tremble from my hands to my chest, sending my heart pulsing harder.

I could not hear any others around me as I grabbed for the ring of keys strapped at Keyon's belt.

Though, as soon as I had them in my hand, he knocked

them away. They went flying across the floor. I felt the intensity of Keyon's gaze above me, then met his eyes. Both of us were still straining to hold our weapons against the other. I let mine drop, curving the blades behind me.

Before he could swing again, I yanked my dagger up and cut across his ankle. Thankful for the adrenaline dulling the stab wound at my side, I refused to stop moving and crawled across the wood slats of the floor for the keys.

Corinna grunted while fighting the crowd behind me. Women pulled children closer, tucking closer to the wall, not having expected to bear witness to their sacrifices fighting back.

The Viking who had manhandled me down to my cell stepped out to grab the keys before I could.

I launched at him, barely getting away before Keyon could take hold of a fistful of my hair. I would not leave him unchecked.

The Viking went to draw a weapon from the sheath of his belt but wasn't quick enough. I didn't blink or allow myself to hesitate. I kept my eyes wide to ensure my aim was true as I slammed my blade across his wrist, severing it from his arm.

I grasped the ring of keys, tucking myself into the wall to unlatch my cuffs. Though I kept myself alert as the Viking cried out. *"Þú óhreinn dýr!"*

The children moved ever closer to their mothers. Men turned their heads to see what had happened behind their backs.

The cuffs fell away from my wrists, and the collar around my throat soon followed. The moment they did, I allowed the itch under my skin to spread. I was still weak—exhausted—from fighting at every turn, but I was stronger in this body. I was something to fear.

And at this point, I was convinced cuffs were pointless.

Corinna moved through the crowd effortlessly, panting while swinging a dagger and a sword. Everyone in the room seemed to press ever closer. It made tension crawl across my skin, cording every muscle, readying myself to spring.

For the sake of putting the man out of his misery since he would never be able to pick up a weapon again, and in revenge for how he spoke to me, I latched my canines to his neck, puncturing deeper and deeper with every panicked movement. While my breathing was ragged, his cries quieted. Blood flowed from the deep marks left by my canines, falling to the floor in puddles.

Another Viking was foolish enough to get in my way.

Keyon was my intended prey.

He seemed to accept his fate, as he chose then to come up behind me with his ax. A scream to know where Riker was crept up my throat. The sound a battle cry.

In an act of blood and instinct, I dug my canines into Keyon's arm before he could register what was happening, dragging my teeth down the side. He wrenched back, sending me to the ground. My bloody fur smeared across the floor, leaving it tacky. When I looked up, Corinna was whirling to meet the next attacker, sending him to the ground with a mere kick.

Keyon looked as though he was doing every damned thing not to cry out as he stared at the torn flesh. Crimson drops flowed to the floor from his arm and my muzzle.

The room erupted.

There was so much rushing around. Flashes of weapons and shields. Men pushing and practically climbing over each other and the dead in an attempt to reach us. All of them desperate to be the first to slaughter a shapeshifter. Others — women, children, and cowards — fled.

The next moment I looked up, my eyes met Corinna's. Only a few stood in our way of each other. And even less between us and the door of the ritual house. Our escape.

I didn't need Corinna to read my mind for her to know to run. A familiar glint sparked in her eyes, and I knew she would kill as many as she could on our way out. Right now, our last conversation did not matter.

My teeth sank into a leg, forcing the person to their knees.

Keyon and Slate were lost in the crowd behind us.

We didn't look back.

Corinna swung out and threw the last Viking into the doorway, embedding her blade into his throat before we pushed passed with the others fleeing.

My paws hit sand, and I was immediately flooded with relief. A howl made its way from my throat, reaching the endless stars twinkling above the sand dunes.

"Nei! Þú mun ekki hann finna!" a voice followed us—Keyon calling after us.

The crowd poured from the ritual house, hurtling through the sand to catch up to us. Corinna and I ran side by side, sticking close like we did whenever I went on a hunt.

Neither of us paused. We ran faster. Sand kicking up from under our racing steps. And I could not have been more relieved to have my friend running—escaping—beside me.

Neither of us dared glance back. I didn't want to know—didn't want to see the arrows heading straight for us or the clan racing to catch us. I swallowed against my dry mouth, fighting to push back the fever snaking up my leg.

Closing my eyes against it all, I pushed myself to keep going.

I didn't know how long we ran for. It felt like forever and no time at all. I didn't know. My mind was hazy, my legs quaking. I couldn't hear anything.

Shift, I encouraged Corinna when I glanced to her. *Get as far away from here as you can. Don't look back. Warn Haiden and the others.*

One of us had to make it back to Waylria.

When she shifted and could hear the echo of my words in her mind, I repeated them to her.

She spread her wings with a caw that echoed off the dunes. *Make it back to Waylria alive.*

Her words brought a cold dread—a promise that my curse would not go unatoned for.

I slowed once it was safe enough, breathing heavily, overwhelmed with the feeling of having to cough up my last meal as I watched Corinna's raven skin grow smaller and smaller in the distance. But there was nothing in my stomach to retch up.

Silence enveloped me. My wolf ears detected nothing among the dunes.

It was not until that moment that I realized how alone I was. Riker was gone. Corinna was flying back to Waylria with her warnings. And I was miles upon miles away from everyone and everything I knew—torn about where to go now.

MY HEART THUMPED FASTER with each blink as I took in my surroundings. Sand upon endless sand, with the wide expanse of sky overhead. I had no sense of where I was going, and I couldn't bring myself to care. I no longer had anything to prove to those in Waylria. Nothing pulled me in the direction of home. Back to my realm. No, my heart desired another home.

And that left me at a loss, because Riker was lost to me.

My fur sank into my skin; fabric brushed against my skin with the reappearance of my clothes. With shifting back to my human skin, I reached into my pocket. Blood dripping from my mouth, I hesitated at the jagged feel of the wood piece when I clutched it. Riker had dropped it right before they had taken him from me. Even under the endless stars, I could still feel the phantom press of his lips against mine.

The copper taste of blood coated my teeth. I used the hem

of my shirt to wipe away the thick gore. Heat flushed my cheeks as I wiped at them, still struggling to catch my breath.

To fight back the tears welling in my eyes, I bit the inside of my cheek, and then, when I went to clench my fists and allow my body to crumble in on itself, my hand tightened on the rough long wood.

Gaping down at the wood in my palm, I ran my thumb over the carvings on its side.

ᚺᚢᚷ ᚠ ᛘᛖᛁᚤ ᚠᚢᚲ ᛘᚲ ᛘᚢᛏ ᚲᛟᛘᚨ ᚦᛖᛁᚤ ᚨᚨᛏᚱ

I had no way to read the message, but I knew the piece held something deeper than their etchings.

We had broken so many laws between our realms just by walking beside each other. When I had failed to follow orders. When Riker had failed to kill me when he had the chance. His absence was an ache—a gaping hole—in my chest.

Riker knew what lay ahead and how to stop his father and brother. If he was alive as his brother had hinted to, Riker was the key to stopping Keyon. Because something larger was simmering beneath the surface of what had already happened. Something much, much larger.

Breathing against the searing in my leg, I went in search of tracks.

Riker was the answer.

Perhaps finding the oracle again wouldn't hurt either.

Once I could run on my leg again, it would be without stopping. For now, I had eluded my enemy, and I had Riker's words with me. I stared down at the runes one last time before limping and climbing the dunes of Sandire, eyes set on the horizon of dark trees ahead.

Rune Translations

For the sake of avoiding spoilers, rune translations have been included in the back of this book. The Elder Futhark (or Fuþark), also known as the Older Futhark, Old Futhark, or Germanic Futhark, is the oldest form of runic alphabets. This was commonly used for writing Proto-Norse, and it consists of twenty-four runes that often are arranged in three groups of eight, each of which is referred to as an ætt.

- ᛞᚢᛉ – in Old Norse, this translates to**dýr**, which means "animal" or "beast." In terms of using Elder Futhark Runes, this translates to *∂ýr*.

- ᚺᚢᚷ ᚨ ᛗᛖᛉ ᚨᚢᚲ ᛖᚲ ᛗᚢᚾ ᚲᛟᛗᚨ ᚦᛖᛉ ᚨᚠᛏᚱ – in Old Norse, this translates to "*Hygg á mér, ok ek mun koma þér aptr,*" which then can be translated into Elder Futhark Runes. In English, this translates to "Think of me, and I will find my way back to you.

Acknowledgments

Thank you for reading *Forbidden Captive*! Writing this book was a whirlwind when I wrote the first draft almost ten years ago. Redefining my characters, further establishing the world, and then rewriting the story was a journey that made me fall in love with every aspect even more.

If I had not met my critique partner, Alyse Cline, during a beta read of the first or second original draft of this book almost a decade ago, I likely would never have picked up this story again. *Forbidden Captive* would have collected dust in a drawer if it wasn't for Alyse's continued obsession with Riker. When I shared character art, the book cover, and every change I intended for this massive rewrite, she was (somehow) more excited about every step than me.

My fiancé's endless support, encouragement, and reading and rereading of this book pushed this into the hands of readers. You are my ray of sunshine and my biggest supporter, always. Whenever an ounce of doubt enters my body, you are there to defy it and help me regain the confidence to keep going. That in and of itself is indescribable magic.

To our puppies, Nova and Starry, for being right by my side while I would brainstorm and for how they always hoped I would share one of my snacks. But most of all, thank you to Nova for rolling on every piece of paper and notecard I laid out. Y'all were the best fluffy assistants to have around!

Thank you to my amazing character artist, cover artist, and visual supporter Meghan at Wolfe Fantasy. I truly could not have brought this book to life without you. Being able to email you with my wild ideas to have you bring them to life shortly thereafter was amazing and everything you have created has been stunning.

A massive thank-you goes to my parents for encouraging me to follow my dream from day one, even when it sounded idiotic to everyone else. Not only would I not be where I am today without you, but I would not be who I am without you.

A thank-you to the other two members of Bat Girls, Hannah and Grace, for not only chatting books but for being bookish cheerleaders. Hannah, this book is fantasy and not horror and serial-killery this time, so you can read it without feeling the ick.

Finally, to my editor, Dee's Notes, for helping spice up my lines and catch those last-minute errors that didn't catch my eye.

About the Author

Ashley Earley grew up in Georgia, where she spent most of her time running wild in the woods of her backyard, building forts to create her own fantasy worlds, obsessing over books, and experimenting with her writing.

Today, she lives in Kansas with her fiancé and two pups. She still spends her time devouring any book she can get her hands on, writing, and editing for her clients at Earley Editing, LLC. In May of 2021, she graduated with distinction from University of Colorado Boulder, receiving a Bachelor's in English with an emphasis in Creative Writing. She also enjoys snowboarding, exploring, annoying her dogs, constantly eating chocolate, and sharing her writing adventures on Instagram.

Her Thriller/Suspense short story, *Chasing Hair of Gold*, won first place in the 2016 Writer's Digest Popular Fiction Awards.

As a writer, she leans into fantasy or horror due to her love of all things creepy. As an editor, she loves a little bit of everything when it comes to fiction. Give her that steamy, forbidden romance, give her vampires, or even that young lovey-dovey stuff with all the twists and turns!

Author Website: ashleyearley.com
    Instagram: @ashley_earley
    TikTok: @ashley_earley